YES, *and* BACK AGAIN

YES,

and BACK AGAIN

SANDY MARIE BONNY

thistledown press

Thistledown Press Ltd.
410 2nd Avenue North
Saskatoon, Saskatchewan, S7K 2C3
www.thistledownpress.com

Library and Archives Canada Cataloguing in Publication
Bonny, Sandra Marie, 1978-, author
Yes, and back again / Sandy Marie Bonny.
Issued in print and electronic formats.
ISBN 978-1-77187-052-8 (paperback).--ISBN 978-1-77187-088-7 (html).--
ISBN 978-1-77187-089-4 (pdf)
I. Title.
PS8603.O62Y47 2015   C813'.6   C2015-905167-3
C2015-905168-1

Cover and book design by Jackie Forrie
Printed and bound in Canada

Canada Council for the Arts   Conseil des Arts du Canada

Canada

Thistledown Press gratefully acknowledges the financial assistance of the Canada Council for the Arts, the Saskatchewan Arts Board, and the Government of Canada for its publishing program.

YES, *and* BACK AGAIN

1921 Canadian Census

Census Place: District 216, Saskatoon area: Twp 37, Rg 6

Subdist-40 Sutherland Town Page 12 Family 67

Household		Sex	Age	Or	Birthplace
head	Thomas Tanner (marr.)	M	34	Ind.	Manitoba
	Occ: freighter		Rel: Church of England		
wife	Margrite Agnes Tanner	F	28	Ind.	NW Territories
			Rel: Catholic		
Madeleine Ann Tanner		F	10	Ind.	Saskatchewan
			Rel: Catholic		
Robert Joseph Tanner		M	8	Ind.	Saskatchewan
			Rel: Church of England		
Phidelma Agnes Tanner		F	4	Ind.	Saskatchewan
			Rel: Church of England		
Alexander Moise Tanner		M	inf	Ind.	Saskatchewan
			Rel: Church of England		
Thomas Laurie Tanner		M	inf	Ind.	Saskatchewan
			Rel: Church of England		

1941 Census of Canada

Census Place: City of Saskatoon, Province of Saskatchewan

Detached Family Dwelling

Household		Sex	Age	Or.	Occ.	Rel.	Birth
HEAD	Robert Tanner	M	24	Can.	Draft	Protestant	SK
SIB.	Phidelma Laurie	F	20	Can.	HK	Protestant	SK
	Cecilia Agnes Tanner	F	8	Can.		Protestant	MB

2016 Statistics Canada Mandatory Short Form

Location: City of Saskatoon, Province of Saskatchewan

Single Family Dwelling

Household	Sex	Age	Ethn	Birth	Occupation	Rel.
1) Tanis Jane Campbell, m.	F	27	other	AB	Student	other
2) Neil Allen Cameron, m.	M	28	Can	SK	Education	other
3) Jesse Campbell Cameron	M	1	other	SK		tbd

» Prologue

At the corner, past a bend in the road of close and leaning elms and a little before the electrical station, there is a whitish two-storey house whose view of the river is blocked by a green concrete four-plex. Before the apartment was built, a person standing on the front step could look out past what was a young and spindly tree toward a swath of wild grasses that reached for the river.

The bank, with its tangle of bushes and the papers that blew down and snared in them, was out of sight. Grass met the swirling back of the river and the water's movement was catching. The steps were adrift; the house slid with the current, and only the far bank — white with snow, orange in fall, green in spring — anchored the scene. A come-and-go sandbar gestured forward, tapering to point downstream.

It could not have been this spot, exactly, where Marguerite's father's cart once tipped. The river courses deep, out in front of the sandbar, and Marguerite always told the story as "by the ford." A shallow crossing. So it could not be this exact place on the river where her story belonged — but as the house settled and the current ran past, Phidelma, who'd heard the story enough times, felt water at her feet.

It was a single-axel cart Marguerite's father had. Light enough to be drawn by one horse, and the cart box doubled as a raft once the wheels were eased off and lashed to the side. It was fun to travel with, easier than walking, and he had taken it across the river before. This time, with his wife and children and every possession on board, a strap binding the downstream cartwheel loosened. The wheel caught the current, yanking the cart box sideways as it came away. Icy cold water flooded the plank floor and the children, Marguerite and her two sisters, scrambled for the high, dry end of the raft. They clambered over crates and blanket rolls, and their parents leapt into the water to level the cart box with the weight of their bodies. It steadied, but spun behind the horse, who strained and then, with their father by its head, tracked for the bank. The river pressed over the raft, pushing it lower and lower until the girls' dresses were floating around them. They clung to the cart rail, feet sliding against the submerged boards, and the water reached Marguerite's chin — just as the cart touched bottom. Right close enough to the bank for their mother to catch and carry her in.

Their father let the horse free and it followed the children up the bank and stood close while the eldest made a fire. The river hung on, cold and clammy, until the girls stripped and threw their wet clothes up into the bushes. Then they were suddenly light and naked in a late summer afternoon's warmth. Beside their fire the bushes dripped with saskatoon berries, deep purple and delicious. Their parents mucked in the water, pulling tools and bedrolls and everything else worth saving out. The girls worked wet knots open — it was heavy work to lift and hang the soaked bedding over the berry bushes, but the three girls worked together and their shadows danced across the quilts. They crossed their wrists, linked their thumbs, and made a shadow play of butterflies, maemaengwaen.

"Hey!" Their father called, "Tanfants!"

Their parents had sat, and rested finally, beside the fire with their salvaged belongings. They shaped their girls' hands. She curled their fists, he lifted and bent their fingers, and they ran back to the quilts with a full theatre of birds, and dogs, and rabbits.

They'd needed the baths anyhow, the sisters joked, telling the story. When the water sloshed into the cart box Marguerite had peed herself, then climbed right onto Angélie, warm and dripping. She never lived that one down. Her sisters teased about it enough that Marguerite took to telling that part herself, rather than having it pulled out on her. Even away from her sisters, that confession snuck in.

When her grown daughter, Phidelma, stood looking from the front step of the house she usually wound up smiling. That story set her down safe among her mother and aunties, laughing down along the bank that the view didn't let her see. The past was safe-kept, hidden in plain view. It was only the moving water, the turgid current, that sometimes made Phidelma feel she was sliding away.

The house has stood through many changes. There is the boxy apartment beside it now, and beyond that the grasses are tame and the river parkway well lit, with an asphalt bike and jogging trail. The little elms have grown and their branches arch over the street. Their roots work into clay water pipes, and need annual routing. They buckle the sidewalk, and the cement has heaved, and broken, and been re-poured time and again. The city tends the trees, trimming deadwood, but they are aging and branches have twice fallen on the front eave of the house in storms.

The neighbourhood fights an uphill battle to keep picket fences white. Most of the landlords have switched to posts and chain-link, which sag once they've been kicked in or climbed over. Gangs claim open space. There is a spray-painted tag marking each back lane. There is a tag on the weathered garage behind the house but it is difficult to make out the letters. They are royal blue, three indecipherables crammed together in a stamp that looks vaguely Arabic. A foreign creature drawn to the white board siding — unexpectedly caught, pressed, and pinned.

»One

A character home with great potential, the house had newish shingles and no water damage visible in the upstairs rooms. Its ugliest feature was a back-angled plywood wheelchair ramp that split the backyard, rising above the height of the entryway then descending to the sill on a piece of pressboard steadied by a stairway of stacked breeze blocks. The elderly renter had gone through a series of strokes and this was the property manager's response. No good tenants willing to stay had been noted on the listing. There had been a few other houses, rental units, which Tanis and Neil had shied away from buying partly because the houses weren't right, but also partly because they were uneasy at the idea of evicting the good tenants.

This house's tenants had already been forced out. There was a hairpin turn at the landing on the stairs to the second floor that would've been some feat for a wheelchair, and was also too narrow for a queen-sized bed.

"You can buy split box springs. Even box springs that fold," the realtor, Gary, told Tanis and Neil as they followed him up the stairs. He twisted his body sideways in the tight passage to fully convey the amazement he seemed to think they should feel. "You'd never know the difference once they're flat!"

You would know the difference, though, if you'd been the one to buy the bed and carry it, folded, up the stairs. The idea of your mattress as the open palm of a Venus flytrap would, Tanis imagined, stick with a person.

They followed Gary into the master bedroom, one of his selling features which, at 11x9 feet, took up a full half of the upstairs of the house.

"You're right, it's roomy," Neil said, turning to Tanis.

The room had plenty of space. Even with a heavy colour of green paint pressing in on the walls it was airy compared to the stuffy feeling she'd had on the main floor where the tenant's things had congregated in recent years. The bedroom had an old-fashioned double sash window that looked out at the sky and neighbouring elms. "Does this open?" Neil asked, heaving on it.

The window squealed and jerked open an inch, just enough to pull a draft of fresh air, and the rustling sound of the elm leaves into the room.

"It's a great window, original," Gary enthused. "They get sticky when they're not used, but with a little sanding, or lead graphite . . . " and while he cornered Neil with talk of dry lubricant and air returns, Tanis crossed the hall, creaking over a slat board floor that had been thickened by layers of dark brown paint. The walls in each of the two smaller rooms were a pale greyish taupe she'd learned from Gary to call "the landlord's special" — all the leftover paint mixed in together. The "office" had book-sized shelves built into a recess beside another, narrower sash window whose frame butted the wall. She yanked at the sash but this one had clearly been painted shut.

The "nursery" had a sealed window too, but beside it, instead of shelving, there was a mosaic of gold-flecked mirrored tiles. Tanis examined herself divided into eight small panes. Unless the tiles were distorted, the stress of house shopping seemed to be keeping her slim. She pushed dark bangs back from her face, leaned in to her reflection, and then turned to inspect a vintage brass switch plate that caught her eye. It looked original, dark brass with an egg and dart pattern stamped into the long edges — almost obscured by grey paint. They hadn't even bothered to remove it, and lower on the wall they'd painted right over a socket plate. Tanis bent to scratch at the paint. Maybe underneath it was original too?

"Plenty of plug-ins," Gary said, appearing in the doorway. He kicked out at the wall. "See here, and over there. Two plugs in all the upstairs rooms, so you've got space for computers, chargers, a TV in the bedroom — "

"Why are they upside down?" Tanis asked. The sockets were flipped, with the third prong hole at the top.

Gary shrugged, "Just a style thing. I gather this would be your work space?"

"Yes," Tanis said, liking the idea. Gary talked up the feasibility of building more inset shelves on the outside wall and Tanis waited out his sales pitch. It was true she'd need shelving in her office, but now she wanted to ask Neil about the plugs. And she was wondering if there was a way to buy replica brass plates, or a way to strip them without wrecking the dark patina that made the upstairs switch plates look so cool.

Ten days later Tanis and Neil still didn't know if upside down plugs were a problem. Everyone they'd shown pictures of the house to thought it looked cute, but warned them to make a home inspection a condition of their offer, and it was a condition for the mortgage from the bank. Gary had recommended an inspection agency, but Neil contacted another, recommended by a friend and fellow teacher, Declan, who tipped them to the "fact" that realtors and inspectors worked on kickbacks. Honest

Abe's Home Services sounded reliable, but it seemed unfair to Tanis that the inspection they were paying $400 for would be non-invasive. Even routine medical exams involved poking and prodding. Tanis and Neil weren't even allowed to watch, and had been sent to wait in exile at the Tim Horton's up the street.

"Seriously?" Tanis asked, startling Neil out of an engrossing re-read of the flat screen coffee menu above the till. "We pay four hundred dollars and he's not even going to touch anything?"

"Well," Neil equivocated, "He'll open the panel box but he won't move anything. That's what non-invasive means."

"We should have broken in to pull back some paneling in the basement before he went through."

"Hm . . . and maybe we could have broken a few of the rattlier windows to get them replaced before we buy it."

"Rattling windows?"

Neil nodded. "The upstairs window, it kind of buzzed when you and Gary were going down the stairs. The glass must be loose." He grinned, wrapped his windbreaker around a hand and mimicked punching through glazing. The woman ahead of them in the coffee line shuffled a step away and Neil smiled more mildly, unwrapping his fist.

Tanis frowned. "How loose?"

"The kitchen ones shook too when you were walking around upstairs, it's probably just a matter of caulking. But, you know me, babe . . . " Neil dropped his voice, edged in close, " . . . give me the word."

Tanis shook her head. They'd reached the front of the line and a display of assorted muffins and doughnuts. She pointed. "Crullers!" and Neil stepped up to the counter to order coffee for himself, green tea for her, and crullers for them both.

Tanis grabbed napkins for the doughnuts, and watched Neil as he bantered with the girl behind the counter. Yes, wasn't it a nice day. No, she didn't mind being stuck at work. No, she didn't get to take doughnuts home . . . the girl was about the age his students would be that fall, fifteen or sixteen. She was complaining now about wearing her uniform home, or being hot, something like this, and Neil was smiling, laughing back.

Tanis turned to look for a table out of the sun. Despite the line they'd stood in, the place wasn't too busy, and she found a roomy table to wait at.

"Hot," Neil said, when he came over with their tray.

Tanis frowned. The drinks or the server?

He sat down across the table and passed her the green tea. "Very hot."

"Yes, okay." Neil was the one who was always scalding his tongue and complaining about it. Tanis pried the lid off her tea, blew into the steam, and sat back. "So, basically, once Abe is done we know if we've bought the house?"

Neil nodded. The inspection was their last obstacle, or their last out, depending which way they wavered.

"Our house," Tanis tried it on for size.

"723 Avenue L. Love it or leave it." Neil said.

"723 . . . " She echoed. There could be anything behind those paneled basement walls. Mold, or asbestos. If they were to start a family —

"It will be good to be able to walk to work," Neil said.

Their once-all-terrain Forester stalled in the winter, despite the block heater, which they always plugged in. It would be nice for Neil not to be relying on it to get to the high school. Tanis didn't need it so much. Most days she'd probably work from home, depending on the clients and contracts she was able to pick up. If she had to go out, she could walk too. It wasn't far to get to the library downtown. A bit farther to the University library, but she'd need the exercise. It was too easy to fatten up and hibernate when you worked from home.

"Tanis?" Neil said.

"What?"

"Nervous?"

Tanis smiled and shook her head, *no*. "I found pictures of the street in the city archives, did I tell you?"

"You didn't."

"There are pictures from before the houses were in. Just huge trenches dug for drainage, because the neighbourhood is kind of on a flood plain, you know."

"Yeah. The realtor said we'd need to put in a sump pump. That can be a condition."

Tanis nodded. Neil was the details guy. The floodplain, she'd been going to say, was thick with wolf willows and berry bushes, right up to the end of the newly cleared lots. There'd been some large rocks too, which a series of photos showed being levered onto pallets, getting dragged away, and reinstalled for erosion breaks around the new bridge pilings in the river. But in the pictures Tanis found of Avenue L they'd only just started clearing lots, cutting drainage lines through scrub with a horse-drawn digger. The workhorses were front and centre in the surveyor's shots; standing in harness, tails to the camera, heads together and tilted in so that their ears met. Their breath was coming up, white steam, between them.

They'd been a matched pair, Tanis told Neil, huge, bright white, and apparently oblivious to the men bent over the chains and digger piled behind them.

"Maybe we'll have to frame it," Neil suggested. "Is that the kind of thing you can get prints of?"

"I don't know."

Neil had inhaled his cruller and went for a bite of Tanis' before she snatched it back. He had downed his coffee too and began creasing the rolled lip of the cup, preparing to inch up the rim, when Abe appeared in the glass doors.

He was a farmer, keeping busy with home services in retirement, but he still wore coveralls. His briefcase was an all-weather steel clipboard that had seen better days. It was in his hand now, their inspection report presumably inside.

Tanis gave a small wave. Abe crossed over to their table, drew in a giant breath, and eased himself into the fixed seat beside Neil. It was a tight fit.

"Can I grab you a coffee?" Neil asked.

"Sure," Abe said cheerfully, clapping the clipboard down on the table, "Double-double would be nice." He opened the clipboard and pulled out forms and folders while Neil went back to the coffee counter. The man's hands were enormous and Tanis found herself staring at them. His thumbnails ended in crescents of grime. He smudged the $400 paperwork as he set it out, and thumped his paws down on the table to either side. His hands made the large-sized coffee Neil brought look dainty.

The tagged garage had never been issued a building permit, Abe's inspection revealed, though it had stood there going on fifty years. An automatic door had been installed sometime in the 80s, but the framing had sagged and now the door grated against a support post as it opened. The retractor motor was powered by an extension cord that stretched at garrotting height across the yard, wrapped tightly around what had once been a laundry wheel.

The whole set-up was a giant lightning rod, Abe told them. Not a potential heritage site, as Tanis had secretly hoped, having read of a garage in the city that had turned out to be the oldest building remaining from the original settlers' colony. But, the inspector said, factoring a cost of $800 for demolition into a new single car garage package at $10,000 would no doubt be fine and dandy with their bank. He mimed some kind of turning a wheel motion.

"Crank up the loan?" Neil guessed.

Abe winked. "Then there's the wiring. You'll want to be upgrading that, for sure. A lot of ungrounded sockets upstairs."

Tanis and Neil met eyes. Neil nodded, "We'll ask to split costs for an electrical upgrade with the sellers. Gary said that would be reasonable."

Abe agreed.

"But . . . other than that?" Tanis asked.

Abe sipped his coffee and set the cup back down, "Otherwise it's a go, kids."

» Two

Phidelma and Robert were running back and forth, panting with laughter — they had discovered a new spring to the emptied floor after the men carried the beds and the cabinets out. When Robert jumped on a length of board, bowed against the packed earth, it jumped up, bouncing Phidelma across the room. She lost her step and stumbled onto the quilt Marguerite had laid out to roll their clothes in.

"Robert — " Marguerite snapped. He shrugged, and then grinned to Phidelma, who giggled and ran back over the loose boards.

"Can you be useful?" Marguerite asked, half seriously. They were young, and she couldn't blame them for being excited, but she was nervous about getting the packing done in time.

"How, Mama?" Phidelma asked. How indeed. Marguerite pulled a winter jacket from the pile of clothes the men had emptied out of the cabinet and laid it flat and tidy on the quilt. She pointed to the children, then to the quilt, and turned away to stack the pots and dishes into the crate Thomas had brought. The stove had gone already and Marguerite missed the sound of it, hissing and popping, the kettle rattling to a boil. She'd have loved tea about now.

The boards under where the stove had been were grey, and the rest were brown. Over the years she had scrubbed the floor under there just as often so it must have been the heat, Marguerite supposed. Or ashes worked in. She bent to look and the boards moved.

Robert called, "Look Mama!"

They'd finished laying out the clothes and had started jumping again. The floor moved enough beneath the quilt that it looked like a pile of little children rolling on a bed and in it, Robert's blue wool coat for winter. Meline's school dress, Meline's flannel gown. Robert stamped down again and the ladle was in Marguerite's hand already for packing — it came down on his shoulder fast enough to surprise them both.

He gave a yell and bent down.

"You want to do that twice?" Marguerite asked.

Robert straightened and stared at her. Phidelma had jumped too. Now she was circling the quilt in a crouch, pulling the edges straight as they'd been when she and Robert had begun their helping. Robert reached up to feel his shoulder and rubbed the fingers of his other hand together, as if they'd gone numb. He gave his arm a shake.

"You've helped enough," Marguerite said. "You can keep outside."

The boy turned for the door, Phidelma trailing after, and Marguerite crossed herself. She closed her eyes and listened to the children — Robert gave some kind of a whoop and Phidelma answered, sounding happy enough. They'd be back when they saw Thomas coming for the rest of the things. Marguerite knew her children. She'd had five in the house. The twins died at a little under a year, but it was her oldest girl, Meline, that Marguerite missed. And here they were moving away from the home she'd lived in.

Marguerite had set Meline's clothes aside for Phidelma. Now she bent over the quilt to collect the two dresses and the nightgown. She'd sewed them new, and altered each five times over as her girl had grown. The little one, Phidelma, had always worn Meline's things, hand-me-overs. These would be the next size up, but with a knife in one hand and the hem of the fabric in her teeth, Marguerite tore the clothes to strips.

Phidelma came back to the door and watched. When she understood, she came and knelt beside Marguerite, passing in lengths of cloth when the ends of the braid got short. They worked Meline's dresses into a cord and knotted the ends. Then they folded in the edges of the quilt, and rolled it up, and bound it tight.

Phidelma stepped away along the length of a loose board, heading for the small pile of things she'd kept apart beneath the window. Her book, a ribbon, her hat, and a favourite sweater. It was a bright afternoon outside but light came through the oilcloth like a candle through a fog. Phidelma picked up her book and took it to sit in the brighter light of the doorway.

Marguerite shook her hands at her sides. The braided cord had pulled against her fingers as she cinched it tight and she willed the heat away. "At the house, there'll be glass windows," Marguerite said. "Lots of light for your book."

"I know."

"Papa will take up the floor in here."

Phidelma nodded.

Board by board, Thomas would get what he could for the floor. Then the walls. They'd need all they could get to finish the new house. It was bare bones inside; but it had a title, which meant taxes. Thomas was happy to have Robert and Phidelma starting at the Protestant school his taxes would pay for.

These ones would not go to the nuns, the Catholic sisters who walked Meline home themselves, that first day of school, when she'd been so little and forgotten her way. They'd come around when Meline fell sick, bringing a book of prayers that Marguerite couldn't read. But Meline had got Phidelma started reading, and this girl was a page ahead of Robert, now, even with him four years older.

"You glad to be going to your new house?" Marguerite asked.

Phidelma shrugged.

"And that's going two miles away. You remember about Grandpère, and the river — moving his whole family in a cart?" This time the girl nodded and turned eagerly — when Marguerite told this story she always made it funny, full of jokes to bury the part where she'd felt the river fill her mouth.

"I'm not scared," Phidelma said. She stood up and crossed the room to lean against Marguerite's shoulder, trusting the part where the aunties gathered together on the bank.

» Three

On possession day the realtor arranged to meet Tanis and Neil at the house to transfer papers and keys. They arrived ten minutes early, sat in the Forester out front of the house, and Neil tried to plan the rest of their day. He would go with Declan to the Re-Store to look for some shelving for the front room, Tanis would start the move by ferrying their houseplants over from the apartment. One of them would have to pack the kitchen. "Tanis, after we've got the keys," Neil asked, "what do you want to do about lunch?"

"Let's wait in the yard," Tanis said.

Neil peered out through the windshield at the lilac hedge in front of their house. "Yeah, why not." She hadn't heard a word he'd said, but when they got out of the car she held an open hand out to him on the sidewalk. Neil took her hand, gave it a squeeze, and then let it go so she could lead the way through the opening in the hedge.

"Hello, our house," Tanis said, and walked up to the front window.

Neil stepped up to look in through the quarter pane on the front door. He was tempted to knock, but the house was clearly empty. A big square of leaf-patterned sunshine was the only thing in the front room. Pretty, but a blurred line ran through the middle of the crisp outlines of leaves and Neil looked over to the front window to see if there was a piece of tape or something on it. Tanis tapped at a cloudy line.

"It's cat snot," she said.

"What?"

"Their couch was here, right? This is, like, nose smearing from that cat. He must have looked out at birds or something."

Neil remembered the cat, fat and orange and very old. It had sat like a bag of groceries on the front mat when they'd first toured through. Tanis had bent to pet it, then wiped her fingers off on her jeans.

"How long would that take to build up?" Neil asked, eyeing the streak. Tanis replied with a face. The arc of snot didn't seem like a great indication that the house would be clean.

Neil peered in through the door pane more critically and caught a flash of movement across the house, outside the kitchen window. "Oh, hey, Gary's here. He's must've pulled in the back."

"Yay!" Tanis said, and hurried to the side path, not waiting for Neil this time. But it wasn't Gary. It was a lanky black haired child, maybe six or seven years old, who was spinning around on the grass beside the wheelchair ramp — lost in some private game of dizziness that left the child staggering when Tanis gave a surprised, "Hello."

The black hair swung at chin length and a dark T-shirt and green shorts didn't give gender away. The child squinted at Tanis against the sun.

"My name is Tanis," Tanis said. "We're going to move into this house. Do you live near here?" The child couldn't have come far, because it had bare feet. The black T-shirt had an embossed character that caught the sun, Hello Kitty. A girl, then.

"Yeah," she said, "I live here."

"This is Neil," Tanis said, turning to gesture back. Neil waved from the side of the house and the girl took off in a quick jog, heading for the back alley. She stopped at the end of the yard, turned, and said, "Bye."

They waved.

"Cute," Tanis commented.

"I wonder who the other neighbours are." Neil said, looking over a low wall to the back of the apartment next door. The girl had headed that way. Neil counted eight parking stalls, which would make for quite a few neighbours.

After Gary arrived, recommended Molly Maid's services, and left, Tanis and Neil stood together in their new kitchen and looked out at the yard.

"There's our new friend," Tanis said. The girl had reappeared, and was shuffling through the back alley across the end of their yard with a partially inflated red gym ball. Tanis opened the back door and waved, and this time the girl scowled and gave the dust a kick.

"What was that?" Neil asked, tossing and catching the new house keys.

"I wonder," Tanis said.

"Kids," Neil said, sarcastically.

Tanis smiled. "Whatever."

"Whatever?"

"Whatever, Mr. Cameron. But anyways, Neil — we need to change the afternoon plans. You and Declan can go look for shelving, but good thing we're in first because that tiered shelf you saw online is not going to fit. We'll need to mount shelves up high so the couch can fit under, right?"

"Yeah, you're probably right."

"So you guys go get shelves, and I'll leave the plants at the apartment for now. I'll go to Superstore and buy some bleach and rags. What is that stuff Gary said we could find for the wall? TSP — is it safe?"

It wasn't until that evening, after Tanis had gloved up and scrubbed the cat snot and yellow grease deposits from the main floor walls, and Neil and Declan had bought and piled shelves on the living room floor, that they found the child's den. A worn haven beneath the apex of the wheelchair ramp, whose underside was decorated by rainbows and stars and happy faces and hearts drawn in Sharpie marker. Black on brown pressboard, the sepia sketches were hand-tinted pink, blue, and yellow with sidewalk chalk.

Declan had gone out to examine how the supports were held together, and called Tanis and Neil out to the yard to see.

"Oh, it's so cute!" Tanis gasped.

Neil rested his arm on Tanis' shoulders; they were both exhausted. It'd been a day. Time for a beer, and bed. They'd got the keys at eleven and here it was nearly nine. Declan listed the tools they'd need to get the ramp out. The truck he could borrow, the sledge they'd need to separate the breezeblocks. The little girl, at that moment, seemed to be watching a cartoon with a kung fu soundtrack that drifted over through the open second floor window of the apartment.

"Shouldn't she be asleep?" Tanis asked. "I hate that we have to wreck this, it's obviously her playhouse or fort or something."

Declan grabbed the lower lip of the ramp and gave it a shake, demonstrating how rickety the thing was. If they wanted to be good Samaritans, Neil pointed out, it was probably better all around to clear the backyard and make it safe. But from the way she'd been playing in the yard earlier, it was clear to Tanis the little girl felt at home in their yard. Safe as houses, Tanis thought, looking up at the back of hers.

"It's going to take a bit to get this wonder out, though, Neil," Declan said. "When do you want to get some guys together?"

"Well — " Neil yawned. "As soon as we can, I guess. It would be easier to move our stuff in with this ramp gone. By the weekend even? Tanis?"

She'd sunk back into a crouch at his knees and was twisting her body around the flash of her phone camera. Saving what she could.

BARGAIN
Cent-a-mile
TRIP to WINNIPEG
ROUND TRIP FARE From SASKATOON $9.10
Low fares from other stations
Good going November 8-9
Return until November 12
GOOD IN COACHES ONLY
No Baggage Checked
Apply Ticket Agent
CANADIAN PACIFIC

***

A FEW THINGS YOU SHOULD BUY THIS MONTH
at B.R. Hendry's Post Office Store
HEADQUARTERS FOR FAMOUS NAME BRAND NYLONS
*Phantom * Orient * Kayser * Corticelli*
feel the comfort of beauty and quality . . . all the best brands!
PRICED RIGHT
Save on Valentine's Day
GIFT NYLONS * 51 GAUGE

» Four

The house didn't quite feel ready to Tanis, but they'd be moving on the weekend and Neil was right that it made sense to get the boxes in Thursday afternoon, before their extra hands took off for the lake. Tanis dropped him off at the U-Haul rental and went ahead to finish cleaning the walls. It didn't make sense to clean the floors yet, not when they'd be tromping in and out. But she opened the windows and got a good breeze moving through before the U-Haul arrived in the yard. The truck doors slammed and Tanis heard Declan holler, "This thing ain't gonna unload itself!"

Neil and their other teacher friend, Andrew Puller, were working open a slide lock at the back of the U-Haul. The yelling came from the back of the yard, where Declan was clapping to hustle four teenaged boys out of his minivan. The U-Haul didn't unload itself, but this crew threw themselves into the task so wholeheartedly that at first it seemed to. Tanis scrambled up and down the stairs calling directions, flattening herself against the walls to let the boys past, and most of the furniture ended up in the right rooms. The boxes of carefully padded junk mostly landed in a pyramid, crowding the front room. Unpacking was overwhelming, and as the house cluttered up Tanis escaped to the yard, where the wheelchair ramp now lay on its side, disassembled, like a dog waiting for a scratch. The afternoon sun lit the arch of the ramp, the exposed belly.

Tanis pulled her phone from her back pocket and had another go at preserving the child's artwork. She loved the sun and the stars, out together in the little girl's improbable sky, with two rainbows. And Tanis saw new details, tight against the rough joist, tulips and a parade of small brown animals. Bears or dogs, or maybe caribou? Reindeer. They were reindeer, the lead had Rudolph's red nose. Summer flowers and Santa's helpers. This was a collection of every best thing.

Declan crossed the yard to join her. "It's pretty cute, all right."

Tanis lowered her phone, suspicious. "It is, right?"

"Yes, sure is. So, I think this crew is getting hungry. Do any of those boxes have food?"

"Ah," this was what he was after. Somewhere in the middle of the living room box pile there was definitely food, but Tanis wasn't sure it was food for teenaged boys. And, as Declan wiped his face with the hem of his shirt, Tanis realized that they didn't even have glasses unpacked to offer the kids water. They'd probably been putting their mouths on the kitchen faucet.

"Declan, why don't I make a run to the store? Do they drink pop or Gatorade?"

"Hey, please, either one," Declan said agreeably, then gave a fake-looking pout. "Is it going to be okay with you if we take this work of art apart while they're here to help?"

Tanis pocketed her phone. "You bet."

She cranked the AC and radio in the Forester and drove to both Superstore and the liquor board store — buying beer, chips, and pop — and a giant bag of McIntosh apples in case anyone else felt like they needed something fresh and healthy.

She came back to find Declan leading what appeared to be an actual football team now — the original group with another four boys in their late teens — in a noisy demolition exercise. She dodged through with her bags, set them down in the sink, and divided drinks and snacks between the wash and rinse basins. The rest of the counter was piled high with boxes. Through the kitchen window, Tanis watched Neil fling a fractured pressboard strip into the truck. Declan had lifted breezeblocks, one to a hand, and a couple of boys were attempting to follow suit. Beside the action, a small shadow moved along the stone wall dividing their yard from the apartment's parking lot. The kid. Tanis sighed. Neil was right that scrapbooking the girl's scribbles for her would be a little weird. Tanis would have to make friends, and amends, with their little neighbour another way.

She stowed the beer in the freezer, out of sight of the teenagers, and the men — she figured kids probably shouldn't see their teachers drinking. Then she worked open three boxes and finally found her mixing bowls. She shook the chips into two and carried them outside with the bag of apples and flat of pop. The feast disappeared and, just as quickly, Declan banished his football players with a combination of over-the-top thank yous and threatened consequences if he didn't see them at practice that evening.

Andrew Puller wiped chip crumbs from his hands onto the chest of his shirt, smiled, and mumbled, "Totally welcome, you're totally welcome," when Tanis thanked him for his help. She liked Andrew. He was one of Neil's more grown-up friends. He owned a house and a dog with his girlfriend, Noreen, but had baby blond hair and a tiny frame and would probably be asked for ID in the bar forever. He taught Phys Ed.

"Totally, thanks," Tanis said again, extending the comment to Declan too. The men exchanged glances of the *but of course* variety, then Declan went to his car at the back of the lot, and

Andrew to the U-Haul, which they had to return, and Neil to the Forester, taking the car as well as both sets of house keys.

Tanis realized that she'd turned the lock on the kitchen door before Neil pulled out of the yard, but rather than chase him down the alley, she licked a finger and mined some residual chip crumbs from the bowl in her hand. He wouldn't be long.

She contemplated the bare earth revealed from beneath the ramp, then collected the crushed pop cans and apple cores the teenagers had thrown in the grass around it. The backyard was a mess but the front — was also a mess. When Tanis took the cans around to the blue recycling bin in the front of the apartment she looked back at her new house and saw nothing but hedge. A solid lilac wall, except for the little gap where concrete bricks tiptoed through leading up to the door. The strips of grass and weeds on either side needed mowing, and the lilacs definitely needed trimming, but the upper leaves had been gilded by frost, which had started coming at night already. Tanis raised her phone and took a few quick photos, cropping closer and closer in on the leaves that curled and cupped tiny blue pockets of sky.

As Declan pointed out, the hedge obscured their entryway, contravening home safety police tip number one. But it also provided privacy and a sun-dappled front living room that would otherwise be plainly visible to the street. Tanis didn't mind looking out at the street but she knew how Neil felt about people looking in. The blinds would inevitably be kept drawn. He would insist on it so the flat screen wouldn't be on display. Tanis imagined the argument. Her counter, *TVs are not that expensive anymore*. Theirs was only thirty-two inches. Yet, it was a newer flat screen. And Neil had props, floor speakers, and an amp. Tanis could see Neil frowning, a hand up to draw the blinds on the last precious light of a late December afternoon while she argued against it — and rather than feeling annoyed, the scene sent shivers through her. She could barely believe the feeling of rightness she had about them settling into this house. Into a right cadence of quibbling. It was her house, his house, and their first.

Around back, the U-Haul had left muddy ruts in the grass and the garage sagged, plotting its collapse into the back alley. Tanis stepped on to the springy, rotting back step that had emerged from beneath the wheelchair ramp and examined the security stickers on the back door. They'd been stuck on, year after year, several layers deep. Beside the door was a tall thin cupboard that opened on both sides, or had once, before it had been glued closed by exterior paint. It was a milk cupboard, Abe Klassen had told them, and Tanis imagined the lady of the house putting empty bottles out, carefully rinsed in the evening. And the milkman, early the next morning, opening the outer door to set fresh bottles in. And nary the two would meet. Until the milkman knocked at the door one day. Or the two of them opened their sides of the cupboard unexpectedly at the same time. Tanis smiled.

There was a little tumble latch on the outside of the milk door and she gave it a wiggle. It turned. Lifting her foot up to the frame, Tanis pulled at the tiny knob and managed to yank the outer door open. She lifted a foot through, leaned her weight in, and was rewarded with a cracking sound as the door broke free of its seal.

These old fixtures were security risks, Abe had said — but only for thieves able to squeeze themselves through a portal less than eight inches wide. Tanis had broken the cupboard open, but she couldn't even reach around to the back door lock from the opening. Who could possibly fit in?

The lease had obliged the tenants not to smoke in the house, but they'd obviously taken liberties in the tiny back entry. A sour smell of cigarettes wafted out through milk cupboard and there were black smudges on the bottom ledge of the opening where cigarettes had been butted out. Everything needed to be cleaned, but for now Tanis pulled, pushed, and finally shoulder-checked the double cupboard closed.

Neil and Declan had been talking about options to replace the front and back doors with something wider, steel or fibreglass and energy efficient. Tanis agreed, but when she went back around the house to settle on the front step she relished the feel of the old wooden door against her back. Flakes of peeling paint caught in the weave of her sweater, tugging at her. Claiming and welcoming. The lilac hedge rustled and shushed, and there was a late hum of leafcutter bees. Tanis closed her eyes to listen, and heard the Forester turn into the back lane.

Out of curiosity, she went to meet Neil by passing around the house's north side, where the narrow lot pressed up against the neighbour's fence. This passage had evidently been neglected by the management company and was waist high with fireweed. Tanis charged through and surprised Neil, standing with keys at the door.

"Hey!" she called.

He tilted his head, "Hi."

"We have a very small flower garden down that side," Tanis announced, glorifying the fireweed. She crossed the grass to plant a kiss and welcome Neil home.

» Five

The plaster was drying yet and smelled of the riverbank. Of a warm fall morning, after a cold night's frost had knocked the grass down, flat and soggy. Marguerite had last seen the doorway lead to open framing and now the house had grown flesh. Thomas grasped his wife's hand and tugged her forward by starts.

Robert and Phidelma tiptoed ahead over sanded, blond pine floors. The windows that Thomas had bought from the new school were seconds, cheap, with the lead glass rippled. The sunny rectangles that shone through them on to the new floor were beautiful, marbled, something like light at the bottom of a clear lake.

"Castle for my princess," Thomas said, and in a room ahead Marguerite heard Robert boasting to Phidelma. "See that part, there," the boy said, "that'll be hot water anytime we want it."

"It's a real nice castle," Marguerite said, and she stepped up behind Thomas to run a hand after his over the plaster, still damp, in the front room. She touched the open brick where the chimney ran up through the house like a spine. In the kitchen, Thomas shooed the children and opened the cupboards one at a time for her to see. More space than they had dishes for.

He'd tacked her flowered curtain over a corner shelf, and he'd set one of his glass windows over the washstand so it could light them to the outhouse at the back of the yard. Past the outhouse, willows shook together, lined up green at the edge of the drainage ditch across the back of the lot.

"Is there going to be another house right there?" Marguerite asked.

"Across a lane. We'll have a front and a back way," Thomas said. And he turned Marguerite around by her shoulders to admire her new wood range. "You'll be able to cook for an army," he said.

Marguerite eyed the hot water reservoir, nice, that. And she eyed the fat pipe climbing up to meet the chimney, ready for the wind to gargle down. She reached out and felt a framing post beside the range, then shook her head. "Walls won't even blow," she said.

Thomas grinned. It had been a while since that smile cracked his face. He picked his wife up, light as a feather, and spun her once. Then he kissed her, full on the lips, with the boy right there, crept in behind them. Marguerite gave Robert a smile and pulled him over. They all could hear Phidelma in the front room, stepping around and singing what the girls had been singing lately, "Johnny rapper-tapper, rapper-tapper" — something about the bluebells. That fall she'd go to school and learn the proper words.

That fall they moved in and got cold quick because the walls hadn't been quite finished. There'd been hay that Thomas arranged for insulation, then the early frost left it too wet to use. He moved them in to live just on the main floor, in the two rooms where the walls were in and the plaster set. The glass windows frosted up like oilcloth when winter came, letting in just enough light to keep all those new edges soft — and the house felt close enough to what she'd always called a home to Marguerite.

When the children went upstairs, though, fetching tools Thomas had stored up there, they pulled on their coats and they hurried. It was cold and with the windows boarded there was little light to run their errands by. Their feet sounded strange overhead, to Marguerite, like birds in barn rafters. But they tapped and shuffled, something like if angels were to land on a roof.

» Six

Though their friends had made moving easy Thursday afternoon, the next three days of unpacking dragged on and on. Tanis worked randomly, turning to whatever task was closest at hand — which led to a sprawl of half-emptied boxes and semi-organized piles to trip over. Every time Neil bent to a task Tanis seemed to discover a newly urgent thing she needed help to lift or fix. His back and shoulders weren't used to the work. He threw his hands up Saturday night. "I quit."

"What, Neil?" Tanis called down from upstairs.

"I quit!"

"Quit what? Can you come here for a sec — do you remember how to switch the phone jack? Are we supposed to turn off the power?"

"Yes, and no!" Neil shouted, a foot on the stairs. "Do we have to do this now?"

"Please?"

"I'm quitting tomorrow."

When the landline connected Sunday morning with a month's free unlimited long distance, they called each of their parents in turn. Neil was ready to vent, but Tanis got her mom on the line first and gushed away, mostly about the tiny door in the spare room, three feet high, which led to a triangular tunnel under the eaves. Camping stuff would be shoved in there, Neil had thought. Now Tanis divulged an elaborate plan to carpet the space as some kind of a skull-cracking playroom for the not-yet-conceived child Neil became increasingly aware they had bought the house for.

"It's so nice for kids to have a yard . . . " Tanis said. "Totally, I agree, Mom. A garden is definitely the best way to learn about food. At least, a healthy way — No. Well, of course I would have loved a yard. No." Neil groaned, Tanis' mom loved to lay on guilt. Nostalgic guilt had to be a new category. He tapped Tanis' back in solidarity, and rolled a pillow under his achy shoulder.

It would be good to have a yard, if they had a kid. They already had a kid in the yard, actually. Which was fine with Neil because, even if the street was pretty, it wasn't the kind of neighbourhood a kid would necessarily be safe roaming more widely. Drowning in the river would be the least of her mom's worries.

When Tanis finally escaped her mom, she dialled Neil's parents and read aloud from an ad for pantyhose she'd found on a newspaper stuffed in behind the coal chute door in the basement. Whoopee. Neil had barely been able to breathe down there, the basement reeked. The tenants' cat had used the half-dirt floor as a wide-angle litter box and Neil had literally gagged when he knelt to connect the washer and dryer.

"Give me the phone," he said, waving a hand. Tanis shrugged and passed it over. She stretched out alongside him on the bed, resting her head on his chest for the first part of his more accurate report.

The original hardwood under the industrial carpeting in the living room had been replaced in patches, and splattered liberally around the edges by dark green paint meant for the baseboards. The showerhead was over-screwed and the fixture cracked when Neil tried to adjust it to stop it from dripping. It was so old he was sure there wouldn't be parts. It was cheap plastic anyways, they would have to replace the whole thing. And the fuse box in the half basement was a, " — What, Tanis? Right." She'd interrupted to remind him that the knob and plug set up wasn't technically beyond code.

They had made splitting the cost of electrical upgrades a condition of their offer but hadn't considered the holes they'd need to bash through the walls to run the new cables in. It was going to cost a fortune unless they did it themselves.

"Tanis told us the floor joists are fir, though, Neil?" His mom chirped from her end of the phone. His dad was on the second line, "And it's got the old framing, Neil? Not 2 x 6 but 2 x 8? You'll remember the house on Maple Crescent aunt Muriel had, that house could have stood . . . "

Tanis rolled away and off the bed, escaping Neil's litany of complaints. Now his dad would filibust the conversation to a cheerful end. It wasn't a litany, his complaints were reality. Neil rubbed a hand over his face. "This house — " he interrupted his dad, strategically loud enough for Tanis hear, " — this house has *great* bones."

The sink plug spontaneously jumped free of the plunger when Tanis washed her hands and Neil was on his knees again, before breakfast, setting it back in.

"Thanks, sweetie," Tanis said. She blew on a cup of coffee. "Oh, look, the tiles are lifting there. Behind the toilet. Can we grout them back in, do you think?"

Neil scowled at the tiles, tiny white pentagons. "Probably," he said. "You can probably grout them back in. Do you realize that I have school starting Monday, Tanis? I don't even know where the math banners are. Where's my coffee?"

Tanis blinked, then passed him the mug. "They're in the living room. The chalkboard-looking one, and the quotes, and your toys. By the door."

Every fall since he'd started teaching Neil had hung up a green numerals banner with white-dashed stripes in his classroom, the kind that elementary students use to learn to print numerals. It was supposed to make his high school students feel safe and homey. Last fall Tanis had made him a second banner, with quotes about math as a language, Einstein saying he was no good at it either and that kind of thing. The "toys" were Neil's manipulatives. Beads on wires. Tessellation tiles. Magnetic fraction apples.

"Did you unpack them?" Neil asked.

"Yes, why?"

"They were packed for my classroom. What did you do with the rest of the box?" Tanis met his eyes silently. He had packed a bowl and spoon and travel mug, a set of gym clothes, socks. Everything he usually would have organized in his desk by now. "You have no idea, do you?"

She had no idea, but made them toast while he looked.

» Seven

Monday the radio alarm woke Neil to international news, hostage takings, and suicide bombs, and at home rising unemployment, missing and murdered First Nations women, an inquiry the government wouldn't make — and beside him Tanis began rambling about decorating the bedroom. Their mattress was on the floor for the time being, and a stack of boxes blocked the cold air return. Neil sniffed. The funky smell had lifted the day before, when they'd had the doors and windows open. With the house closed all night the smell from the basement had crept distastefully upstairs.

"Yellow," Tanis was saying, sleepily, "and white on the closet part. It'll have to be glossy I think, to be washable, and then — " The radio cut her off, beeping a panicked line of Morse and a robotic voice read world's fortunes, TSX, NASDAQ.

"What should we have for breakfast?" Tanis asked.

"Shit."

"What?"

Neil stared at the ceiling. There was no reason to take this out on her, but he did not feel ready for the school year, at all. "Coffee's fine, but I'll get it on the way."

Walking up the hill, hefting the box of things that he'd normally have set up in his classroom the week ahead, a slight ache in Neil's right foot got worse and worse so that he arrived at school with a full-fledged limp. Tanis' oak desk had caught its weight against his instep when he'd moved it to another wall for her. The foot had ached a bit Sunday evening, but not badly. Now it throbbed, Neil's calf ached in sympathy, and when 8:40 rang in Math nine he felt wrecked.

Twenty-seven kids filed into the desks. Neil stared at them, then rallied and listed their names off the attendance sheet. So much for first impressions. He looked at the notes he'd jotted down the night before. He'd written a few ideas to introduce himself, and some standard lines about the importance of learning math.

"You might wonder why you need to learn math when there are calculators," Neil said. "Well, I say, tools can only ever be as good as the minds that use them."

A kid at the front raised two fingers. He had a black hoodie up, but had tucked the edges in behind his ears. It looked weird. Neil checked his list. "Heath?"

"Did you rip that off Ayn Rand, Mr. Cameron?"

"Wow. I don't know, did she say that? I haven't actually read her work."

Neil turned to his desk, embarrassed to feel himself actually blushing. What was he, twelve? They were the kids. He was supposed to be making their life hard, not the other way around. He lifted the box of manipulatives, still unpacked, and turned around.

Heath was getting congratulatory knuckles from Jennie behind him — great.

"Okay Math nine," Neil called them to attention. "I'm going to pass some items around, and I'd like you to think about what each of these sets can be used for, what mental tools they represent, because math really is a mental tool. That's what Ayn Rand says, right Heath?"

"Wrong, Mr. Cameron," Heath said, and got a laugh.

A second fist bump with Jennie.

The students left their desks and clustered into noisy groups around the toys. They spun the bead rods across the tables at the back of the room, and pretended to eat the magnetic apples. Someone threw a tessellation tile across the room and Neil moved quickly to keep the rest in the box.

At quarter past nine he got them back in their desks and passed out some math puzzle sheets the last math teacher, the old-liner he'd replaced, had left in the top drawer of the desk. They worked on the puzzles, and on generating equations that could produce 8008, "BOOB", on the ancient AOLSI Corp. calculators stacked on the back table. Throughout this "work" electric chirps and vibration shudders signalled tweets and texts. So much for the school's social media ban.

Some schools that had given up the fight and actually had a BYOD policy for math classrooms, bring-your-own-device. But that would make its own problems here where half the kids probably couldn't afford data plans. For today, Neil left them alone, and when the buzzer sounded the kids seemed pretty content. They didn't run out of the class at any rate. Math ten followed, and Neil walked his second crew through the concept of proofs in a reasonably engaging way. He spent his prep period, and lunch, relocating and downloading a reasonable diagnostic assessment quiz for the Math nine group in the afternoon. That was how Neil had begun his classes last year, and he felt nostalgic about the little window of mental clarity that brought it back to mind. It had been a truly helpful start, to know off the bat where the students were coming from.

"What's this about?" A student challenged, kicking her seat back and waving the stapled sheets at Neil when he handed her a stack of them to pass back down her row.

"It's a diagnostic exercise," Neil repeated, turning to speak not to the one attention-seeker but to the whole class. "It will be good to know where we're beginning, but there are no expectations here. I know you've come from different grade eight classrooms, and we'll have a range of experience. So don't be nervous."

"Well, how come the morning class never had this?"

"They'll have it tomorrow," Neil assured the group. "This may not take the whole period, so if you're done you can take some time to explore the materials on the ledge, over there." That was what they'd heard about, they'd come to play. During lunch hour Neil had set the manipulatives decoratively under the windows. They looked bright and cheerful, unlike his students. One of this group, Neil was sure, would tell him where to go. They didn't, but they ignored his request to turn off their phones, which buzzed through the quiz, and they left him with magnetic apple slices scattered on the windowsill and latched to the radiator casing. His final class of the day was Life Skills and Neil did not feel qualified. Luckily that class had a binder, and he just had to flip to Day One.

"So, how was it? How many kids, what was it like?"

Neil collapsed against Tanis at the door. It was nearly five o'clock, and his foot was so sore that he'd thrown his knee out favouring it on his way down the hill.

"Well?"

"Well, I think maybe we should celebrate tonight."

"Yay! It went good!"

"No," Neil corrected, "it is over. Today is over."

Tanis looked no worse for the day. He peeked around her but didn't really see any changes to the stacks and piles. "Tomorrow," she said, pulling him into a cuddle, "is a long time away. We can go out to celebrate!"

"Or order in while I ice my foot?"

"Really? That bad — we can order in."

The Secret
by Jody Bear

The ground is damp. The hole less than two feet deep. Water will soak quickly through the cloth, bleed the ink which has held her words so long. In a day it will soak through, in ten years it will be gone. This is what she is imagining, anyways. That a secret cannot hide in the ground forever. That is not the point this time. She brushes dirt off from her hands then moves into the light to wipe her fingers on a clump of grass. It has grown up from a mound of dirt in the broken yard and, the way it is getting blown around, it looks like it is reaching around for her hand. Reaching up for her. Her hands burn cold. She draws her fingers through the grass and even though there is no one to hear her the ground feels alive and so she whispers, 'And this time the pages are seeds.'

[3/5 Very good descriptions, Jody. Watch for sentence fragments. "Which" requires comma use. Dialogue should be set apart with "double quotation marks". The idea of "suspense" comes through well, who will dig this "secret" up?]

» Eight

The Math nines arrived expectantly Tuesday morning. They'd heard about the diagnostic quiz from the afternoon class and took the papers up without a fuss. Most of them spent the full period working at it. A few added doodles in the margins, and after a reminder of the device ban came over the PA system Neil heard only two vibration mode shudders.

The Math tens came in with attitude, but it was mostly aimed at each other. The girls slouched forward against their desks so that the rather loose tunic tops they wore gaped open. The boys sat back, hands hidden beneath their desks, where Neil couldn't see their phones. He followed the advice on the superintendent's morning blog. The same advice had reached all the teachers, all the schools, and the students would soon be sick of answering, but Neil spread his arms welcomingly. "So, what did everybody do for their summer vacation?"

His interest was supposed to show how much he cared. They looked skeptical. Neil sent the two quietest girls, Jody and Alexa, out of the room to collect atlases from the library. They would be learning about perimeters and irregular volume calculations this year, so to get their feet wet Neil had each student measure their summer trips and calculate their total distance travelled, with the added element of difficulty converting kilometres to metres, centimetres, miles and inches.

It was amazing to Neil that you could make it to your second decade of life without understanding how a scale bar worked — but atlases went over much better than the apples. Maybe it was something about the paper, the true tactile realm of math for institutionalized high schoolers. Rulers, pencils, and little "x"s for converting units. A lot of the kids caged their answers in little square boxes, something they'd learned in grade nine, maybe. From the old-school teacher. Neil didn't mind. They worked on their worksheets and talked mostly on topic. Hands went up, almost politely, "Hey, Mr. Cameron . . . ," how many weekends were there this summer? I'm trying to see how many times I probably went to the lake. Which highway would Kolton have been on, going from Saskatoon to Winnipeg? Yellowhead or Trans-Canada?

Most finished with a bit of time to spare and Neil let those with devices go online to compare the distances they'd travelled with animal migration routes. Only one student had travelled father than a monarch butterfly, a girl who'd spent her summer with her dad on the pow-wow circuit. West to BC, east to Ontario, and south as far as New Mexico.

"That's a heck of a lot father than I got this summer," Neil said. "Wow." He looked up at the clock and caught the principal's bald head popping in at the doorway. Bornstein gave a thumbs up, and as the buzzer went Neil clapped his hands together and shouted, "Time!"

"Hey," he said, as they kids filed out, "you guys have a good afternoon."

"You too, Mr. Cameron."

Neil did like teaching, and it sure felt better when he was at least half prepared. In his third period prep he reviewed Monday's Math nine diagnostics and liked what he saw. His Math tens had had a good time with today's class, and tomorrow he could use the momentum to lead them into complex perimeters. He surveyed his room. Thirty desks in five rows of six, textbooks and calculators stacked on the back tables under the corkboard across the room. The manipulatives were tidy again under the windows. Once the banners were up behind his desk, above the whiteboard, the class would be perfect.

A little rap came at the door. Then a louder knock. Neil pushed his chair back and tested his foot. Not too bad, but he hopped to the door.

"Hi, girls." Two of his Life Skills students stood in the hall, one with a mug. "What can I do for you?"

"We saw you were having trouble getting around, Mr. Cameron," Melissa Arthur said. "We brought you a coffee." She held up a mug that Neil recognized from the staff room drain tray. Taelur Anderson, a step behind, reached past Melissa and offered Neil a creamer and a crumpled package of Sweet 'N Low.

"Wow. Thanks, girls." Neil accepted the coffee, creamer, and fake sugar, and limped affectedly back to his desk. The girls giggled. "Thank you," he said. "D'you mind closing the door?"

Neil set the coffee on his desk leaned his weight into his sore foot. It still hurt, but nothing like the day before. How had they known he liked one cream, one sugar?

"Don't let them like you too much," Karen Smith, the Language Arts teacher, cautioned at lunch, when Neil mentioned his free coffee. She'd sat down between him and Andrew Puller on the sectional couch. A trio of younger teachers. The experienced ones filled the seats at the rectangular table, or ate in their classrooms, Neil supposed. There were twenty-four teachers and twelve chairs.

"What do you mean, like me too much?"

"Just, like you. Whatever," Karen said.

"They'll expect favours, or they'll start 'disclosing' shit," Andrew Puller clarified, and Karen wrinkled her nose. Disclosure sounded unappealing, but was probably a more of a problem for Phys Ed and Language Arts instructors. Knowing where his Math ten students had spent their summers had made Neil more curious to get to know them and it seemed to build classroom rapport. He'd never known, or understood exactly, what a pow-wow singer did or how far a butterfly could travel. It felt cheesy, though, to try to explain that to Karen and Puller.

"I kind of have to get to know the Life Skills 20 class, don't I?" Neil said. "To supervise their work placements? The binder says that I need to establish trust and open communication."

"That class bites," Karen said, through a bite of sandwich. "They'll get away with everything on those placements, trust me." The chunk of bread disappeared into her mouth and Neil stared. It was always new teachers that got stuck with Life Skills, but Karen was only on her second year in the school. She'd ditched it after one go, then.

"Well, it seems okay, so far. Day two," Neil said. "The course binder makes it pretty straightforward. When they're back from their work placements it looks like it's pretty much online unit after online quiz, repeat."

"It's too easy, that's part of the problem," Karen said. "They cheat."

"Yeah, I've certainly never had a student cheat in a math class," Neil countered.

Andrew snorted.

Karen took a swig from her water bottle. "You'll see."

She patted the coffee table meaningfully as she rose to leave and Neil nodded, "I guess so, eh?" He peeled the lid off the giant blue Tupperware Tanis had shoved in his bag and examined the contents. Chicken breast strips, niblet corn, cherry tomatoes, three kinds of lettuce, and bacon.

"Wow," Andrew said. "You pack that kind of lunch everyday?"

"No, I don't," Neil answered. He hadn't known that Tanis had even bought stuff for a salad. Groceries must have been part of what she'd done yesterday. He lifted his fork in one hand, and his phone in the other and sent a text: *Thnx for lunch T, you the best!*

That afternoon Neil paired the Life Skills students off for the two-month work placements that made up the experiential portion of the course. He paired Melissa Arthur to Jody Bear, rather than to Taelur Anderson as they'd requested.

"But thank you for the coffee, girls," he said, guiding Taelur over to her partner, Stephanie Mithra. That, Neil thought, would do a good job of keeping them from liking him too much, or at all.

»Nine

The two children were upstairs, clomping their heels, running and sliding. Marguerite pictured Robert and Phidelma grabbing one another's arms and waists, and spinning on the planks Thomas had laid down so smooth. She had half a mind to do what he'd done the night before and hit the underside of the upstairs floor with the broom handle. Except that'd left a mark on the boards. Like someone pushed a thumbprint right into the fresh lines of the ceiling. Nothing you'd see once it was finished, Thomas said. A dare for them to mark it up until the spring got warm enough for plaster to dry and set. Robert at least seemed to be taking it that way.

It used to be you'd only hear a person tromping over your grave if you were in it — the thought gave Marguerite a grim little smile and she put her fork down on a dollop of lard. She pressed the tines in, turned them, and pressed again, working the fat into a bowl of flour. Overhead the children's noises switched from happy and wild to complaining. Marguerite lifted her fork, pinched it clean between her palm and thumb, and set it down to roll up her sleeves. Quiet set in above. Let 'em be, she'd said often enough, Kiiyaam. *Thomas was set to train Robert like a dog. Broke to work and listen.*

Marguerite was used to children being out of sight, out of doors, not to this getting spied on from up above — and from the bend of the stairs where Phidelma had taken to sitting with her school readers so that you never knew what she'd heard or when she'd come or truly gone.

Marguerite pulled the dough together, then pressed it out flat to cut apart. Six good-sized pieces — and this was another thing, the range cooked more food than they could eat before it went hard as a rock. Make less, Thomas said, but it took the same wood to heat, didn't it?

Marguerite closed the oven with a rag and tucked the tins of soda and flour back on the corner shelf. She was glad that he'd moved it with them. The flowered curtain hung across it was something Meline loved, way back in their first place. He'd called that house a cottage — they'd made two rooms out of one by hanging up the quilt her sisters-in-law gave them for a wedding present. It was heavy and grey, made for warmth. What Meline reached for as a baby was the yellow flowers on the little curtain Thomas nailed up to hide the dishes their first winter married.

With Thomas freighting and the baby so small it hadn't be easy to travel or go visiting. Marguerite had sung up company, her sisters who were too far to come even when she missed them so much. She rocked and bounced and sang their songs to her tiny daughter and her sisters shone right out of Meline when she learned to talk and smile, her little bird.

Marguerite had held Meline up to feel the flowers on the cloth that she wanted so much. And she had held her at the oilcloth window to feel the wind rattling and the snow brushing by. That first little house, and the second, then the third — every one of them shifted when the weather froze or thawed. They'd wake up to find the oilcloth loose where she'd tacked it up tight, an old draft sealed and a new crack opened. Tear one of those little houses down — with moss in the roof, and bark chinking, and the spring pollen weeping in — it'd be so full of life it would change right back into the dirt it came from. Just give up its ghost and grow new.

Marguerite was waiting on the biscuits, caught up in remembering, when Phidelma tromped down the stairs. A colt on a plank barn floor was what Marguerite heard coming at her. The girl hit the bottom of the stairs and ran headlong, ploughing into her mother's skirt and rocking her backwards.

How many times, Marguerite wondered, rubbing her floury fingers against each other behind Phidelma's head, how many times had she told Meline that she wasn't a train? A brick wall. An ox. This child was gripping Marguerite's knees, hiding her face in Marguerite's thighs. Little bits of dough fell into the braided hair. Marguerite put her hands on the child's shoulders and pushed her back.

"Mama," Phidelma asked, "is there biscuits yet?"

» Ten

Jody Bear was meant to be drafting a letter to the phone company for their support of the school cafeteria's healthy snack venture, but instead had followed two other girls, Melissa and Taelur, onto the roof of the school. Taylor spelled wrong. This is how Jody thought of Taelur, as the girl whose name is spelled wrong. From the roof the girls could see boys on the grass below, jumping and hacking. Hacky-sacking. Hooting. They were unaware of the girls, and if their positions were reversed, the boys would be calling down. Mooing and barking, throwing butts. Or maybe these white girls she'd followed were above that kind of treatment — Jody wasn't sure. The girls did not call to the boys. They sheltered themselves from view and a strong wind by huddling down beside a ventilation box on the gravel over the gym.

Even with shelter the second week of September was cold and they crouched down, pulling the fronts of their bunnyhugs over their knees. There was a crawlspace beneath them, Jody knew. Right under the roof — and kids or whoever, teachers maybe, crawled in there to release balloons and confetti snow during school dances. There were rumours about a musty pile of band uniforms stored in there, piled up like a mattress. Initiations. Lost virginities. Jody shook her head — *no thanks* — to the cigarette that Melissa held out toward her. The tip of it glowed, drawn by air from the vent beside them. Taelur took the cigarette to set it daintily against her lips, sipping smoke. Jody watched the steady embered end, the line of smoke that rose up uninterrupted, and she studied Taelur's face.

When Neil returned to his classroom, having toured the library, commons, and restrooms to check on his Life Skills students in their independent work projects, cigarette smoke was wafting in through an open window. The same stink that had lingered on his fleece jacket, ever since he'd left it hooked overnight on the handle of the milk door in the back entryway at home.

Neil's classroom was on the second floor, but he heard a short, high cough outside the window. Voices rose more distantly from the lawn below; "Piss off ya mudda-f---er, yeah!" Boys laughing. The roof beyond his open window had gone quiet but Neil stood, inhaling nicotine, until he heard a girl's giggle. Then he closed it quickly, slapping his palm against the glass for good measure, intending her to hear.

Returning to his desk, Neil sent an email to Melissa and Jody, asking for the letter that they were meant to have placed in his empty mailbox. He copied the email to their parents, thinking *the roof is flat as a pan, they aren't about to fall off it.*

While Jody sat trapped on the roof with Melissa and Taelur, Neil pulled a blank page from his recycling stack and mind-mapped his Math ten lesson plan. He had taught the course only once before, during his internship, and this fall had vowed to review equations and proofs days and weeks before, rather than the mornings of the lessons, this time around. To make math look easy, it had to *be* easy.

From his desk, Neil could see the shadows of crouched bodies cast on the gravel roof. The sun was low, and the shadows stretched. He finished outlining two week's Math ten lessons. The window latch had clicked, he was sure. Beneath Neil's fingers he had felt the mechanism catch and lock into place. But when he finished, and rose to turn off his classroom lights, the shadows outside were gone.

›› Eleven

With Neil busy in his second week at school, Tanis was supposed to be unpacking. But she'd slipped with a box cutter and opened her thumb in a fairly serious way, which kept her from working on setting up the kitchen. Instead, she held paint cards up to the walls with a bandaged hand, and in the afternoons made shopping trips for things that she suspected were lost in the depths of the pyramid of boxes in the living room. Thursday morning she took a few hours to work, trying to keep pace with a research and report writing contract.

Neil hadn't found time to assemble her office chair, so Tanis set up shop in the bedroom, placing her laptop on a box in the middle of the mattress. She managed to get a bit done, finger pecking around the gauze on her thumb, but when the afternoon sun hit the window, the bed became a puddle of warmth and she melted. Leaning back into the pillows Tanis unwound the bandage and rotated her hand in the sunlight. The cut looked gory but was mostly still numb. The feeling would come back quicker if she massaged it, she'd read that somewhere, but she wasn't sure she wanted to deal with feeling it, and wrapped it back up instead.

A nap would be unfair, when Neil was away working for the world's youth, so Tanis fought temptation, rose foggily, and tried to whip herself awake in housecleaning mode. Down in the basement, emptying boxes of odour-busting baking soda over bricks and dirt floor alike, Tanis got chilled. She carried their dried laundry resignedly back up to the bedroom. To bask.

She moved her makeshift desk off the bed and dumped the laundry out in the beam of sunshine to sort and fold. She began with one of Neil's T-shirts, lifting it and shaking the creases out, before pinning it with her chin to smooth the fabric against her chest. Halves lengthwise, sleeves folded back, and then three folds vertical. Retail quality. Tanis looked around and set the folded T-shirt on the top of a closed box under the window. She bent to grab a second shirt, then looked back to the window.

There were two kids sitting on the sidewalk across the street. The little girl from next door didn't usually venture so close to the road, but Tanis watched an extra minute to be sure neither of these kids was her. They weren't sitting properly on the sidewalk, but crouched at the edge of the curb, with oversized bunnyhugs pulled up over their heads and down over drawn up knees. They had pulled their arms inside too, and the empty sleeves blew back behind them, shadows ribboning the pavement in a strange way. Round, headless, and limbless, the kids seemed intent on something at the edge of the road. Tanis was drawn to the stillness of their bodies and the contrast of their shadows on the bleached sidewalk and was reaching for her phone to take a picture when a hood blew back, releasing a tangle of blonde and pink hair.

The girl laughed, high and loud enough for Tanis to hear it. The other kid's sleeves reanimated, dainty fingers spread out from the cuffs and reached up to push back her hood. A black ponytail swung forward, which the girl caught and smoothed against her neck. She was smiling. They seemed pleased, excited even. Gangly legs stretched down from the front of their hoodies and out into the road and Tanis saw that they were older than she'd guessed. Not children but teenagers. She drew back from the window, embarrassed to be seen standing there, still in pyjamas and folding clothes in the middle of a weekday afternoon. She waited and then, curious in spite of herself, peered out and saw the two walking off, strides matched against the sidewalk.

They were heading south, toward the river parkway, and they disappeared under the elms just as an orange school bus pulled up to stop at the corner. 4 p.m. already, it was hard to believe. The street's five children spilled out onto the sidewalk, the school bus pulled ahead, and the kids scattered, noisy as they called their goodbyes, like a flock of birds startled off the highway. The year's trendy fluorescent schoolbags bounced on their backs as they ran to their doors.

Tanis set her forearm against the sash and watched the apartment block girl run up the sidewalk and turn in at the path next door. On the cement step of the apartment, the child turned to face the wind, shaking her hair back from her face. She squinted up at Tanis' window and waved. Surprised, Tanis waved back, and the little girl heaved open the apartment door.

The street was empty for a minute, quiet, and Tanis set her forehead against the glass. The sun beamed in but the glass itself was cool. She rested against it, opening her eyes just in time to see the old man with the crazy yellow beard come past on his bicycle, large black garbage bags dangling, balanced weights, from either handlebar. He was familiar now, after a week in the hood. She and Neil had seen him rummaging through the bins in the back alley, looking for bottles they assumed.

The school children had run against the wind, but the old man caught it in his sails and coasted double speed past the house — a haven that suddenly felt stale, when Tanis could be out with the brush of wind on her cheeks, too.

Neil would be home soon, and his classes had finally started to take on their own pace. Or so he had texted at lunch: *Classes are rollin', rollin', rollin' xox*

His students were paying attention and almost ready to come down from summer, though Tanis guessed they would be working themselves up for the weekend ahead, which was supposed to be the last gasp of warm weather. Depending on how his afternoon had gone, Neil might be convinced to come for a walk by the river.

Tanis folded the laundry more quickly, then turned her focus to the kitchen and sorted the mugs and glasses so that at least they didn't have to wash their cups every time they wanted another drink. "Coffee and juice make a terrible mix," Neil had declared, somewhat accusatorily, that morning.

Tanis met him at the door, shoes in hand. "It's gorgeous, the trails will be dry. Let's go!"

The muddy trails that they had mucked their way through on the weekend would have cured in this week's warmer weather. They'd be hard-packed now, scattered by the leaves that had begun dropping — falling to crunch under the twinned tread of the teenaged girls that Tanis had envied earlier. The girls would be weaving and laughing along the river bank. She pictured them walking, still side by side, except where the trail was really narrow. Because that is how you walk when you're young, and in tune.

"Babe," Neil said, "Check this out." He held up a red box, *Piss-off Pet Stain Remover*. He'd found it in a strangely crowded hardware store up by the grocery.

Tanis examined the box. Neil had purchased a toxic, carcinogenic, liquefying powder that might just tackle the basement. Tanis' baking soda campaign had certainly not worked yet.

"Fingers crossed," Neil said, and Tanis passed the box back and held her fingers up, tightly crossed.

She'd never heard of this product, and didn't quite share Neil's sudden conviction that it would work. But she set the river and walk aside without a second thought. This was Neil's first permanent teaching contract and he had been planning and worrying all through the distraction of the move. He was relaxed now, and jingling a new set of house keys, which he'd also had cut at the hardware store. A set to hide in the garage, as they'd each been locked out once already.

"I'll hide them well," Tanis promised as she tucked them in the back pocket of her jeans.

Neil bounded down the basement stairs with his magical powder. Tanis followed him as far as the kitchen, then threw her runners down on the pile of flattened boxes in the back entryway. The stack of those was growing, it really was. Progress, all around.

» Twelve

Friday morning Tanis woke before the alarm and tiptoed quietly down the stairs. The air on the stairwell was fresh — it smelled like toothpaste in the kitchen, a mint-and-pine smell. Tanis opened the basement door to poke her nose in. The cat smell was thicker, but not overly gross. When the alarm brought Neil downstairs front and back doors were open and the house smelled like coffee and pancakes.

"Do you have time for breakfast today?" Tanis stood by the stove with a bowl of batter, the first few pancakes steaming on the pan.

Neil grabbed his wife in a morning squeeze. "I don't have long to eat, but yum! Hey, what's this?" She'd set plates on the table and a legal pad between them. Neil picked it up and read: *1) Clear living room to make one relaxing space.* They hadn't wanted cat pee permeating their things so everything meant for the basement was still clogging up the living room. Now Tanis had written *2) Buy Rubbermaid totes for under stair storage.*

"Good, and good." Neil commented. *3) Organizing options for the closet.* The only closet in the whole house was in the hall upstairs. It made an inconvenient L-shaped dent into their bedroom and Declan had suggested knocking it out and buying a set of wardrobes. "What's *organizing options*?" Neil asked.

"We need that closet for storage space, for more than clothes. I thought maybe we could we get one of those wire systems, with hanging shelves? They look easy to put up."

"They're sized for modern closets, though," Neil said.

"Can we measure it then — so I can research options?" Tanis waved her ladle over the bowl of batter. Breakfast would be a minute.

"Now?"

She doled new rounds of batter onto the frying pan and wiped her hands on the dishtowel. "Come upstairs?"

For the time being, Tanis had been stacking things on the closet floor. Yoga mats and winter boots topped the mound, incongruously squashed against wallpaper patterned by tiny yellow bears carrying nosegays and fishing rods. "I love this wallpaper," Tanis said. "Some lucky kid — this must have been expensive, back in the day."

"Why only the hall closet?" Neil asked, that being the extent of the wallpaper. "Did they lock a kid up and spoil it in there or what?"

"No . . . " The bears were a vestige, a little leftover in the closet after the nursery had been redone. First for an older child, and then for a refined teenager. "They wouldn't have — "

"It's something like four feet by thirty-six inches," Neil interrupted. "Smell that?"

"Smell what?"

"Burning pancakes."

The morning was as crisp and fresh as the afternoon the day before, and after breakfast they poured the coffee into travel mugs and Tanis walked Neil part of the way up the hill. He kissed her goodbye a few blocks short of the school, and she walked four blocks west, then south, to extend her walk and loop back to the house by the river parkway.

Down along the river the leaves had just begun turning, handfuls in each tree, and Tanis had her mind on the upstairs rooms. She had been favouring a lighter yellow, *Acacia*, but maybe something brighter — an ochre, or gold. With a russet highlight wall, *Bold Sienna. Carmine.* Flipping through the paint cards, Tanis had fallen in love with half of the names. *Kaydance* was the name of their friendly little neighbour. She'd introduced herself to Neil over the stone wall. Her mother, who Tanis had now twice seen out waiting with Kaydance for the school bus, looked about their age, maybe even thirty, it was hard to tell. She dressed kind of young, but maybe the yoga pants were just pyjamas. The school bus came early. Tanis wondered how to go about introducing herself — just knock?

»Thirteen

Friday night, while Neil and Declan and Andrew, now dubbed "the Puller", began crashing holes in the walls to prep for the electrician coming to update the wiring, Tanis knelt before her new cupboards. They'd mostly been emptied, but there were leftovers in the back recesses that she stacked on the kitchen table. There was also an ancient cast iron pan stuck on one shelf, glued in place by a circle of rust that Tanis broke only by hammering a putty knife between the two surfaces. She banged, and echoing crashes upstairs sent tremors through the kitchen floor and into her shins. The kitchen felt like a train car rumbling, and Tanis bounced sideways when the pan broke free. It pulled up a wide strip of paint on one side and left, on the other, a ridged crescent of rust that needed sanding down.

The gauze around Tanis' thumb stained orange and black and she unwound it gingerly, but the cut hadn't opened. A reddish purple line ran up the side of her thumb pad and over the tip, still gross but mostly painless. The rest of her thumb felt naked though, out from the bandage, and she pulled on dishwashing gloves to wipe, dry, and finally prime the lower cupboard shelves. The house continued to shake as the men stomped around the second floor so Tanis propped the cupboard doors open with paint rags wedged around the hinges, to keep air moving over the shelves.

While the primer dried, Tanis evaluated the questionably antique dishes she'd found — 50s ugliness mostly, tiny dishes with drippy glaze and, on their undersides, an imprint from JAPAN. Post-war and full of chips. Not treasures. She bagged them with the gloves, paintbrushes, and the rusted iron pan and took them outside with the bucket she'd used for the primer.

The sun was newly down and the evening still warm, but Tanis' fingers and cheeks prickled cold as she rinsed the bucket in the stream of the garden hose. Milky-white water ran off the grass into the gravel alley, and snaked over to the apartment's parking lot to smear Kaydance's chalk art. Upslope, under the apartment's back door light, three stick-legged ponies and a yellow smiley-face sun survived. Downslope a dark meadow of either kites or diamonds swirled away. By the garage, where Tanis carried her bag of kitchen discards, the gravel was marked by lines of chalk and white acrylic primer. It looked like something was leaching up from the puddle at side of the alley, which, rainbowed by oil, was suspect enough.

Tanis didn't notice, until she reached for the handle and missed, that the door to the garage stood open about a foot. She peeked inside. It was very dark. Had Neil forgotten to latch it? Had he stored anything important there? He'd been talking about winter tires and rims and — Tanis startled at a sound from inside. A kind of a brushing sound against the ground, like someone trying to slide something heavy.

"Neil?" she ventured, "Hello?"

There was no answer.

"Kaydance?"

Tanis stood at the door, the weight of the old iron pan pulling heavily on her shoulder. She shifted, it clanked against the ugly mugs, and she heard the shushing sound again. Or did she? Her ears had been full of crashing and banging. Maybe it was quiet that had her unsettled now. "Hello?" she tried again. She wanted to throw her garbage into the dark and pull the door shut, but if someone was hiding in there she'd be locking them in. But how likely was it that Kaydance would play in the dark, or that her mother would let her? "Boy, oh boy," Tanis called in a sing-song voice, "This is one heavy garbage bag."

Shh-crick, the dark garage replied.

Reaching blind through the doorway Tanis flipped the lid of the garbage bin open. "In you go, and that's that!" And after the smash of dishes in the depths of the bin, the garage seemed as still as the yard. "I'm going in," Tanis said apologetically. It was her and Neil's house now, but it was and wasn't their garage. The siding had been claimed, in practiced strokes of blue spray paint, and with the back alley so close to the garage door it was practically public property.

Tanis stepped back to the grass, and then spun around as the kitchen door banged open. "Yo!" Declan called, "Come up and see!"

"See what?"

He opened his hands to present, with a flourish, the door. "Okay," Tanis laughed, stepping into the shadow he cast over the empty yard. "You know, I thought I — "

"Super cool house you guys got," Declan said.

"Oh yeah, thanks — "

"Gotta see it upstairs, come up."

"Okay." It was a relief to be back inside, and also nice to be included in the manboy-action that had taken over, finally. There were holes in the walls of every room now and the socket boxes had been pulled out and lay among their wiry entrails in drifts of powdered plaster. "It looks like things are — coming along?" Tanis ventured.

"Oh yeah, really good, come see what we're doing upstairs."

"Okay."

They climbed the stairs through an eerie blue light cast by the LED lanterns Neil had bought from the hardware store to fill in before their new fixtures were installed. They'd punched a hole through the upstairs hall ceiling where Neil planned to set a frosted sconce, and the plaster dust footprints that tracked in and out of the bedrooms and office seemed like a sign of progress in those rooms too. But the footprints were weaving in and out of everything she'd piled in the hall closet, the only closet. Everything she had tucked out of the way been pulled out. Tanis saw it heaped in the shadowy third room, the nursery. "What, um, did you guys — ?"

Declan put a hand on the small of Tanis' back and guided her out of the doorway, and she was suddenly aware that Neil and the Puller weren't there. Declan was tight enough behind her that he pressed into her when she stepped backwards.

"Want to see what we're doing in the closet?"

"Where's Neil?" Tanis asked.

"Look in the closet," Declan said, and gave a little smile. He was really big, Tanis realized. Not just tall and broad but heavyset.

She stepped away from him, across the width of the closet, and from that distance peered into the dark rectangular space papered with teddy bears. They'd pulled her brand new metal shelves down. "What is this?"

Declan loomed towards her, stomped a workboot and sent plaster dust swirling up. *Bang! Bang!*

"*Arrrrrgh!*" a muffled groan came through the closet wall and as Tanis watched, transfixed, the wall of the closet pulsed and heaved. Then the wallpaper tore, separating along the join of the right side and back wall. *"Help!"* Neil shouted. *"It ate me! The house ate me!"*

The closet screeched, *"Arrrgh! Rawr!"* and Puller's hands appeared, clawing zombie-style through a widening, wedge-shaped opening. The closet wall rocked, and chirped, and finally opened with a rusty squeal.

Declan fell back against the hallway wall, snorting and giggling as Neil and Puller shoved one another out through the wall, coughing and covered in bits of insulation foam. Tanis was the audience for whatever this was. But what was it? She squeaked out a laugh, and then slipped through the men to the gaping hole in the closet. "What is this?"

She felt hands on her hips, pulling her back and blushed, half expecting Declan before the familiar rub of Neil's stubble drew in against her neck. "We've got an attic, babe." He rocked and she leaned back into him, confused.

"Sorry," Neil whispered, "Did we scare you? It was supposed to be funny."

"Wow," Tanis said finally. "How did we not know about — whatever this is?" A set of steep iron stairs angled up into blackness, and Tanis imagined Neil and Puller packed tight in the narrow space between the foot of the stairs and where the closed wall had been. Waiting how long for her to find them? Just as long as it had taken Declan to lure her upstairs. "How did you get in there?" she asked, turning in Neil's arms.

"There's another hatch in the bedroom, the normal ceiling kind of attic access. I'm guessing it was put in to blow in this insulation." Neil brushed bits of grey-blue foam from the front of his shirt. And more from Tanis' shoulder.

"You guys still have Gatorade?" Puller asked. Tanis said they did, and he and Declan tromped down the stairs, making new space in the hall. She examined the unbroken wall stretching from the stairs to the bedroom door and looked back to the closet. "Why would they close those stairs off?"

"Drafts, maybe?" Neil said. The attic access did seem to be creating one. There was a cement smell, like a car parkade, and the flagged ends of the ripped wallpaper were fluttering.

"Is it a real attic?" Tanis asked, and reached up to pull another chunk of foam from Neil's hair.

"There's a wall, actually, at the midline of the roof, with a sliding door." Neil mimed opening a panel. "So the insulation doesn't go all the way through. Over these rooms and most of the hall, there's a proper floor up there. Same as this." Neil tapped the painted hallway with his foot. His sneaker was coated in powdery grey something. Tanis stepped into the closet, but when she put a hand on the ladder Neil tugged her back by the waistband of her jeans. "This crap on my shoes," he said, "it's something like fifty years of dead bugs. Seriously, yes. Moths and flies. We need a Shop-Vac."

"I'm not a princess," Tanis protested. "I don't need to wait for a Shop-Vac."

Neil kept her, hugged in tight. "There's not much to see, and it will be better in the morning." He kissed the back of her neck.

"Is there a window?"

"So curious. Yes, there's some venting — so there should be some light. Or we can use one of the bigger lanterns. But I'm wondering about the air quality now. All this dust — you must have heard us coughing up there?"

"Actually, Neil, I was in the yard and — "

"Yo!" Declan's voice came from downstairs. "We hungry, N-man!"

"N-man?" Tanis stifled a laugh that became a cough that took on a life of its own. She hacked into Neil's shoulder, shaking her head at "N-man". Guys bashing holes together. "Do you want me to cook you something?" she asked.

"Pizza, man," Neil said, mimicking Declan. He shouted down the stairs, "Yo, yo for the dough!"

They left Declan and Puller cheering over a football game on Tanis' laptop, and set out to walk five blocks to TJ's, streetlight to streetlight, to save the delivery charge.

Away from the boys Neil held Tanis' hand, and kissed her at the first crossing light. Then he stalled in the middle of a giddy soliloquy on the relative costs of paying the electrician to remove socket boxes, $450, and the $60 he'd be dishing out for pizza. He took a sharp turn, pulled his hand out of Tanis' and walked up to a light pole.

"Shit," Neil said. There was a yellow poster, the edge of which was lifting in the wind of traffic on the street — a busy thoroughfare to downtown.

Tanis saw the header, MISSING, and two headshots. Teenaged girls. "Do you know them?" she asked.

"Yes." Neil kept his hand on the paper, flattening it so that Tanis could step in for a better look. Melissa Arthur on the left, Jody Bear on the right. The poster had good contrast in the streetlight's diffuse orange glow, and the girls looked . . . happy. Melissa was grinning boldly, teen flash, and Jody had a shyer smile, dark hair hanging over eyebrows plucked to a pencil line but raised over wide, alert eyes.

"You know them?" Tanis asked again. Neil nodded, and maybe it was just because of the uniformity of teen fashion, but they looked familiar to Tanis too. A lot of girls wore their hair like Melissa, in ponytails with the bangs slicked back. And like Jody, with angle bangs on one side, the other side tucked back behind an ear. The kids both wore hoodies. One white, one First

Nations, these two could have been the girls laughing on the curb across the street. Jody could be, with her wide, shy smile, a time-lapse image of Kaydance half grown up, a plausible older sister. A cousin.

"Are they friends with each other?" Tanis asked.

Neil considered that. This was weird. He'd made them work together. But he'd also seen them texting together in the commons hall, half hidden by a pair of open locker doors. "I think so, friendly at least. Jody's in my Math ten and they're both doing those Life Skills work experiences — "

"And?"

"And today there was a tweet in the afternoon. Totally bogus — a fake Amber Alert thing. But the kids were freaked out."

"These kids were freaked out?" Tanis asked.

Neil couldn't remember. Jennie had shown him her phone. The tweet just said students, two *#AboriginalYouth.* Jody had been at school, though. At least at the start of Math ten that morning, when he'd taken attendance. It was afternoon when one of the kids had shown Neil a Facebook post that urged everyone to contact the authorities if they had information pertaining to the "locations of the girls" — but there'd been no names. There'd been no call, much less Amber Alert, received at the school. Bornstein hadn't heard from the police, not by the end of the day.

"Did Mr. Bornstein follow it up, though? Did he call parents?" Tanis wanted to know.

"I doubt it," Neil said, shaking his head.

"He didn't take it seriously, then?"

"Didn't buy it? I don't know. I didn't, there were no names. He couldn't just call the parents, I don't think. It's Friday, there were a lot more than two absent kids."

"Maybe they ran off together," Tanis said. She had begun shivering, and Neil put an arm around her shoulder.

"Hopefully," he said, and he checked his phone to be sure that he hadn't missed a notice of some kind. There was nothing. The poster they'd found didn't look that official either, actually — Neil frowned. "It's strange there's no number on here to say who to call, if we did see them or know something."

"Just 911, I guess?" Tanis ventured, crossing her arms. What felt strange to her was that Neil had come home excited about weekend demolition. About wiring, and making sure there was beer in the fridge. He hadn't said anything about missing kids. Puller and Declan were teachers too and none of them had said a thing. And then there'd been strange sounds in the garage, like someone was hiding in there. What if it — *stop it,* Tanis told herself. She rocked up on to her toes beneath Neil's arm and he squeezed her shoulder.

"Melissa's not really in my classes," he said. "I'm supervising her work placement for Life Skills. But Karen, you remember that English teacher from the BBQ?"

Tanis remembered Karen, the too-friendly brunette.

"Karen told me Jody hasn't got any real accountability at home, a mom working shifts and a dad two weeks in, two weeks out, or something like that. Broken home."

"That's more *the norm* than broken, Neil."

"Yeah, maybe," Neil said warily. Tanis was the single child of divorced parents, but he'd never heard her reminisce about smokes on the roof. And he'd never heard her complain much about her parents. Jody's were apparently absent, and Melissa's seemed heavy-handed. They'd replied snarkily to his email about the overdue letter, anyways — it was *his* job to supervise *his* students, they'd written. They'd offered no excuses for their daughter, either, though.

The Twitter thing, and the Facebook post, had spooked some of the kids. It'd gone viral between their phones, outpacing the teachers, and some of the students had called their parents — too scared, or eager for an excuse not to make their own way home. "Beaming in their helicopters," Karen had said, commenting on the exceptional line-up of minivans at the curb. Neil hadn't known what to make of it, but now he remembered closing the sliding window of his classroom. He raised his hand to press the poster a final time against the wind, willing it to stick down.

The rest of the way to the pizza place they scanned the alleys, half-hopeful that the girls might appear — just amble casually back, from missing to found.

On the way home Neil balanced two extra-large pizza boxes and Tanis carried chicken wings and two litres of Coke. As they came around the house to the kitchen door Tanis looked back at the dark garage, and thought of calling the girls' names into the blackness inside. She didn't. She did glance up at Kaydance's lit bedroom window as they went in, though. The little girl was up late, it was a Friday, and her window was bright and reassuring.

"God, the poor parents," Tanis said.

"Oh, it's not that late," Neil said, misunderstanding. "I'm sure Michelle will win the battle soon." He had balanced the pizza boxes on his head to free up a hand for opening the door and Tanis laughed in spite of herself when she turned around.

"Michelle?" Was that Kaydance's mom?

"Mommy," Neil nodded, manoeuvring himself and the pizza through the door. The handle of the bag suspending the two litres of pop had twisted like a tourniquet around Tanis' fingers and she followed Neil into their blue-lit LED kitchen to shake her hand free.

In the front room, taking up the couch and sparse legroom, Dec and Puller alternately swore and cheered at the football game.

Tanis and Neil ate their pizza sitting on top of the kitchen table, feet on their chairs, a free events magazine open on the table between them. She was tempted by the listings — concerts, movies, lectures — she wanted to get out. They would try to wake up in time for the farmer's market Saturday morning but that might be it for weekend adventures, as Neil would have to go in and work on lesson plans at the school.

"I'm buying us something real to cook from the market tomorrow," Tanis announced.

"Okay," Neil said. "Where are the pots?"

"One of those," Tanis mumbled through a mouthful of pizza, pointing to a stack of dust-frosted cardboard crates.

Neil grabbed her hand and traced the tip of his thumb along the red sealed wound on hers. "Does it hurt?"

"Not really," Tanis demonstrated that it worked fine, flexing her hand, then reached for a second slice of pizza. "Do you realize how much plaster crap you guys got all over everything?"

"I'll find a Shop-Vac first thing tomorrow, Tanis. It's a project, we bought a project."

She bit into her slice and chewed. "A good project?"

"Yes." He smirked and pointed. "But the flowers . . . " The kitchen's wallpaper was actual paper, not acrylic sheeting, and someone long ago had glued it perfectly flat against the wall. Brown and yellow flowers had been bleached out by steam over the stove and faded by the sun along the side wall.

"Yeah, I agree. That has to go, top of the list. After the shelves . . . " which were in still stacked against the baseboards, waiting to be mounted in the front room. "After the wiring . . . "

The electrician had promised to do "his best" to come Monday but that promise had a lot of wiggle room.

"And the lilacs." Neil chimed in.

"What about the lilacs?"

"Puller knows this guy who's got a root grinder, who'll rent — "

"They're staying."

"Tanis, they're overgrown, and they're kind of weeds."

"I like them."

"They take up half the yard and they catch garbage."

"You'll like them in the spring," Tanis promised.

That night, though, the wind in the lilacs grew so loud that Tanis got up and looked out the bedroom window. There was a garbage bag caught and flapping around in the hedge. The apartment flood lamp shone down into the depths of the bushes and reflected from the bright bellies of disposable coffee cups. The branches were waving, and the shadows under them, and the wind was moving inside the house too. A palpable draft leaked in, tasting like rain.

RCity News — Online — Monday, September 17

Police Issue Alert for 2 Missing Teen Girls

City police are urging the public to come forward with any possible information pertaining to the location of two missing teenage girls. Melissa Arthur and Jody Bear have not been seen since leaving their west side high school, Russmere Collegiate, following an afternoon volleyball practice on Friday, September 14th.

Melissa Arthur, 16 years old, is described as Caucasian, 140 lbs., 5'7" with long brown hair, worn in a ponytail, which has previously been dyed black, blonde, and pink.

Jody Bear, 15 years old, of First Nations descent, is 110 lbs., 5'3" with brown hair falling past shoulder length.

While there is no immediate evidence of foul play, Saskatoon Police Detective Ray Hamilton says that, in releasing this alert, he hopes for a swift and safe return of these girls to their families. Peter Robinson, a superintendent with the public school board, notes that the Police Incident Response team will be sent to Russmere Collegiate this afternoon, where a section of the large gymnasium will be set up for students and parents to share relevant information and to receive counsel.

Comment Board (4)

1) *Missing for the weekend? Probably slept over at their boyfriends'. But glad to see the police on it quickly, let's hope they're found soon.*
2) *Note "west side". Not where I'd send my kid to school.*
3) *Check the mall.*
4) *I am close family with Jody Bear's aunt. They are very worried for her and if she is safe. If you have anything please contact the police or RCMP.*

» Fourteen

"They'll probably turn up at school," Neil reassured Tanis as he left Monday morning — "hung-over, of course." That was supposed to be a joke but she looked back at him, annoyed and squinting because her glasses were an old prescription and she hadn't popped her contacts in yet.

"Call me if there's anything I can do, okay?"

"Yeah, I can. If they tell us anything."

"Kay."

"What've you got on? Will you be here?"

"Yes — um, who were you going to get a Shop-Vac from, though?"

Saturday they'd gone to the market, then got caught up with shopping for second-hand couches. She'd wanted a settee to put under the window in her office. Sunday Neil had gone biking and come home to find Tanis grimy from attic explorations she'd not been able to hold off on. Cleaning that muck would keep her from worrying about missing girls all day, for sure it would, so Neil dug out the address of an old friend of his dad's. A man from the generation of men who always have Shop-Vacs, as well as gas mowers and power wash hose attachments, battery chargers and spare rims. Mr. Lyons promised to drop his Shop-Vac off after lunch, but before coffee.

"What time is that, do you think?" Tanis asked.

Neil considered the question. He didn't know, but he liked the idea of coffee having its own time.

"Two thirty?" Tanis guessed. "Three?"

At three Neil received a series of texts: *The vacuum is here! — Coffee o'clock, I win. — He called me ma'am* ☺

These chimed out while Neil walked back to the school from a doggie salon where Life Skills students Trent and Jay were learning the ins and outs of grooming, and flirting with the trainee groomers. A pair of closely shorn poodles panted on their leads and the boys were flexing their muscles sweeping up fur when Neil arrived, but the shop owner had completed an observation form and checked boxes for timeliness, mannerliness, and following instructions. She'd added that Jay was a "natural with terriers" in the comment line.

The boy was lighting one of the pretty intern's smokes when Neil ducked out the back door. Technically, Jay was on school time. Technically, Jay was not on school property. Neil shook his head and index finger, and the boy mumbled, "Sorry Mr. Cameron, sir." Sir and ma'am.

Thanks, sir! Neil texted to Tanis. She replied *??*, and he followed their regular pattern and hit the phone icon to chat. "Hey, ma'am."

"Hey, yourself — oh, I get it. Hey — sir. And, hey, sir, how do I get this Shop-Vac up into the attic?"

"Balance it on your head?" Neil suggested

"Right."

"Actually, what about your big grocery bag. The sling thing. That would be safe — or just wait for me to get home."

"When do you think you'll be back?"

"Four, four thirty?" Neil guessed. But when he signed off on Tanis, Neil found two notices from Bornstein. The principal had called an emergency staff meeting and Neil picked up his pace. He'd been taking his time, winding his way back to the school looking at houses and cars. Now he had an eye out for the girls' posters on the corner street posts and instead saw adds for bands, a lost beagle, and a basement apartment for rent. The rental ad had a fringe, tearaway contact information. Neil tugged a strip off and folded it as he walked, just to have something in his hands.

The staff had gathered in the library, and with nearly everyone attending the circle of chairs had to be a double row. Neil found a spot in the outer circle between two of the older teachers. Lynn Enns, gym teacher, on the right, and Bo Patrenko, chemistry and physics, on the left. In front of him a there was a brown head of hair, traced through with white. Neil racked his brain and couldn't place her.

Today was good, today was fun. Tomorrow is another one. It was a Dr. Seussism and Doug Bornstein repeated it twice to his staff. He was concerned for Melissa and Jody, but seemed more concerned about the rest of the student body, who were brewing with rumours, split on whether the girls had been abducted, killed outright, or had just run away.

"I overheard one of my students saying they'd seen blood in the bathroom." The voice came from around the circle and Neil couldn't see who'd spoken.

"I can't confirm that," Bornstein said.

"I can," Lynn piped up beside Neil. "Anne McIntosh took a volleyball to the bridge of her nose." A laugh ran through the teachers and Bornstein raised his hand.

"That's the kind of thing we need to keep on top of. Rumours can run wild and — we don't need added drama to this situation. I've already had to ask Yanis and Kipland to create a stronger police presence, parents have been worried."

Yanis and Kipland were the school police liaisons, present semi-regularly. They were meant to establish trust and student confidence, but usually got called in to deal on the spot with drugs in a student's locker, and sometimes fights or bullying.

"The hashtag *#MissingandMurdered* is getting linked to the notices." The same faraway voice piped up, with mumbles of agreement.

Neil pulled his collar away from his chest. He was warm from rushing back for the meeting and fanned himself with his shirt. Jody was First Nations, visibly, but not particularly traditional that Neil knew of. Melissa didn't look native but apparently had ancestry, somewhere back, and the original tweet had alerted everyone. *#AboriginalYouth.* Lynn Enns had glanced Neil's way, and now seemed to be staring at his chest. He shrugged sympathetically.

"We have no reason to think they've been racially targeted," Bornstein said. "But you're right about the hashtag and the parents of our First Nations students are especially, and naturally, concerned. So we've got the police presence. And we'll be flexible about smoking."

Lynn gasped. She was the health and lifestyles head and had kicked the school year off with a serious anti-smoking campaign.

"We can't have students purposefully taking themselves out of sight to smoke and keep an eye on them at the same time," Bornstein explained. "The police have suggested the cement pad by the main doors as a smoking area. It is full in plain view of the front office, at least from Adrienne's desk."

Adrienne, the head secretary, looked up from a notepad and nodded.

"Does anyone have a problem with that?" Bornstein asked, in a voice that tempted someone to dissent, or second the motion. Lynn scowled but kept quiet.

Neil had been at schools where students disappeared before. Usually they just stopped coming, had mixed up priorities or a temporary situation that made school too hard. But Melissa and Jody weren't your typical retention risks — Jody had great grades and Melissa, though definitely not academic, was active in the life of the school, playing volleyball and fighting hard for live bands at the seasonal dances.

There'd been one in Vancouver, and one in Edmonton. There'd even been one in Saskatoon, though he had been caught years ago. Those guys had supposedly targeted First Nations women living high-risk lifestyles, but Neil knew that wasn't universally true of the victims. He'd seen a documentary.

"*Tomorrow is another one,*" Bornstein repeated ambiguously to his staff. Bornstein suggested that the teachers ground their students' fears with opportunities for proaction. Adrienne had typed up a memo with questions suggested by the police, and tomorrow, at the beginning of each period, classroom teachers would read them aloud. The papers were passed clockwise around the inner circle, counter clockwise around the outer circle. They converged, rustling through silence, at Neil and Patrenko.

Do not respond now, but please consider these questions carefully:

Did the girls, or another classmate, seem upset in any way last week?

Are you aware of older friends, or friends from other schools, that either girl may have been in contact with since the beginning of the school year?

Were you aware of any plans either girl had to travel?

Were you aware of any grievances held against their parents or guardians?

Neil read the list and wondered, why not be direct? Why not say, *do you know where they are?* And why couldn't the kids answer right on the spot? He'd have to read this list, explain what grievances and guardians were — and then there'd be no way to know which students might or might not trickle down to the gym to share information with the police at the end of a fifty minute math lesson. Would that be something they'd want to do, a thrill, or a breach of teen solidarity? You'd want to be a hero but not a snitch, Neil considered, and sighed.

"Neil — " Lynn broke into his thoughts. The meeting seemed to be disbanding, or at least the person in front of them had risen from her chair. Neil felt a tap on his knee. "What's this about?" Lynn asked, a hand open and waving above her heart.

"I'm worried, I — "

She leaned over and, scrunching her face in distaste, pulled a clump of fur off Neil's breast pocket and held it up. "You skinning something?"

Neil opened his mouth to explain and felt himself rock sideways as Patrenko slapped a hand on his shoulder. The science teacher pitched his voice low and mock-growled, "It was a full moon last night, Lynn."

"*Chh-ck,*" Lynn clicked. "Running with them, Neil?"

"Ha. I've got kids at Doggy-Dos," Neil explained. He plucked the bit of fur out of Lynn's fingers and rolled it into a ball against his palm.

"Doggy-Dos." Patrenko laughed. Lynn kept her face wrinkled, lines spiking out from around her mouth.

"What was that sound you made?" Neil asked. "That click — it sounds like my laptop when I drop files in the trash."

Lynn, mouth still smooshed, raised an eyebrow too. "That's the sound of somebody feeling sorry for you," she said. And she relaxed, lifted her chin and gave another "*Chh-ck,*" out of the side of her mouth. "Prairie thing, eh?"

Neil grinned and tried it, clicking out of the side of his mouth. He saw that the seats around them had emptied. The student questionnaires had been left behind on a couple of chairs and Neil pointed. "What the hell."

"Oh, never mind," Patrenko said. "They'll be back tomorrow. Mark my words." He stood up and scratched at his belly, working a finger in between buttons on one of his standard plaid shirts. Neil looked down at his lap and stared between the paper in one hand and a ball of dog hair the size of a gumball in the other.

"Why?" Lynn asked, her voice flat. "Why mark your words?"

"Attention," Patrenko said. "And that's what they'll get."

» Fifteen

While Neil delivered the police survey to his scattered Life Skills 20 duos, Tanis began with the closet floor, vacuuming up the brittle flakes of teddy bear wallpaper. Then the grey insect bodies that dusted the iron stairs. They were captain's stairs, a ladder almost, and Tanis vacuumed each step as she ascended, bracing the barrel-shaped vacuum canister against the wall. The floored part of the attic hadn't been blown in with insulation, but Neil and Puller had tracked enough through from the unfinished space over the bedroom that Tanis had to empty the vacuum canister four times before the floor was anything close to clean.

Slashes of sunlight came in around a roof pipe and in from a vent under the eaves, behind which Tanis found a window casing. A frame of glass had been detached and laid to rest on the floor. The vent had been a window once and, peeking through narrow wooden slats, Tanis found herself looking directly into the second floor apartment. Kaydance and Michelle's living room. No wonder the window had been sealed off. But why the room wholesale? Too drafty as Neil suggested, or someone had something to hide — you heard about finds, in old houses. Setting LED lanterns in the angled corners of the rectangular space, Tanis looked around for hiding spots and found several.

Between framing there were box shelves, but these were empty. Beside the chimney bricks there was a little metal box, perhaps casing for wires, also empty. Anything could have been hidden in there but nothing was.

The cones of lantern light converged in the centre of the room, leaving a flat, dark shadow that Tanis ignored until she stood on top of it and saw her socks illuminated fully by the too-bright LEDs. The floor was stained, not shadowed. Evidence of water damage — or a spill? Something dark and hard to clean. Stepping away from the stain, Tanis brushed her hands against her thighs and shivered, then felt silly. There'd been nothing in the garage. Now she was imagining things.

Scanning the angled ceiling Tanis saw no evidence of the water stains that should have been there if something had dripped through. Abe Klassen had assured them the shingles were less than ten years old, and good for another five, but he hadn't said anything about the roof being replaced and Tanis thought the wood looked old. Original. Something, clearly had been spilled —

The front door opened, and Neil's lanyard of keys jangled as he dropped them. "Tanis?" he called, "I'm home!"

"Neil, come up here!"

Neil sat on the couch to pry off his running shoes. He'd expected to find Tanis waiting in the front room, or maybe the kitchen — busy priming or steaming the flowers off the wall. But it looked like she'd been working at something online, and from a camping spot in the living room. Boxes were pulled up to one end of the couch to make a desk and her laptop was open, but powered off. The coffee beside it looked thick and old.

"Coming up to see the crime scene?" Tanis called.

"What are you talking about?"

"There's a — a giant bloodstain in the attic!"

Neil climbed the stairs, repeating, "What?"

"An ancient, giant bloodstain!" Tanis' voice wound its way out of the closet, which Neil approached, glancing into the office where her contract boxes sat unopened and coated in dust and plaster chunks from the removal of the ceiling fixture.

"Did the electrician come today?"

"What? No, nobody came. Was he supposed to?" Her flushed face appeared at the top of the captain's stairs.

"He said today, or this week," Neil answered, kicking idly at exposed lath and plaster. He looked up to see the bottom of the Shop-Vac descending " — what, I'm supposed to grab that?"

"Thanks, yes, couldn't lift it this time." The vacuum cylinder slipped, unexpectedly heavy, through Neil's arms and crashed down. Tanis came behind it, stepping clumsily over a loop of hose for a hello kiss. "I emptied it five times already," she said.

"It seems like you had a busy day," Neil agreed. "Is supper pretty much all ready for me?"

"Yes, and no. I didn't quite get to the kitchen — come up and see the murder in the attic." Tanis grabbed Neil's hands and pulled him to the stairs. She let him go at the ladder, and Neil watched her climb until something fell and hit his face. Insulation, mouse poop. He shook his head, brushed a hand through his hair, and followed her up.

It was dark. At a little past 4:30, it was still bright outside and the bedroom window had lit the hallway, but only thin strips of grey worked through the attic venting. The LED lanterns cast an eerie blue light and the splotch that Tanis led Neil to see was purplish. The stain was darkest in the middle, where it spread over a good two feet, and it trailed to a ragged smear in the direction of the vent.

"That could be anything." Neil said.

Tanis raised her shoulders, "Like what?".

"I don't know. Paint or wood stain, maybe. Or water." Neil crouched to examine the blotch. It was smooth, no different in texture from the rest of the floor. He twisted to look overhead.

"There's no stain on the roof," Tanis said. "I checked when there was more light in here. And also, with more light it looked more reddish brown."

"And that," Neil pointed to the smeared end, "that's supposed to be where somebody got dragged through it?"

Tanis snorted, "Or tried to clean it up."

"Gross," Neil said. "And who would do that bad of a job of cleaning up a pool of blood? Seriously."

"The murderer, obviously!"

"As if." Neil looked around the floor while Tanis giggled. She'd done a good job of clearing out the dust and foam, and it was neat to see the lines of the roof, vaulting in.

The stain was pretty much in the middle of the floor and Neil could only have taken a few steps in either direction without ducking. Tanis circled him, switching off the LEDs. She paused by the vent. "Oh, that's funny."

"What?" Neil asked.

"Come see."

Neil ducked and saw Kaydance in the window of the apartment. She was tucked in between the curtains, pulled closed, and the big window in their living room. Hidden near the meeting of the two drapes, she peeked through the panels, watching something inside — and she was wriggling and bobbing up against the glass, excited, or laughing. "Cute," Neil said. "I think she needs to pee."

He stepped back on to the stain and straightened his back. "So, you couldn't have found a stack of mature bonds, or mature whiskey, or anything like that?"

Tanis had a great imagination, but never for the dinner's-ready role play. For the fourth time in their two weeks since moving in, Neil ordered TJ's extra large Hawaiian, delivery this time. When the deliveryman arrived Tanis was resting cross-legged on the attic floor, exhausted from heaving the Shop-Vac around, and Neil was on his knees, prying one of the stained boards up with the back end of a finishing hammer. It was the first time they heard their own doorbell and it scared them both, buzzing close underneath like a vintage oven timer. Neil's first thought was that he'd tripped a wire. Then they heard knocks and the man gave the doorbell another run of quick stabs — *Bzzt-bzzt-bzzt.*

"Pizza, pizza," Neil said, sliding the hammer across the floor to Tanis before he dropped down the stairs.

She picked the tool up and felt the warmth of Neil's hand on the handle. She set it down on the stain, creating a scene straight off the cover of a mystery novel. Gross for sure. And they ate, once again, by the light of LED lanterns, both ham and pineapple greenish blue.

It was Tuesday afternoon before the electrician came, raised his eyebrows at the attic access stairs, " — makes my life easy." Said it was a shame that they'd smashed out all the socket boxes. "Could'a refit a lot of them, eh?" He identified Tanis' crime scene as an oil spill. "Amazing the place never burned down with oil and paper casings on the wiring up there, eh? I've seen some houses where you get a short with mice or whatever, eh? Voosh! Right up. Yeah," he grinned back and forth between Tanis and Neil's horrified faces.

Four-hundred dollars on a home inspector who hadn't identified the attic room, much less a hazardous spill.

"It's a thing with older houses," the electrician continued. "Never know what another person's done in it. Seen all kinds of things — like you think a plug's grounded, got three prongs, but really they just set it in there, not connected to nothing. So maybe it's a good thing you took out them old boxes. What I put in you'll know what you've got, eh?"

You don't have any idea what I've got, Neil thought.

"Amazing it never went up," The electrician repeated, shaking his head.

"Well, I'm very glad it didn't," Tanis agreed.

The attic floorboards had been laid tightly together, and it took some pounding for Neil to get the chisel end of the hammer in. He wasn't expecting the cavity between the joists to be filled with bugs and lint. And mouse poop. The house had once had a lot of mice — they could add hantavirus to the lung hazards.

"That's why they had a cat, I guess," Tanis said, leaning over Neil's shoulder.

"Cats, or mice, your vote."

"Dogs," Tanis said. "Stop, okay? I haven't returned the Shop-Vac. I'll clear it out."

And while Neil took himself out for fresh air and a bike ride along the river, Tanis sucked up a cord that caught on something under the boards. The vacuum whined, the broken edge of the floor knocked, and Tanis turned off the suction and drew the metal end bit of a shoelace out of the Shop-Vac hose.

It wasn't that wide a cavity, and crossbeams ran against the joists, but Tanis fought imagining a body in the floor until Neil came home, pried up a wider section of the floor, and pulled out a pair of boots.

» Sixteen

"Hello, is Cecelia Mazer there?"

"Who shall I tell her is calling, dear?"

"Oh, well my name is Tanis Campbell, and if you could tell Mrs. Mazer that I — well, I think she used to live in the house that we've just bought."

"Oh, yes?"

"At 723 Avenue L South?" Tanis was calling from upstairs, and she stepped nervously between the bedroom and office as she waited for the woman's answer. There was a cough at the other end of the line. "This is Cecelia Mazer you're talking to now. Celia is fine."

"Okay, oh — hi," Tanis tripped over her words. "Well, I'm just calling because we found out that there'd been some dangerous building materials upstairs we had to take out. And then when we did we found some things we thought might be yours."

"Well, they'd probably belong to my tenants there before you."

"Oh," Tanis said quickly, "there were some things of theirs left in the kitchen, but then there's some older things. In the basement, and under the floor in the attic space."

"In the cellar and in the attic, you say?"

"Yes, in the basement we were sealing up where there was a coal chute, I think."

"Oh, a coal chute?' The woman sounded mystified. Tanis wondered when she'd last visited the house. The tenants had dealt with a management company — really, it could have been years. "We found some papers folded in there," she said, "shoved behind the inside door of the coal chute."

"That's the one with the dragons on it?" Celia asked slowly.

"Leaves, I think," Tanis said. "A kind of a scroll pattern, it could look like dragons." Close enough? She curled her toes under and pressed them into the hallway floor.

"And what kind of things are you finding?"

"Well, in there, some clippings. Ads somebody saved? Then there's also some kind of a book with a ledger in it — just numbers. I don't know what it is, but maybe you would."

"And you're living in her house now, you say." Celia mused, "Are you a researcher or something? At the university?"

"No, no, just it's our house now so, you know we're — "

"Lots of people probably lived in that house so I probably don't know anything about those things," Celia cut in.

"Well, the dates on the clippings, they're from the thirties, around then, so that would be your mom maybe? There's three ads for nylons and I know in the thirties they were hard to come by. Some kind called The Phantom Orient — and then there's a clipping for a round trip shopping train to Moose Jaw and I know it was bigger than Saskatoon at one point, and another ad for Winnipeg." Tanis paused and the woman sighed at the other end of the phone.

"My aunt lived there, I lived with an aunt."

"Okay, oh — you lived in this house with your aunt? Was the house hers?"

In the background at the other end, Tanis could hear the Mrs. Mazer rattling something, maybe cooking or putting away dishes. It was hard to get a handle on how old or infirm she might be.

"Is it a busy time?" Tanis asked. "I'm sorry to have interrupted you. If you're not interested I can just file these things away, it's not a big deal. I only thought it would be interesting to know about the house — "

"No, no, dear, it's interesting, I suppose it is. I never saw my aunt in nylons, that's for sure." There was the sound again, the faint rattle. Something swirled in a saucepan maybe.

"I'd love to hear more about her," Tanis said. "If you have time, or if you'd like to see the house, we could have coffee or tea or something like that, I'd really like to — "

"So, what was so interesting in the attic?" Celia asked sharply.

Tanis turned in the hall and faced the opened closet. "Well, we thought there was no attic, and then we were going to do some wiring upgrades and we found out there's two access points to under the roof. And there's an attic. Someone blew insulation all over it from the bedroom. Maybe that would've been you?'

"I don't think so, dear."

"Okay. Well, if you go in the hall closet there's another access and Neil, my husband, found this old set of metal captain's stairs sealed up in there. Do you remember stairs going up to the attic?"

"I was pretty young when I lived there."

"Really? Well there were stairs and it was finished up there once, with a floor, but only part of it and there's — "

"See, though, I don't remember there being an attic, and no stairs either."

"No, I don't think it's been open or used for a long time, but there was a floor laid up there so we thought — " Tanis took a breath, paused, then dove in. "We thought maybe it was for smuggling something or hiding, you know, like Al Capone in Moose Jaw or someone like that."

A hoot of laughter shot over the phone. "You don't know much about my aunt."

"Well before her, you know, maybe whoever built the house used it — "

"Oh no, no. It was my grandfather who built that house."

"Really? We've been wanting to know who the owners were, you know, and when it got built and all of that and — "

"Of course you would be curious," Celia said in a practiced, placating tone. "So what did you find up there then? Bottles?"

"Bottles?"

"For bootlegging?"

"Bootlegging?"

"That's what they say Al Capone went in for, dear."

"Oh, right. That's so interesting too — "

"Well, now you young people might think it's interesting but I think it was pretty much hell on Earth for the lot of them back then. My grandpa could sell a tail to a horse but he wasn't much for taking care of his family, from what I know. My grandma died of TB and her kids had everything to kill them, typhoid, scarlet fever, Spanish flu, it never ended. Can't blame people set on like that for making money where they could, but living outside the law is no life for anyone. You know when polio was coming through in the fifties my aunt was like a — "

"What was her name?" Tanis interrupted, to keep Celia on track. "I'd love to hear more about her."

"She was mostly just a woman of her time, like they say."

"Mazer. Was she Ukrainian?"

"No. No, that's not a Ukrainian name, and it's my husband's, you know."

"Of course — what was your aunt's name?"

"Phidelma Agnes Tanner, and then she used Laurie later, that was her mom's name, but her dad, Grandpa, he was a Tanner. My dad was a Tanner but my aunt put me in school with Allary as a surname and that was my mother's people."

"Your mother's people?"

"Red River Métis. I think it was common, then, using a mother's name for a daughter. But you see, she died when I was very young."

"Oh, I'm sorry. Of TB as well?"

"Could be."

"So many people used to get sick, it's — "

"Well now, my daughter did look for her death records, you know. My father was missing-in-action in the Second World War, so we never buried him. I thought I'd find her burial place, my mother's, but we never did. Just my birth certificate came, blue, because of how they used to do the carbon copying, you know."

It struck Tanis that Celia could be the child who the little bears on the wallpaper were for. She'd probably slept in the nursery, and maybe the mirrored tiles had been hers too, in the house built by her grandfather. Tanner, Allary, Laurie. "I do know, actually, " Tanis said. "I do genealogy work for a lot of families. Sometimes it can be very tricky to trace."

"That what you're after, then?"

"Oh no, no," Tanis tried to explain that she wasn't after work. At least not in this case. She'd traced ancestry for a few Métis families though, who wanted to apply for membership cards. There was a hush, a silence not filled by movement or anything else at the other end. "Celia, um Mrs. Mazer? In the attic, what we found up there, it's a big stain. The electrical guy thought it might be old paint or linseed or — some kind of furniture polish stuff — so we had to take out that part of the floor because of the fire hazard."

"I see."

"He said it was lucky the house hadn't gone up in flames already — but the attic is really well-ventilated. It even has a window. Anyways, we took out the stained boards and Neil found boots under the floor."

"Boots? Were there any feet in them?"

"No feet, no legs! That's the first thing I thought of too." Tanis leaned back against the wall, relieved to hear Celia laugh.

"Old boots, I suppose. Maybe they'd be my grandpa's or something like that, then?"

"Yes, that's what we thought. They're not terribly amazing, and actually they had a bit of a nest in them. Shredded up insulation and, well, droppings — mouse stuff. I don't know if you'd like them, but they're in a bag. And the newspaper clippings too, of course, if you're interested."

"I wonder what they'd be doing up in an attic floor," Celia said.

"It's strange, isn't it?"

"And you've gotten curious now, about that, I suppose. And now about Phidelma, my aunt?"

"I guess I have, kind of, yes."

"Well, my daughter too, you know. She's done some looking but hasn't found much. Maybe they didn't keep many records for the women, in the wars."

"There's very little," Tanis agreed.

"They weren't invisible then," Celia said. "They ran the world, practically, as far as I knew. My father, like I said, he'd gone MIA. So it was just her, Delma — that's what I called her — taking things in to keep us. Sewing and ironing, then we had boarders for a while, some girls in for school. Then after the war, oh, I was ten or so, she sold the half lot. And that was to build the apartment for the veterans, the men. They'd been the ones out of sight out of mind, to me."

"I never thought of it like that," Tanis said, jotting details down. "I thought the veterans got houses when they came back, or homesteads?"

"That would've been the married ones. Delma cooked for the bachelors, they got the suites. We took in clothes for them sometimes too. She knew how to make money, my aunt." There was a smile in Celia's voice as she told Tanis how her aunt had marched her off to school, and kept her in it right through grade twelve, when a lot of girls were pulled out to work after grade eight.

"She sounds like a really amazing woman, doing all that and raising you too," Tanis said.

"Oh yes. But a woman of her times, you know. She never moved out of that house, just died in her bed there, in the middle room. The big one was for the girls, when we had them. The little room, that one was mine."

So the aunt had died in Tanis' office. "Did she die, um, peacefully?"

"I suspect so, dear. The certificate said failing, and whatever failing is, it was quick."

A murder in the attic had been funny — unbelievable and quirky. A quiet death in the office felt sad, though deaths at home must have been common. There used to be births at home too. "Were you born in here too, Celia?" Tanis asked hopefully.

"I haven't a clue where I was born, dear. That birth certificate my daughter found is from Winnipeg but it says registered at six-months-old."

"Not in this house, then."

"No, but I grew up there. I have lots of happy memories."

Lots of all kinds of memories, Celia thought, but she does not, at this moment, let them back into the house. It's flattering the way young people are interested all of the sudden in the past, not only this young woman but Celia's daughter and her granddaughter too. Celia would like to tell Tanis something important, but what she remembers now is boot leather, rich and black, and the task that was hers, to rub the leather smooth with tallow. Pa père's socks stepped softly up the stairs. Phidelma rattled wood into the belly of the range to fuel the simmer and chirp of the aluminium percolator. The metal left a taste in his coffee that Pa père complained about, and Celia remembered falling asleep with a metal tang on her own tongue from the pan that warmed her tea.

"I'd be grateful for those boots, actually, Tanis." Celia spoke carefully, using the girl's name for the first time.

They arranged to meet at Tim Hortons since the house was a mess. Celia said that she hadn't been back to it since she took Corinne there to meet her great auntie. Phidelma had served tea and jam sandwiches, and held the baby, and burst into giggles when Corinne spat up all over the front of her blouse. "You know, that white chunky stuff," Celia elaborated. "The kind you see with formula babies?"

"I don't really know babies, actually," Tanis said.

"Well, you've got rooms to fill now. We'll see you next week, dear."

›› Seventeen

The day the house went up was cold. Workers gathered on site, called up from the pool of day workers, and Robert and Phidelma went along. Their father bossed, his children watched. Thomas shouted that the house would go like this or that, and his voice took up the whole cold space of the street.

When Phidelma told this to her niece, years later, she slapped at a support post in the kitchen wall. The plaster had been torn out and Phidelma had paid a man to put a hot water pipe through to the washroom — she was excited, and slipped into her father's accent, choppy English, softened by Gaelic and Cree, hardened by volume, "I'll pay no one prawn to sting aroun' smoking!" Phidelma said and encouraged Celia to give the post a kick. There was nothing dainty about the house. But there was something magic in hearing Phidelma tell about the pretty blonde boards at the construction site, stacked up and waiting. And how the house rose up out of the mud like a picture from the reader Phidelma had shared with her sister Meline. Two boxes, climbing each other, and a triangle on top. The siding to colour it in.

The windows waited three weeks for their framing. They sat in a crate at the back of the lot and Phidelma peeked at them every chance she had. Her father had bargained them off the school board from a building site across the river. Phidelma told Celia how her dad, big brother Robert, boasted that he'd be going to that new school. It had technical courses, for radio operators and trades. That fall they'd both just got started on the first level reader:

One morning Jerry and Jane
Took their sled to a high hill.
They sat down on the sled,
And away they went down the hill!

Meline was older than Robert and Phidelma. She had gone to school for two years, but then fell sick before school quit for summer. Marguerite expected the nuns to collect Meline's school things after she'd been taken to the hospital. They visited her there, but didn't ask for anything back.

The children called out,
"Please, please,
Get out of our way!"

Phidelma said that Meline glowed while she was dying. Her face lit up in her fevers, like a cloth window hung tight enough for light to melt through.

"This is the hill
Where we want to play!"

Meline held the long spoon, and rapped Phidelma's knuckles when she stumbled learning the words. Marguerite shook her head over her two girls playing at school, but she sat beside them sometimes and Phidelma liked to trace the lines of silver that ran through their mother's black hair where it wrapped around itself, winding into a knot. The white hairs sparkled when she moved. The aunties used to pull on these, teasing her, "Aren't you supposed to be the youngest one?" and when Phidelma copied them, Marguerite laughed and pushed her gently away.

"The next one?" Meline poked Phidelma with her spoon. "Are you stuck?"

At the foot of the hill
There was a road.

Meline coughed yellow and bits of red. It was like an egg cracked open and something already started inside. Phidelma reached over to take the cloth, to hand Meline another. "Are you stuck Delma — no? Keep going, then." Poke, poke.

Marguerite steeped the auntie's tea to help Meline's cough. Both girls drank so much of it that their smiles turned a kind of golden brown, but Meline's skin faded until it was something close to the colour of the paper in the reader. The pages where ink leaked into shapes, and shapes into sounds. Meline's hair was black as ink, spread out smooth against the folded blankets that propped her up in the day.

» Eighteen

Thursday Bornstein called another staff meeting, and this time gave the kids an early dismissal. "How come, Mr. Cameron?" Math nine wanted to know, and Neil looked at his class, at Jennie in the seat that would be empty next period, in Math ten, when Jody should have been filling it. He tried to think of an optimistic response.

"Did they find the missing babes?" Heath asked.

"No Heath." Neil snapped, and the boy looked shocked. But that'd been fair, the kid was out of line. Neil took a deep breath and began walking through the rows of desks, passing out the morning's worksheet. "No, the investigation is ongoing and the police are very optimistic that the girls will be located quickly." That was what Bornstein had posted to the teacher's message board and Neil recited it slowly. "There may be a 'stepping-up' of a police presence in the school, however," he added, eyeing Heath, "due to student *behaviour*."

"Whatever. When are we out?" the boy asked.

Neil was tempted to send him out now. "Whatever," he said. "After fourth, 2:10. I need to run down to the office, and we'll take up the first two questions as soon as I am back. You have — " he checked his watch, "seven minutes." He'd be more like ten, with two sets of Math ten worksheets to print and copy, but tapped his watch urgently for them at the door.

After fourth, Neil made his way to the staff meeting through packed halls. The kids were milling around, full of energy and nerves. Neil pushed his way through to arrive as a latecomer, and found a seat with Patrenko again. The man patted a chair beside him — they'd set up a third ring in the library circle this time. There were more police. Neil recognised two officers, Malhiot and Sawatsky, who'd been around the school. But not an older man and woman — maybe their bosses, he didn't know the hierarchy. Kipland was there too, in uniform, and he blushed and fidgeted with volume controls on a hand-held mic while Bornstein gave his introduction.

"Looks like he's about to go on *American Idol*," Patrenko whispered. Neil snorted into a suddenly quiet room, and tried to cover the sound with a cough. More stage coughs sounded around the room as Kipland laid out recent "progress" in the investigation. Taelur Anderson, third and neglected wheel to the missing girls, had posted a picture of enormous boobs on Facebook Tuesday afternoon.

"That's a bit random," Patrenko whispered.

The bosoms, as Bornstein later referred to them, were squashed together in a tight black band with the UFC tap-out logo on it and Taelur had typed in her "thoughts", *You pay, I'll buy them.* "Senior gymnasium teacher Mr. Andrew Puller," Kipland read from his notes, "came upon the senior boys basketball team taking up a collection." The room coughed.

"Oh, come on," Karen's voice sounded across the circle.

"Is this common behaviour among the students?" Kipland asked. Was it something that the staff would expect Melissa or Jody to do as well, a fashion amongst girls in the school?

"Well," Declan, in the first ring of teachers, raised a hand and answered for the group, "we're not allowed to 'friend' them on social media so we wouldn't know, right?"

Malhiot appeared to take note of this on her phone. Or maybe she was texting a friend.

"Could you venture a guess?" she asked, lifting her head.

"Probably it's just attention-seeking," Karen answered, a few seats down from Declan. She went on to share that a week ago Taelur had been kind of excluded by a growing friendship between the missing girls.

"What did you notice?" Malhiot asked.

"Well, like Taelur saved them spots they didn't come for at a lunch table."

"I see. And this seemed significant to you?"

"Well, no. Not at the time, of course. I just thought they might be breaking up with her and I was watching out for her a bit, I guess, because of that."

"That's very caring of you — anyone else?" Malhiot scanned the room and Kipland shook the mic, ready to sprint around the circle collecting comments or questions.

They were all teachers, Neil wanted to remind him. They all had teacher's voices. He surprised himself, raising his hand and speaking. "I noticed that, yeah," Neil said. A couple of heads turned his way, but mostly the comment was met by nods. Neil wasn't sure if he should mention that Kolton Dueck had taken Taelur's place, hanging around Melissa and Jody instead.

"Thank you very much. Taelur downloaded the image from a spam link she followed out of Melissa's Facebook page," Kipland said, then added pedantically, "We are interested to know about whatever social influences the girls may have been responding or reacting to," which drew a few coughs out of the group.

Melissa's Facebook profile was a space where the student body had been taking opportunity to post elegiac quotes and pleas for her safe return. It wasn't private and even Neil had gone on, just to look. He didn't recognize a lot of the posters' names, but they'd have online aliases if they didn't want their parents friending them. They posted to each other mostly on Instagram and Twitter, but hashtags linked the content — Neil had tried to explain that to the kids. Nothing online is anonymous. Jody might have listened, because her Facebook page had fewer comments, she'd restricted access to her wall posts.

In the library, Neil took out his phone and loaded the Facebook app. He wasn't the only teacher doing it and wasn't the only one to find that Taelur had reposted the boobs as her profile picture, melon-sized water-balloons. He flashed the phone at Patrenko, whose eyebrows went up.

A collection of the offers in Taelur's comments feed would add up to nearly a thousand dollars, Neil saw, scrolling down. But they weren't real dollars. Taelur had been wanting to upgrade her phone and needed eighty-nine dollars to bridge the gap from a current parent-sponsored plan, Kipland explained. But clearly, Malhiot stepped in to emphasize, clearly the act was a plea for attention that could attract the wrong kind.

Neil swiped the app off his phone and checked for tweets. There were police-issued missing persons alerts for Melissa and Jody circulating now, but the original posters Neil and Tanis had seen a week ago were still up too. Neil saw them on his walk up to the school and they were starting to look worn. The wind hadn't let up.

The rapid appearance of the posters was still a mystery and the police polled the school staff with a number of time-related questions. When had this or that class been out? Who was in the copy room when? Who had been seen in the gym and bathrooms? The tone of the meeting eventually became so mundane that Neil began chatting with Patrenko about yard equipment, and arranged to take a leaf blower off his hands free, an old gas lawn mower for fifty bucks.

With the fall evenings getting dark earlier and earlier Tanis was trying to make her after-school run a routine, instead of the after-digestion run she'd gone for in the summer from their old apartment. From there she'd run around a big park filled with dog walkers and soccer players. She and Neil both liked the river parkway better, but it got a bit sketchy later in the evening — Tanis liked jogging when commuters were there, biking home or idling along on the river road. She had taken to heading out running right when Neil arrived home hungry.

"You order better than me anyways," Tanis had said that morning, when Neil asked about suppertime. So today he planned ahead and picked up a tin of Italian tomato soup, a fresh loaf of bread, and wedge of applewood-smoked cheddar from the uphill bakery on his way home, surprising a clutch of his students who had apparently spent the early dismissal afternoon there. "They don't buy anything," the teller grumbled, then winked. "At least I keep a good eye on them here."

Jody and Melissa watched over the students too, from their MISSING posters on a bulletin board beside the door. A week ago the teller's comment would have seemed creepy, but this afternoon Neil had bent over the counter instinctively whispering back to this small, round, bald man, "Thanks."

Melissa and Jody's contemporaries were passing and flashing the flat faces of their phones back and forth over sticky buns. A social media campaign had been launched, tips tweeting in for all to see, but in real life the teens here were quiet — engrossed by small text rather than talk. In his class that fall, Neil had seen kids a desk apart send each other instinctive LOLs before making eye contact and laughing. Here each kid had frowned at their phone, breaking when they noticed Neil's presence, to elbow one another and stare at him in turn.

Neil walked home and found Tanis still there, at the kitchen table, one hand inside a boot and the other raised and holding a toothbrush.

"Is that my toothbrush?"

"Hi, to you too," Tanis said, looking up, and then at her hand. "Yes, this is your toothbrush. But I'll buy us both new ones. I already trashed mine on the other boot."

The other boot was drying on a square of newspaper on the other kitchen chair. Neil set his bag on the floor and picked it up. It looked quite different, clean and shiny. Old, but not even very worn. "I wonder who it belonged to?"

"It's Celia Mazer's boot," Tanis announced. "Probably, anyways — " and she shared what she'd learned, and also her embarrassment at Celia's suspicions that she was a university researcher digging for material, or that she was looking for money to do genealogical research. Which was kind of ironic, Neil pointed out, since Tanis did actually work on contract doing genealogical work, and was also dying to extend her credentials with a graduate degree.

"But I'm looking into this just for us, really. For the house," Tanis said, bending over her boot to toothbrush the eyelets. "Though Celia seemed interested to learn more about her family history if she could."

Neil recognised the beginning of a project. He flipped the clean boot in his hands, looked for a size under the tongue — 44 — and sat it back on its newspaper. "Maybe you could write something up about the house and then sit on it. Get into grad school with a thesis in the top drawer."

"That's not how it works," Tanis said. "You have to apply and write up a proposal, and get ethics approval, all with a committee of professors — "

"Sounds like you've been looking into it?" Neil asked.

Tanis smiled and shook her head.

"What time is it?" Neil asked. "Didn't you want to go jogging?"

Tanis went for a run and Neil pulled the cheese and bread, a prairie kamut loaf, out of his backpack and set them down on the counter. Tanis' phone rattled on the countertop and Neil picked it up to look, but it was just an offer of a new text plan. Asides from his lunchtime habit of sending updates, Tanis mainly got messages from her mom. Beside her phone, Tanis' laptop was open, her star voyage screen saver hurtling through space. He hit the space bar and it opened to a document file.

It could have been a milk door, I suppose. There was a milk cart at one point you know, but most of us would've used canned. Oh that was sweet stuff, oh yes. There was a reason teenagers didn't keep drinking milk like they do now, you lost your taste for that with your sweet tooth. But you know, that door, it could have been an ice door. There was an ice man who came around when I was young, with a big cart full of ice blocks, all covered over with woodchips to keep them from melting. That would be in the winter too, when the woodchips kept them from freezing together — mind you also there would be the coal man. He had a truck, but like you say, that would've gone right into the basement, not into the kitchen. My aunt, you know, she didn't keep one burning thing from another. // No I mean she'd throw coal right into the woodstove if there wasn't wood, or wood into the furnace on the other hand. // Yes, there was just a note we'd put out on the back door, then he'd know and leave a bill behind. Nothing like now, you just left something saying what you wanted and it would be there when you got home, and then again — sometimes maybe it wouldn't. // If you'd paid up you'd get your coal. But she didn't like being home when he came around. I heard said of him, not from my aunt, from another girl's mother, that every village has its idiot but they should've turned that one out long ago. He stayed back from the war for one reason or another and didn't live it down, I suppose.

Tanis' work, but she'd excused herself in this transcription as usual, not bothering to type in her questions. It was a research convention, she'd explained to Neil once when he'd challenged her about it. Neil's students were so eager to express themselves that they peppered even math assignments with "I" — as in I would say the answer is plus or minus eight.

It was seven days now that Jody and Melissa had been gone. Even Patrenko, who'd been dismissive about Twitter hysterics on Monday, was serious now. In the afternoon meeting he made a claim that runaways took three days to call Mom and the police hadn't corrected him.

"So what does that mean?" Declan asked. "They didn't runaway — or what?"

"Certainly," Malhiot had answered flatly. "We certainly have no idea where they are." She'd seemed pissed, not worried, though. And a lot of the teachers, even Neil himself, had laughed instead of gasped at Taelur's attention-seeking.

Neil closed his eyes for a long minute in the kitchen. Maybe the police knew something already. That was a nice thought. He'd rehearsed in his head the casual "welcome back" he'd give Melissa and Jody in the hall, a half-sarcastic voice that they would look up to assess and then they'd see that he was glad they were back, and one hundred percent on their side. Their Life Skills teacher, seriously. Like the church sign board at the end of their block had recently proclaimed: *you got to be the change you want to see in the world, and there ain't no such thing as a penny anymore.*

Neil hunched over Tanis' laptop and re-skimmed her notes. Then he stepped into the back entry to examine the fascinating "milk/ice" door. She'd poured powdered graphite into the hinges and it swung easily now, but Neil still had to heave upwards to close it and came away with greasy fingers.

The portal would be a handy place to set a stereo for a yard party once he got a deck in. His mom thought that the door, and the whole back entry, might actually be a laundry cupboard — a place where the laundry line would have once come right inside so ladies could hang underthings up safe from public view. Neil asked why bother, if the laundry was going out to dry anyways, and had been informed that knickers and slips were dried in privacy, tucked inside more decent pillowcases. This seemed ridiculous, but when Neil pictured Tanis' panties and bras waving around in the yard he missed the start of his mom's monologue on dry starching. Now Neil took a deep breath, tasted residual cigarette tar, and opened the milk/ice/laundry cupboard to let some air in.

The whole house had seemed too small the first week but it was getting bigger all the time. With the wheelchair ramp gone the yard had space for a good-sized porch, maybe with a hot tub when they could afford it down the road. And they had a new room upstairs. Great for storage, at least, going by the preservation of the boots.

Neil was fanning the milk door open and closed, still airing out the kitchen, as Tanis came in the front. He checked his watch. She came in out of breath, but it'd been a pretty short run. "You're back soon," he commented. "You okay?"

"Yeah. I guess was hungrier than I thought." Tanis patted her side, indicating cramps.

"Soup's almost on," Neil said, and stepped inside to lift the tin. She kicked off her shoes at the front door and limped towards the shower. Neil watched her, curious. Had the cramps got her, or the new posters of the girls? They were up on every second post along the river walkway now. Lynn Enns had enlisted her morning gym class, and borrowed the shop teacher's staple guns. Neil worked a finger through the tab on the soup can, peeled back the lid, and gave the bottom a few pats. A gelatinous cylinder slid into the sauce pot, with a sucking noise.

Maybe Tanis hadn't liked the line of cars with plastic taped over gaps left by missing rear windows. Some idiot had taken a bat to the cars parked along the curb. Unrelated to the drama at school, but still not exactly a friendly welcome to the neighbourhood. Also, there had been the girl they'd seen in the alley behind the laundromat on their way back from weekend furniture shopping. A girl, not a woman, definitely a younger teenager, stoned out of her mind and obviously waiting on a ride.

Neil read the side of the soup tin and added one and half cans of water, as indicated. He smooshed the condensed soup down with a spoon and gave it a swirl. Almost appetizing. He put the pot on an element but left the heat off. The sound of running water had started in the bathroom, but it wasn't that uncommon for Tanis to take to the shower to cry.

Neil rapped on the door and elicited a quiet, "What?" He opened the door, then stepped over the jogging clothes she'd dropped on the bath mat. She was wet and naked and, as he'd guessed, crying. The shower *shhhhhhhh*-ed down around her feet in the tub.

"Hey," Neil said. "Something wrong?" Tanis ducked her forehead into the water.

"C'mere," Neil beckoned, and they shared a small wet kiss. He pulled back with damp hair.

"It's probably just PMS," Tanis sniffed.

"That's supposed to be my line!"

"Ha. Could you close the door? I'm getting cold." Tanis rubbed water from her face. She was getting cold, Neil could see. He put his temple against the tiles and pulled the curtain closed around his face.

Tanis chattered her teeth. "You look like you're about to get a haircut."

"Cramps?" Neil asked. Tanis crossed her arms over her nipples and backed into the spray. She wasn't going to talk. Neil squeezed his eyes shut. "Babe, I'm going to go get us some munchies for a movie later, okay? Let's eat when I get back — just don't burn the soup."

» Nineteen

The thought of a smartphone, so essential, had been sneaking up on Taelur at odd times since school began and had often set her crying at the unfairness of it all. It had driven Melissa crazy, Taelur's constant whining about being locked into her parent's stupid bargain phone plan. But Melissa didn't understand. Her parents had bought unlimited texts, no strings. The teachers were totally sympathetic about crying, but they didn't understand either. Miss Enns had cornered Taelur in the change room after gym and handed her this little packet that looked like a condom. It was eye-makeup remover. Helpful, because Taelur had started looking like a raccoon, but then Miss Enns wanted to talk about how she felt about having her friends missing.

"It's pretty scary," Taelur had said.

"It's hard to admit that, sometimes," Miss Enns said. She was short and Taelur could look down into the top of the teacher's hair. It felt weird. Miss Enns had non-colour roots. Brown hair but if she grew it out she'd have hair the colour of dead grass, the colour of the locker room bench that had been varnished so many times the wood was milked up. Miss Enns was rambling on " — it's hard when we feel scared. Or if we feel scared for our friends, or about their decisions."

All the teachers were doing this gentle question thing. "Yeah, it's hard." Taelur said. *Kind of*, she wanted to say. Maybe Melissa and Jody were just partying somewhere and were going to come back and she'd missed it all. Or maybe they had got abducted, but then when they got rescued they'd go on *Oprah* and she'd give them college scholarships and new laptops. At least iPads or iPhones. That kind of thing happened, Taelur's mom agreed, *all the time*. Even Taelur's dad said they should hope for the best.

"Well," Miss Enns said, tapping at the little packet she'd pushed into Taelur's hand, "you make sure you take care of yourself. You can talk to me if you need to, but you've got your parents, and lots of friends. I don't want to find you crying in here again, okay?"

"Yeah," Taelur said, and she'd been almost sorry when Miss Enns left so she could "compose herself". Her mom and dad were okay. They had sat down in the family room to talk, as in *having a talk*, because Melissa and Jody hadn't called home yet.

"I'd feel safer if I had a better phone," Taelur tried. "Like one where I could text anybody, anytime, not just after four o'clock."

"Kiddo," her dad said, "if you need to text in the daytime, for an emergency, we wouldn't say a thing about extra charges. Trust me." He tipped her sideways in her chair and planted a kiss on her head, all understanding, until Miss Enns called to tell on her for going viral on Facebook.

Miss Enns convinced them that Taelur was *overwhelmed* by it all, so her parents took her, the night she posted the big boobs, to Boston Pizza. It was her favourite place. But the best thing was that Taelur's mom, in her mini-lectures, kept calling them *your boobs* the whole night.

"You don't post *your boobs* online," her mom said for the millionth time — but when Taelur laughed, Mom confiscated her useless phone.

"*As if*," Taelur, protested, "as if I even have anything to squish together." Her dad got so embarrassed. It was awesome. But he wouldn't say anything back because Kerri was there, colouring on a kid's placemat.

Taelur helped her little sister with the word find, and looked past her parents as they ate, over their heads to a silenced TV where Jody's mom, Janet from another Planet, and both of Melissa's parents, Mr. and Mrs. Arthur, mouthed pleas for the public to help.

Taelur's mom read Kolton's text, *Yo biatch, where you at?* and powered off the phone.

"Are you girls interested in a free dessert?" the waitress asked, beaming at Kerri and Taelur. Mom glared but Taelur clapped, *yay!*, and chose the chocolate ice cream free to under-twelves. She picked Hello Kitty press-on nails to match Kerri's from the kids' treasure box. They wouldn't even look too small on her nails because Taelur had small hands. She liked that. She liked being fifteen and passing for twelve, but only at Boston Pizza.

"Hey Dad?" she said, when he got up to pay the bill.

"Hey, Taelur."

"Thanks for the pizza, and the night out. And Dad — "

"Yep." He walked away, and Kerri scooted out of the booth to go with him and get an extra dinner mint.

"What did you want to say?" her mom asked.

"Yeah, just I won't post something like that again."

"You're right, you won't." Because they grounded her from the Internet. And they kept her phone, never mind how she'd be *at risk* now. She tried to argue to have the phone at least in the day at school but her dad ignored her, and when they got home her mom went upstairs getting Kerri through the good-night routine and her dad went out somewhere. Taelur got her backpack from the front hall and took it to her room. She took out her math workbook and pulled a blank page out of the back, liking the way the paper tore against the coils. She folded the sheet in half four times and then spread it out and ripped along the creases. She'd have to go old school, and pass notes.

Date: September 21, 10:52 AM — Occurrence Number: 15-15114

Released By: Sgt. Linda Malhiot

Subject: Missing Person – Request For Public Assistance

Saskatoon Police are requesting public assistance in locating two teenaged girls.

Melissa Arthur was reported missing by her family after she failed to return to her residence. She was last seen on September 13th, 2015, in the company of Jody Bear, at approximately 3:45 PM at a school located on the 1500 block of Avenue L South. A photo is attached for media distribution.

Melissa (16 years old) is described as being of a fair complexion, approximately 5'7" in height and weighing 140 lbs. She has naturally brown hair, recently dyed pink, and brown eyes. view image

Jody Bear (15 years old) was reported missing by her family after she failed to return to her residence. She was last seen on September 13th, 2015, in the company of Melissa Arthur, at approximately 3:45 PM at a school located on the 1500 block of Avenue L South. A photo is attached for media distribution.

Jody is described as being of First Nations descent, approximately 5'3" in height and weighing 100 lbs. She has shoulder length black hair and brown eyes. view image

Persons with information on the whereabouts of either youth are asked to contact City Police at 555-8300 or Crime Stoppers at 1-800-555-8477.

» Twenty

"See this, Em?" Thomas smirked, rattling the newspaper. He winked to Phidelma at the stove, but spoke to Emelyn across the table. "You reckon we'll need a plan on Phidelma?"

He is joking, that's all he means his girl to know. But some girls bring their school lunch wrapped in newspapers. Phidelma knows all about the father who killed his daughter, and how he got life insurance on her first. Now here's Thomas joking with Emelyn, the woman who has come to live in the house. They share a bed and have made no secret about it, but when he's away Emelyn is meant also to be some kind of chaperone. There are no other men, despite what neighbours say, so Phidelma supposes Emelyn does belong to her father — that Emelyn is a kind of stepmother, maybe a protector. The girl who was killed — "pulped" was what the paper actually said — that girl had a proper mother and it hadn't made a difference.

Emelyn met Thomas' eyes but didn't laugh.

"I'd be harder than that to kill," Phidelma boasted, and set Thomas' coffee on the table in front of him, not in his outstretched hand. He grunted, but when he lifted the cup it was to cover a smile.

Stepping past Father and "The Woman", as Robert had called her, Phidelma forced a laugh, too. She was supposed to laugh at that silly Ida Dyer getting pounded away into blood and bits of bone and whatnot all over Mr. Dyer's warehouse. He didn't get caught because he'd hired a middleman. A middleman sounded, to Phidelma and Elizabeth, her lunch mate at school, more dangerous than a mean father. It didn't occur to them that the middleman would have been paid, hired for the job. Phidelma imagined something like a boogeyman, beckoned to the deed. Or Wee Willie Winkie, who Meline used to say would light Phidelma's nighty on fire if she got out of their bed.

In this house, nights Thomas had business, men would gather on the main floor and even with raised voices below, it was the brush of her nightgown against the floor upstairs that spooked Phidelma. Wee Willie, the rhyme said, peered through the locks. Phidelma avoided looking at the door from her bed, afraid of that boogeyman's watching eye, no matter how wee he might be.

After older girls explained the idea of a "hit man" to Phidelma and Elizabeth, Ida Louise Dyer's death at her parent's hand felt more grittily real — but awkward as it was to have this woman in the house, Thomas did make a point of giving Emelyn money to take care of his child. And Emelyn was good natured enough about it.

Some mornings Phidelma left the house with money tucked into her shoe to come back with groceries. Or sewing fancies, because Emelyn sewed and she altered clothes. She'd moved in to stay not a month after Thomas shipped Robert to Manitoba, and she'd brought little other than clothes and her table top treadle and a sewing box. The box was red wood, with curved ends and a quilted green satin top that could hold pins. It opened at the middle like an accordion, fanning out to either side, and it was the first thing about Emelyn that Phidelma liked.

Emelyn worked at her sewing machine in corner of the front room, on a table Thomas moved in and set in a place Phidelma could see from the turn of the stairs. Emelyn had black hair, like

Marguerite's, but it was nowhere as thick. The bun she pulled it back into was tiny and tight, and she had wisps of shorter hair at her temples, broken pieces. Her face was long and full, manly almost, but under it she had a round woman's body. Dancing legs and breasts that pushed up, jiggling under her blouse when she laughed or fought with Thomas.

Phidelma was stretching out, but she had a child's body. Her breasts had only just started to swell and ache, she could barely imagine a body like The Woman's.

"Phi-del-ma," Emelyn called, one day, early on. "Let me use your young eyes." She was matching thread to a dress and had pulled spool after spool out of the basket. "Look down in there, do you see another blue? Does this one match, or this one better?"

"This one matches," Phidelma said, rising triumphantly.

Emelyn took the spool from Phidelma's hand and said, casually, "It's a shame about your mother, isn't it?" The woman ducked her chin to meet Phidelma's eyes. "How did she die, little one? He hasn't said."

Until then, Marguerite had run away, as Robert insisted. Or she had been taken, as Phidelma suspected. Either way, she'd been coming back.

"How did she go?" Emelyn asked again.

"Tubercular consumption," Phidelma said, promptly this time. She knew about tuberculosis, and the sanatorium by the river, and how the damp, dirty old shack they'd lived in led to Meline and the twin babies being killed off. This was, at any rate, what she had got out of the school nurse's lectures.

"It was a blessing then, your mother leaving first," Emelyn said, petting Phidelma on the shoulder before she ran away.

Phidelma escaped upstairs, to the room where Thomas stored his daughter and his books and also stacks of fur sometimes if the attic floor got full. There'd been a stack in the room the week before and it was empty now, but the smell of tanned hides lingered. Phidelma sat on edge of her bed and breathed it in and out. Wet smokey wood, like a fire put out by the rain.

She felt angry, not at Emelyn but at Robert who had promised her again before leaving to bring Marguerite home. He'd promised to write a letter too, and hadn't. Robert had his hands busy, Thomas said. Which was how they should be if he wouldn't go to school. Her brother was doing something like Thomas, Phidelma guessed, buying furs, or driving them. What could he know?

The idea of Marguerite being dead, rather than held captive or starting a new life somewhere, made more sense, really. It was a "shame", and Phidelma whispered the word. Not a "blessing", but the sick feeling that had knotted Phidelma's stomach for so long was working its way loose.

Their first time in this house, she and Robert had been excited to run around the second floor. There'd been no walls, just an open space with pillars running up to the roof, and gaps in the floor that you could peer down through. They'd lain on their bellies and had seen Marguerite in the kitchen below them and, overwhelmed by the space and stillness, Phidelma had knocked — just to make a sound. To be sure her mama would look up.

Phidelma heard Emelyn push her chair back and walk from the front room to the kitchen downstairs, and she remembered the smell of Marguerite's skirt. Raw flour and lard, the rough wool against her cheeks. She pressed her face into her pillow, felt the sun on her back, and beneath her feet the rag rug slid sideways on the floor. Phidelma pushed it farther and tapped her shoe.

She dreaded telling Robert the truth. This new and better story left no room for her brother to fix their world the way he wanted to. Phidelma imagined his disappointment, his anger, the storm of words he would hurl at Thomas. But Robert did not come home for a long, long time.

»Twenty-One

Neil rose early Friday without waking Tanis. He showered and dressed, and she slept like a hibernating bear. A stray foot and hand stuck out of her cave. In the night the fitted bottom sheet had pulled up from the mattress and the elastic hem had gathered, cupping the curve of her back. Neil pulled the duvet over the sheet and crawled up the length of his wife's body. Her hair was damp and warm against her neck. Neil couldn't make out the words she murmured, thick with sleep. He bundled the duvet around her shoulders and kissed a naked ear. Safe and snug.

Outside, frost had changed the trees. Neil walked up the hill through a flurry of yellow leaves. They stuck to his shoes and he scraped them against the boot mat at school. His wet soles squeaked against freshly waxed floors. It felt strange to arrive early, alone in a place that was normally so crowded.

Unlocking his classroom door, Neil found his lights already on, but no one inside. He scanned the room for missing things but nothing seemed off. Maybe he'd left the light on the afternoon before — or had the janitor been through? Or the police? Maybe kids had been on the roof again. Neil crossed to the window and checked the latch, which opened easily. You could slide it closed from the roof, but not lock it, so maybe this meant someone had gone out, or unlocked it so another kid could come in to his classroom that way, because the classroom door worked the same way. A kid could get out of but not in through the locked door, without setting off an alarm. Asymmetric boundary conditions. Neil hadn't considered that before.

He stared over the gravel rooftop at the yellow trees and the brightening sky, then set his shoulder bag down on the desk. It was heavy, filled with assignments he'd meant to mark but hadn't the night before. Tanis had mellowed out over supper, babbled about the boots again, and they'd watched a show on Netflix — but then when he'd sat down to work she'd gone to her computer and searched *missing girl Saskatoon* on Google, looking for the police photos of Melissa and Jody. She'd wanted to know what they looked like, really get their pictures set in her head, so that if they were down by the river, among the teens who gathered at the skate park, she would recognize them when she jogged by. But Tanis found too, too many missing girls and women — dating all the way back to the first homesteads. More recently, there had been incidents from the past twenty years. She'd come down to the living room to tell him that eight missing women had last been seen within a ten-block radius of their own house. This house, Tanis stressed, and she'd set a fist against the wall as if it were in some way implicated in the crimes.

"Well, so?" Neil had replied. She'd gawked, then railed. "Well, so? That's what you — "

"Babe, hey, Tanis." Sometimes you just had to wait it out. What he'd meant was that obviously missing and murdered people cases in Saskatoon would be close to their house because it was in an older, core neighbourhood. At first, all of Saskatoon was practically ten blocks away, right? And core areas, with a higher population density, would have more people to go missing, right?

"Still, Neil," Tanis had protested, "we're not talking about a couple of women." He'd wrapped his arms around her and rocked her, "I know." Not that he'd torment Tanis, or his students, with puzzling out the likelihood that they'd be abducted, or murdered, but it was the kind of optimization problem that had drawn Neil into math in the first place. You could calculate optimal conditions for other things. Like job searching, or buying used cars. Murder density was creepy. Neil did understand why Tanis was upset, but he'd worn his empathy down being Mr. Understanding with worked-up kids all week. Finally, Tanis' shoulders relaxed, she had sighed and squeaked out, "I just don't like feeling in the middle of this." Neil had pulled her tight into his chest to hide her view of his face, and answered as evenly as he could, "You're not."

Now, in his empty early-morning classroom, Neil took a minute to honour Jody's desk. Third from the left, far back row, Math ten. Jody was in the middle of this. Jody who'd travelled a total of fifty kilometers during her summer break, according to her assignment, and whose dad had never attended a teacher's interview or sports event in her two years of high school, according to Karen. An "at risk" First Nations youth in a single-parent home — Jody who'd nonetheless attained a very respectable 90% on the assessment test and first unit quizzes.

Smart people get into stupid things all the time, Tanis' mother had told Neil that recently, excusing the six days they'd lived by LED lantern light after agreeing to be fit into the electrician's schedule rather than booking a day and time. That had been fixed, though. Now it was just a matter of plastering and painting things, which would fall to Tanis. "Women's work," Declan had joked. "Work at home work," Neil had replied equitably. But that also included making the bed and laundry, which Tanis wasn't quite on top of.

Selecting a "pen" from his Smart Board tray, Neil pulled out a paper from his shoulder bag and set his morning class's problem up on the board. It listed upwards, so he erased and began again. Repeating a middle variable in the equation, he sighed, switched back to the eraser, and jumped when someone knocked at the doorway.

"Oh, hi, Kolton. What can I do for you?"

The teenager stood a foot back from the doorway. He shrugged under a flannel plaid jacket.

"Do you want come in? Have a question about yesterday's work?"

"So, Mr. Cameron, could I tell you something?" the boy asked, chin raised to make eye contact under the brim of a hat pulled down too low. "You all said if we had to tell you something we should?"

"Yes, absolutely, come on in, Kolton." Neil pulled the boy in by a sleeve and shut the door. Kolton licked his lips, ducked his face and stayed quiet.

"Is this more of an open door meeting?" Neil asked, returning a hand to the knob.

"No, it's not a big thing, just I wanted to tell you, so you know — they're really missing, right?"

"Yes, that's what the police have told us."

"I know, it's just that they're really gone, okay? People are saying they're not but they're not at home, they're actually missing."

"Are people saying that they aren't, Kolton?"

The boy gave Neil a measuring look. "On Facebook and stuff they're saying about some girl in England who faked getting kidnapped. And this guy in Ontario who made an email about being missing, for a joke."

"Some joke. But you know they're really missing?" Neil looked to Kolton's face for confirmation. "Is there anything you need to tell the police, or their parents?"

The boy shrugged. "She would've texted me."

"Jody or Melissa?"

"Yeah."

"Melissa?" Neil racked his mind for the guidelines — boundaries, permissions, the gym. "Have you talked to the police in the gym, the counsellor guys they set up in there?"

"What would I say to them? I just know, right. So you should tell them so they take it seriously."

"I will, Kolton. I can do that. You don't have some idea where they are, do you?"

Kolton looked for a moment as though he were about to cry, or yawn. Instead, he reached past Neil's arm for the door, grabbed the handle and went out, hitching his pants.

Hitching his cool, Tanis called it that. When they postured, pants drooping, then started walking and had to slouch down, hitching their cool saggy pants up enough to move their legs.

"Have a nice day, Kolton," Neil called into the hallway.

The kid wanted to do something, same as the rest. And he was the girls' friend, though Neil wasn't sure it was true that Melissa would be texting Kolton anytime she did something. She wasn't his girlfriend, he didn't think.

He sat down at his computer and opened the staff blog. The update from Bornstein that morning was clear — no news might as well be taken as good news. Their task for the day was to "keep things level". A vigil was planned for the weekend coming up and the police were worried that the students' anxiety levels, and rumour output, would be ramping up. It'd been the students' news — from the ground up — and that had been exciting at first. But now they were ready for the adults to take charge and fix things.

Can't fix what you didn't break, Tanis' mom had often said, a mascot for optimistic parenting. Neil mulled over his encounter with Kolton, then posted to the teacher's circle: *Kolton Dueck is worried that some people are spreading a rumour that the girls' disappearance is a hoax. He wanted me to pass on that he is pretty sure that they are "really gone" and to tell the police and staff to "take it seriously". I think we should encourage the students to attend the vigil. They need to contribute to a solution in some way.*

In the corner of the screen, white hand icons fluttered. Bornstein was still online, live from his office a floor below, and had e-clapped. Neil scanned the members logged in. Enns. Jacobs. Karen Smith's icon went blank while he watched. It blinked out, and other teachers' icons followed as the warning buzzer rang signalling period one. Neil's students appeared in person, filing in, an anxious march of black denim, flannel plaid, silver jewellery.

At noon, Karen appeared in Neil's doorway wielding a data key. He'd had three good morning periods, distracting the kids with the fun of impossible proofs, and almost made an excuse about urgent grading to avoid her, but she looked panicked and guilty. She, along with Dec, Pulley, and Neil, were supposed to be allies of sorts, but they all felt she tried too hard.

"May I show you something?" Karen asked, then plugged the key into Neil's computer without waiting for a reply. "I have to show you something Jody turned in."

"Like an assignment?"

"They're writing assignments, but shit. Neil you have to read these and tell me what . . . you think." She meant *what to do*, that came through clear and Neil turned curiously to his screen where a folder had appeared. *JBear CW10.*

"CW, does that mean Creative Writing?"

"Yes."

"Stories or something?"

"We're going to do stories. But they all have to make this portfolio first, okay? It's called flash fiction. They have the month to do it, then drop the files in to our course site. So I didn't see the last one until I checked today." She frowned. "Just read them, okay?"

Neil opened a folder. *The Secret*, a paragraph about burying some papers in the ground. Tanis would like it. "She's a really good writer," he commented, and pointed, curious, at the grade of 3/5, which seemed low. He raised his eyebrows to Karen.

She shrugged. "They've all got room to grow, you have to push them."

Neil reviewed her comment, getting the gist of the assignments. "So, she had to write a flash fiction story about a secret?"

Karen nodded.

"What's the next one like?" Neil clicked on *Time is a River.*

> You can't walk into the river. You can walk across it. Winter's freezing makes a path. If you walk backwards in your tracks carefully enough you can make a line of footprints that goes right to the edge of the open water. If you walk backwards in your tracks carefully enough they will think that you fell in. At the edge of the ice the water is black. Not blue. It is black. It is swirled and thick like mud. When you stand at the edge of the ice, the water looks like you could walk on it. That thick. That solid. All alone in Time.

[3/5 There is some good description here but I'm not sure that you've captured the metaphor of "Time" as a river. Usually time progresses downstream, carrying the "you" or "I" with it. It is always a good idea to be clear about a metaphor before you begin to apply it in your writing. Next time, see me if you have questions about requirements.]

"See what I mean?" Karen asked.

"Well, okay — yes, it's dark. But it's very descriptive. The assignment was to write about a metaphor?"

"Yep."

"Well," Neil said, "if you're thinking this is some kind of foreshadowing, there's no ice on the river yet."

"Even so, Neil. Last year I had her in English nine and she was writing about fairies and wizards."

"That must happen all the time," Neil protested.

"What must happen?"

"Well, they grow up and wall up. Like Bornstein says, they come to grade nine like puppies. Then they have to test things, and some of them are going to be dark, and this isn't even that — um, dark. She's a happy math student. She puts smiley faces on answers she knows are right."

Karen shook her head. "Do I take this to the police?"

"I don't know." Neil said. "I guess so."

"They're going to want to know why I didn't give them this a week ago — "

"Didn't you forget about it till today?"

"Yeah . . . kind of. Shit, shit, shit."

"I really don't think this is a big deal, Karen. You've put comments and grades in there along the way so obviously you didn't read them today." Neil paused, but Karen failed to look embarrassed. He continued, "If you erased them the police would know that too, right? So just tell them that you weren't and aren't sure if it's relevant to the case, the investigation, whatever."

"You should probably read the next one."

Twenty-Two

The doorbell rang and Tanis went to answer it, half expecting to have to put off another pair of Latter-day Saints. Neil kept encouraging them, taking their pamphlets. But it was police at the front door. A blond boy cop and a woman, much older.

"Hello," Tanis said. She had read online about the door-to-door investigation and maybe should have been expecting them, but she missed most of their spiel wondering if they wanted Neil.

He had come home late the night before, but that was because he was writing emails — trying to communicate with parents before the first meet-the-teacher night. Nothing to do with missing girls. Still. Tanis propped herself up, leaning her weight on the doorknob.

"I'm sorry," she explained, "it's just so sad. My husband is a teacher at their school, and we've been thinking about them a lot. He has to teach, you know, with their desks empty."

The cops stared at her, at her fumbling, and Tanis pressed on, "I haven't seen them. I don't meet his students. Not unless we're out somewhere, say Superstore and we see some. They wave, you know, at him."

The boy cop spoke very clearly, "Did you see Melissa Arthur or Jody Bear at Superstore?"

Tanis shook her head, embarrassed.

"That was an example, then?" he asked.

Tanis nodded.

"Thank you for your time, ma'am," the woman said, and her sidekick reached inside to take the doorknob. Tanis stepped back, he pulled the door shut, and she watched their shadows disappear from the glass. She stepped in to the door, turned the deadbolt, and winced — she'd been so quick, they'd probably heard her lock them out. Ridiculous.

She retreated to the kitchen, ears roaring, and folded her arms on the counter to steady herself. When the police came to the door she'd panicked and they didn't even have anything to hide. When the kitchen stopped spinning, Tanis phoned Neil at the school.

"Is there anything I should know?" she asked. "Is there any reason the police would be visiting us?"

"No," Neil said quickly. "Well a rumour, but I think I've cleared it up."

"A rumour?"

"About student boundaries, the kind of thing, you know, that they warn you about when you start. But it's just that and just a kid who thinks he wants to be involved."

"Involved how? Why would he want that?"

"The girls are kind of celebrities, mysterious for being missing. They have web pages and stuff like that and I guess he was fishing for comments. There's some name for it, online prodding or something."

"Creeping," Tanis supplied.

"I guess he wanted to have more of a connection to the case."

"I think I might actually be involved," Tanis said.

"Why — because of me?"

"You're not involved, are you?"

She sounded nervous, but Neil brushed her question aside. "What do you mean *you* are involved, Tanis?"

"I feel dizzy."

"So sit down. What are you on about?"

"I think I saw them."

"Jody and Melissa? Where, when, doing what?"

"Just outside talking, I think the day they are supposed to have disappeared."

"You think?"

"I think."

"Then call it in."

"Just I'm not sure that it was actually them."

"Well — "

"Or that it was the right day."

"Look, you are not involved in this. If you are, then you just saw them."

"Yes, but they were — "

"Tanis, there is no way that this is your fault. This isn't CSI or something, okay? Everybody's not involved in this. But seriously, call the police."

"Neil." She wanted to tell him that the girls had been going in the direction of the river. The kind of place that kids could disappear. Now the leaves were falling in droves and it felt very open down there but a week before there'd been a screen of leaves. Water, dark bushes.

"Don't wait for me." Neil advised. "Just call them."

When the cops came back, the blond guy and the older woman, Tanis asked if they'd like tea.

"No, thank you," they said, each holding a coffee flask already. For just two people they took up an incredible amount of space in the living room.

"I'll get myself water," Tanis said, making an excuse to get away. Why were they so cheerful? She filled a mug at the sink, then emptied it halfway because her hand was shaking and she didn't want to spill.

"So, you think that you may have met the girls after all?" the boy, officer Kipland, prompted.

Tanis shook her head. "Not met." She explained about seeing the girls huddled on the sidewalk and the woman took note of this unexcitedly. It was a long street, maybe there were more witnesses.

"You can't think of any reason they would want to sit outside your house, in particular?" the policewoman asked, pulling her shoes back on at the door.

"No," Tanis answered firmly. Unless they'd known it was Mr. Cameron's house, had maybe followed him home sometime before. But they hadn't looked up at the house, either of them, not once.

Amnesty
by Jody Bear

One woman disappeared when that door closed. Say that another appeared when it opened. Or that a girl fell through. These are scary stories because we are all moving in the best ways we know but nothing is safe. What if you opened a door, and shit splattered like a can of paint all over your life. Down the street from here they found a girl who went missing in the winter. Not really a girl, she was a mom and already had two small kids of her own. The sky looked down and saw her nestled under some wooden pallets. She was like any other creature, hibernating, until the spring found her body. We can't lift her up to a heat lamp and get her going again. No smell of spring or berries or fat rabbits will wake her up. You didn't see her fall asleep and she won't wake up — you'll have to feel her melt in the sunshine and hear her lick to drink the melting snow. It rains from all the eavestroughs. When she has wet her throat she'll start to whisper. I will too because I heard her, and because only the good die young. Might as well light a smoke, these rest of us need to earn our rest.

[2/5 Touching. You have certainly evoked "sadness". I have deducted marks because you have not cited your sources, Jody. There are numerous echoes of "Lost Sister" by the singer Utinaya here and it would be appropriate to mention this inspiration, e.g. "When she has wet her throat . . . " See your student handbook, page 33, for a definition of "plagiarism".]

» Twenty-Three

When Jody hadn't come home, her mother, Janet McKay, phoned her family, then James, her ex-husband, and his family, and then she'd made her way down a list of every one of Jody's friends she had a number for. She walked the blocks around the school, between the school and her apartment and the condo where Melissa lived. She brought a flashlight to search gutters and backyards, but found herself looking into lit windows instead. Wanting the safety other families seemed to have. Afraid to shine her light anyplace evidence might hide.

Dogs barked, doors opened, and then a police cruiser came alongside her on the sidewalk. They'd received a call about "an individual acting suspiciously".

"Better to wait by the phone," the officer advised, but it was with Janet in her pocket. She'd cut the landline a year ago, no sense paying twice.

When James arrived Saturday, driving in too fast and collecting tickets on the highway, they went out looking again. Janet couldn't think of any streets she hadn't already been down. That left the river, the skate park and public restrooms, and down the slope to the lower trail.

"What would Jody have been doing, coming down here?" James asked. It was dark already, and windy, and the riverbank trees were whipping around. The orange potassium lights over the bike path glowed on the water, lighting it in slivers that rippled and sparked.

"It's different in the day," Janet said. She'd been no nature parent but she'd brought Jody down to the water lots of times. They'd brought slushies down, syrup and ice, beating summer heat on the shaded path. They'd pulled fat grasses up from the edge of the river. She'd shown Jody how to blow on a blade of grass, pressed tight between her thumbs, to make it squeal. "Scare prayer" they'd called it where Janet grew up. Looks like I'm praying, then I scream. Janet bent now to pull a long blade of grass that angled over the path.

"Same sound for a baby deer," James said, taking the grass from her. He pinched it between his thumb and forefinger, then brought his hand up to his face. Smelling summer, ripe in the blade. He didn't make the call, but commented, "It's the same sound you make to get a doe to come when you're hunting."

James was hoarse from shouting down the parkway earlier. His voice rasped as he whispered his questions. Their girl had never done anything like this before. "She been going out a lot, Janet?"

"No," Janet said. The police had asked too, but the handful of times over the summer when Jody had been out in the night she'd been at sleepovers. Movies and sleeping bags.

"She got friends, though?" James looked past Janet to the lights on the water.

He'd been asking that for years. Worried because Jody'd be so quiet sometimes. But she'd always been quiet. So quiet at school, the teachers always said at interview time. She wasn't that way with her friends. "She's always got friends, James. Some different ones now." Janet ran her mind down the list she'd made and explained. "The group from grade eight split up between high schools. She keeps in touch with those girls, too."

"That's Tina, Catherine, them?"

Janet nodded.

"That was a good group."

It had been, not so much anymore.

"You know this Melissa?" James asked. But Janet didn't, not really. The girl had come over once that fall, watched a movie and slept over. They were big girls, and Janet had left them to themselves in the living room, taking a book away to her room. She'd lain listening to her daughter and the other girl laughing loud at jokes too quiet to hear. She'd thought they'd been texting boys, but who knew. They could've been talking to anybody right there in her family room. The other girl had performed a few disappearing acts before, according to the police. Maybe this was the same thing, with Jody tagging along, they'd suggested. Janet shook her head, no. No, she didn't know this Melissa. But Jody'd never been a tag-along.

James stepped in close. It wasn't until he had his fingers on her face that Janet felt her tears. She pushed his hand away. "You don't even know — " she said, stopping herself. *Know Jody*, she was going to say. That was too mean to say aloud.

"You're working hard and all that," she said. "Maybe you don't spend enough time with your girl. Even out at Last Mountain it's your sister's place she ends up at."

"What are you getting at?"

"Just that — just it's hard to keep up. With our girl, her friends."

"I guess it is," James said. He turned on the narrow trail and they climbed the bank without talking. He only had Jody some weekends, Janet had her every night — but she worked night shifts at a medi-centre's front reception. It had been convenient, working shifts, being flexible, when Jody was younger. Now she had to watch sick kids come in, cuddling and leaning on their moms and dads, while her kid was home alone, head in a book it had been for the longest time, now face on the phone. The weekend would come and Jody had her sleepovers, or she took the bus to James. Time with Janet came around less often, but on a weeknight if they were both home Jody would settle in beside Janet's needlework and stream them *Game of Thrones*.

"We still do the crafts, James," Janet said.

He stopped on the path. "She still tell you when you're done?"

Since she'd been small, Janet had let Jody put her nose right up to the pieces, checking how close and tidy the thread and beads came to the lines she'd helped to stencil onto the bags Janet and her cousin sold.

"I'm not sure I'd know otherwise," Janet said.

James gave the smallest bit of a smile. He'd wound the length of grass tight around his fingers as they walked back to the car. Now Janet looked away to let him shake it off and dig for his keys.

He'd always done that, fiddled or tore something up when he was thinking — Jody'd started getting to be the same way. Janet wondered if James had noticed, or his sister. And if it could mean anything. At home, Janet kept glovers needles stuck in the arm of the couch, handy. She'd done that for years. Only this past fall Jody'd started taking them out to weave in and out of her thumb. She pulled the metal bar clear through her skin, and claimed it didn't hurt. The callus on her right hand, where she held her pens and pencils, got marked up. The broken skin collected ink and lead. Accidental tattoos. When Janet noticed Jody lift a needle she'd stop her, but her attention had been split three ways, between her beading, the show, and Jody's hilarious commentary on both.

» Twenty-Four

Phidelma did not finish grade seven after all. There was a snowstorm that would not end, and school was cancelled, and before it opened Thomas had dealings with Mr. Smith. His wife, Mrs. Smith had come over from England after the First World War. She was quite small and looked young until Thomas brought Phidelma right up beside her. Then she saw Mrs. Smith's joints — the bones swelling up under her skin, which was thin and pale and knotted with veins. She needed help with lifting, dusting and cleaning — small jobs separately, but the house was larger than any Phidelma had been in.

They paid her with a coat, first off. She needed it for walking over and it was the nicest she'd had, burgundy wool. But it was built for fashion over function. The coat buttons stopped at the waist, and the skirt caught the wind, flapping over her knees when she crossed the river on the metal truss bridge.

Her first day, Mr. Smith met Phidelma at the door and took her coat. Then he toured her through the rooms, and then into the kitchen where he showed her a blackened double boiler that she could use to heat dry barley on an electric range.

"Can you guess what for?" he asked.

"Coffee," Phidelma answered confidently. But the kernels were to fill a pair of sleeves that Mr. Smith draped over Mrs. Smith's

wrists — to keep down the ache of arthritis. Phidelma had never seen heat therapy, as she came to know it. She'd also never seen a man bend over his wife, caring for her like that. Mrs. Smith's wrists were pinned to the arms of a stuffed chair. She stretched her fingers out from beneath the barely sleeves and Phidelma stared.

"You're lucky to be young," Mrs. Smith said. "A whole life ahead of you, so many things to learn."

Phidelma smiled. That was what her teacher had said, the first day at school in the fall. Phidelma would miss her friend Elizabeth, but not, overly much, the teacher Miss Wilson — although she had let Phidelma run errands to the storeroom. Phidelma had loved to hunt out their class ration of brittle black pigment. There was a pestle to crush it, a beaker and basin to mix the ink for their pens.

"Can you read and write as well a dust, my dear?" Mrs. Smith asked.

Phidelma said that she could.

"Let's take a letter down, then," Mrs. Smith said. She balled her hands, and lifted them our from under the barley sleeves, which she draped over the arm of the chair.

"I don't mind," Phidelma said. She got flustered, though, spelling new words, and spelling through Mrs. Smith's English accent. The first letters took multiple tries. But Mrs. Smith enjoyed herself, and laughed when she made mistakes alongside Phidelma — spelling the words out loud. The letter was nothing special, Mrs. Smith said, just a missive to friends — and by the time it was done Phidelma had finished feeling embarrassed.

"Let's fix ourselves some lunch," Mrs. Smith said. "What do you like for a midday meal, Phidelma? I have ham, and we do have mustard. Do you do sandwiches?"

Walking back and forth across the river, and accompanying Mrs. Smith on errands, Phidelma became a clothes hound for Emelyn.

She reported back that spring on nylons and bias-cut dresses, bows along the back and V-shaped neck. At the ladies auxiliary meeting there were jackets and Chinese tunics with long straight skirts underneath. Emelyn bit her lip. "I have a piece of brocade, Delma."

The silk brocade shift was the last dress that Emelyn finished, swearing over the closure, which had her hand binding Chinese frog buttons. "Does that look even?" she asked.

Phidelma bent in to look, "They look beautiful." The buttons were folded and knotted silk cord, they looked like fancy brass hinges, climbing the breast panel. She pictured the dress on Mrs. Smith, but it was for Emelyn and the panel needed shape to hold the top of her in.

"I'm tacking these closed underneath, even so — I'll be damned if I can't flatten these darts," Emelyn muttered, then sighed. "Your papa had better open his eyes for this one."

The Ladies Auxiliary collected boxes of clothes for the needy, and to send overseas — and by the end of the summer there were already two brocade dresses in the boxes.

"A quick fad," Mrs. Smith commented. "Are there any things you'd like to snag, Phidelma?" It was just them, and Mrs. Evans, who knew just as much about Phidelma at home by then.

"Nothing to be embarrassed about," Mrs. Evans said, turning the girl's attention to the second box. "That wool skirt looks warm now but it would suit you in the winter. We could take it in."

Phidelma examined the skirt. It was good quality wool, and it looked like a nice weight. But when Mrs. Evans held it up you could see where someone had worn it thin across the knees.

Phidelma turned back to the first crate and grabbed at the thing that had first caught her eye. A flowered shawl like the half-breed ladies wore when they came by the Anglican parish office. Marguerite had not had one, but Phidelma thought that if she'd gotten to be like one of those older women, a mother of young men and women, not of babies, Marguerite would have sat still more, like they did. She'd have needed a shawl to put around her shoulders, doing her embroidery. And to pull up over her ears if she walked with Phidelma across the bridge. The wind always blew stronger over the water. It was a long warm fall and Phidelma swapped her cardigan for Marguerite's shawl, folding it in a square and pinning it around her shoulders, until she needed a proper coat.

Thomas and Emelyn had begun travelling, some new business. The first time they left together Phidelma had been at the Smiths' and came home to an empty house. She waited up. They were gone three days, and when she ran to greet them they laughed at her. Emelyn had been drinking, she thought. Her face was flushed, with red patches climbing her cheeks. Thomas, though, stood straight. "What are you now, thirteen, my girl?" Phidelma frowned; he ought to know. "Well, then. Young lady," he said.

"Don't pout, we brought you something," Emelyn gushed. "It'll be just the thing if you grow your hair." The woman pulled a hair clasp from her purse and clipped it awkwardly to Marguerite's shawl. Phidelma's hair was cut in a bob, too short for the gift. It was pretty though. Cream enamel worked through with little spirals of silver, like snow that had caught metal shavings.

The next time they left in the evening, called her down for goodbyes, and Phidelma understood she'd be left behind. But Marguerite was always near. Hidden in Phidelma's own heart, Mrs. Smith suggested. And waiting beside her bed, where Phidelma now made it a practice to kneel and pray. At night the weight of the aunties' horsehair quilt held her safe — the cold satin edging fell across her neck like Meline's arm, fever-moist. The wind at the window was Marguerite's breath, watching out for her dreaming girls.

» Twenty-Five

Tanis dreamt about grocery shopping. First the radio alarm worked its way in — an echoing strain that wound down the food aisles, mysteriously sourceless. Then a clatter and groan came from the back of the store, behind the big metal doors that sealed off the cold storage inventory. Tanis watched the doors heave and shake, dropped a basket full of bagged fruit, and woke to the beeping sound of a truck backing up on the road outside. Something had landed heavily enough to rattle the window.

She'd slept late and Neil was long gone. Tanis reached for her glasses and frowned at the window, which shook again. She rolled to her stomach, stretched flat, and then pushed herself up on her arms, feeling very stiff. She'd alternated computer work with pressing Polyfilla around the new socket boxes for most of the weekend. First wedging the paste in with a putty knife, then sanding it flat once it dried, with spurts of fact-checking service MOUs for a home-based lawyer in between. White borders now reached out around the naked switches, waiting for paint. And her working hours waited for billing.

Tanis rose from the bed and looked down at Avenue L, where a group of workmen had huddled around an iPad on the tailgate of a city truck. They'd been working on the block immediately south earlier in the week — dug up, re-piped, and repaved the road.

Pressing her hands together in front of her chest, Tanis lowered them to her solar plexus. A prayer to ward off carpal tunnel syndrome. She crossed the hall to check email at her desk. She hadn't received any further directions from her legal client, but Celia had replied to confirm their Tim Horton's date — and Tanis grinned, then typed in a quick search of Canadian vital statistics documents. There was a 100-year limit on birth and death certificates, which was frustrating. Information about Celia's aunt was probably there in the database, but screened out of her search as "recent and personal" data. Beyond 100 years, Tanis found a certificate of marriage, Thomas John Tanner of Portage La Prairie, Manitoba (Protestant) to Agnes Marguerite Laurie of Rounde Prairie, Saskatchewan (Catholic). The date, August 9th, 1912, seemed about right based on Celia's age.

> *In the diocese of Saskatchewan, embracing religious mixture enter Thomas Tanner, age 22, Protestant bachelor, and Agnes Marguerite Laurie, age 18, Catholic widow. We determine no cause for which they should not be married at the Sainte-Eglise under agreement that they will remain practicing her religion; and also the natural children of this marriage; so let this marriage commence with economy that it be accomplished as soon as witnessed by Pierre Tanner and Marianne Louise Laurie.*

Their brother and sister? Father and mother? Celia might be interested to follow those names, and to know that her Grandmother Marguerite had already been a widow at 18. That was pretty tragic. Celia hadn't known where her grandmother had come from. Rounde Prairie, Saskatchewan, it said here.

That had been one of the largest French Métis settlements on the prairies, just south of Saskatoon. A quick search for it now revealed abandoned fields, empty except for a cemetery whose roster Marguerite was not on. Tanis scanned through Census records, and found the Tanners of Portage la Prairie, Scottish and Scotch-Métis, farmers and clerks. There were more recent records from the wars, uniform rosters, and a Thomas Tanner from Manitoba had served, though not overseas. His son Robert, Celia's father, wasn't easy to find online. Maybe he'd used another name. Baptized Thomas Robert, but used Robert, Robbie, Bob. Second World War records were still closed, except for those confirmed dead. How long would the government keep a missing-in-action file open before issuing a death certificate? Robert would be something like ninety-five.

It was far-fetched, but Tanis Googled "WW2 Military Boots Canada" next. The pictures that came up had a similar look. They were black, polished and ladder laced with a studded leather sole, but their contemporaries from the attic lacked the iron heel. The combat boots would have been heavy, Tanis reflected, and nearly impossible to wear out. The attic boots, Neil was right — they'd barely been worn.

Tanis started her day, washing her face and making coffee and the beginnings of list, a game plan. She circled through these tasks and came back to her computer, skimming local news, and an article about the missing teenagers. She Googled their names, but all that came up was recent news, the fact of their disappearance, and their Facebook profiles. They were too young to have created a real record.

Tanis searched her clients regularly — because in the now and future world, people created archives everyday — emails, texts, comment fields, and news feeds. You could learn a lot.

You could create and manage yourself online, the same way vital statistics and archival records recreated people from the past. The ancestry sites had sidebars for ads and Tanis had been intrigued by a service that would search, daily, for your obituary, and send a message to your survivors if it got a positive strike. You could archive your own death, you could post your own missing posters; and if someone failed to record you, or search for you, you disappeared.

Maybe Neil was right, maybe all cities are centres for human loss. Where there aren't people, they can't be lost. But the comment boards online were full of analogies to other missing Canadian preteens, and statistics about the over-representation of First Nations youth among these numbers — and the comment boards were not kind. The dismissive hatred that seeped out of them slid so easily into Celia's family story, her missing aunts and grandmother, her father's missing files. People literally not counted.

After searching an alternate database for Robert Tanner, without luck, Tanis dug in to a new contract, fact-checking a magazine article. It was exacting and distracting, and the rumble of roadwork provided a companionable sense of industry. She finished a little before noon and, feeling satisfied, pulled on a jacket to inspect the hole in the street.

The asphalt had been cracked open the length of the block and a backhoe with stabilizers swung back and forth with rubble, brushing up against the elm branches. There was a scattering of broken twigs on the sidewalk. They were making a mess, and Tanis wasn't the only one staring. Beside the sawhorses set out to block traffic and a woman in a green hatchback stared under her sun visor, then rolled down her window and raised a hand through.

The workmen had ear protectors on, and hard hats. Tanis pressed her hands over her ears, jogged wide around the worksite — and was surprised to find Kaydance's mother behind the wheel of the car.

"Hi," Tanis said. Michelle lifted a cigarette, drew on it, then twisted her mouth to exhale sideways. Silver earrings swung against her neck, diamonds made out of tiny metal scales. "Oh, those are so pretty," Tanis said. "Your earrings. They're lovely. Do you know — did you find out what they're doing with our street?"

"New storm pipes. Larger diameter, I guess. They shook the apartment breaking that up." The backhoe was turning between a growing hole and the back of a dump truck, which inched closer in reverse, *beep-beep-beep.* "Doing the whole street, I guess. Block-to-block."

"It's going to be a lot of noise," Tanis said.

Michelle threw her cigarette casually through the window and said, "We'll get rid of these potholes — nice, *shee.*"

"Mm-mm," Tanis said.

"You're in the house next door?"

"Yes, I'm sorry. I didn't introduce myself. I'm Tanis. I've met your daughter in — just around the street — I think you've met Neil?"

"I knew you, sure. I'm Michelle and my girl's Kaydance. No man. You got kids?"

Tanis thought about reaching through the car window to shake hands, that would be way too formal. "No, no kids."

"You got religion?" Michelle asked.

"Excuse me?"

Michelle pointed past the road equipment to a sign out front of the "New Free Church of Christ." A born-again congregation met in a flat-roofed house second in from the end of the block. *God allows U-turns*, the sign board read today.

"Good thing, eh? This mess," Michelle said, and waved at blocked road.

Tanis laughed. "Well, that's the kind of religious we'd be if we were religious, I guess."

"Yep," Michelle said. "I wonder, can you get those guys to move the trucks — they've got one blocking back alley there. I gotta get these groceries in and get ready for work."

"Oh shoot. Yes, hang on." Tanis covered her ears again and jogged over to speak to the men, then jogged back to the car.

"Shit, I'm going to be late." Michelle said.

"Really nice to meet you," Tanis said.

Michelle nodded, and gave a hurried goodbye as the alley opened up. Tanis crossed to the far sidewalk and followed it uphill away from the road crew. Up past the school, where Neil was probably counting down the end of his day. Up to his favourite hardware store, where Tanis found the narrow wooden shelves as he'd described — tight rows packed with an eclectic abundance of gate latches and wood screws, twine and enamel ware. Tanis picked out a bubble wand and solution, sidewalk chalk, a brush and primer, a flannel backed plastic tablecloth, and a sheet of fine grit sandpaper. Carrying her loot home, she rehearsed buzzing apartment 2C and striking up a real conversation with Michelle.

She wanted to invite herself up for tea, or a cigarette — she could smoke one socially if she had to — and then, visiting casually, she could offer that, when it got cold, Kaydance could come and play with sidewalk chalk on their cement basement walls while Tanis worked. She could also do homework at the kitchen table, if she wanted. But her main point would be that, with the weather getting cold, the basement would be a safe place to play inside. Ball, chalk, bubbles. It couldn't hurt, and the offer could be made without criticism, in a friendly way, implying nothing.

But of course Kaydance was at school, and Michelle had been getting ready for work — somewhere. Tanis ought to have expected her ring to go unanswered. She set the bubble wand and chalk on the front step for Kaydance to collect after school and peeked in at the lobby space. They had a book exchange shelf for the handful of tenants. Aside from Kaydance and her mom there was an older guy, some kind of potash worker Neil had met, and an apparently single young woman, a student, Tanis guessed, who drove a Toyota Camry. The gold letters had been repainted recently on the door of *River Crest Arms* and there was a new-looking lock and alarm system. New mailboxes too.

Next door, their house, with a coat of peeling paint that nothing could be done about until spring, had Tanis swallowing her pride. Nothing about her and Neil's home ownership encouraged trust. Especially not the sagging hazard of a garage. Tanis shook her head at how she had romanced it into something older even than the house. A cottage for a pioneer family. One cozy room, with a cold trap under the floor, and a baby in a cradle by the stove. She had imagined it alternately, and this even after they'd moved in, as a stable for the white dray horses in the city archives picture, whose portrait proved that the flood plain had never been a pastoral homestead. In the clear light of a new millennium day, the leaning garage was old, dangerous, and had never been well made.

» Twenty-Six

"They print you yet?"

The voice came around Neil's classroom door and he and Karen stepped back from his computer. They'd been reading Melissa's Facebook wall. Now Bornstein stretched his fingers out at chest height and wiggled them. It took Neil a minute to catch on. "Fingerprinted?" Karen asked.

"And each shall take his part." Bornstein held his hands steady so that they could see the ink smeared on the pads of his fingers.

"Why, though?" Karen asked. "They didn't disappear from school, did they?"

Bornstein pointed to Neil. "I'll take your afternoon class — they want you in the boardroom." Neil dropped his mouth open, then closed it as Bornstein shrugged. "They said to tell you to bring your keys."

"Might want to breathe, Neil," Karen said. "The cops are trained to notice things like that. Also, sweaty hands don't print very well."

Bornstein snorted.

"Oh, come on!" Neil protested, sweeping his keys off his desk.

There were three uniformed cops in the boardroom adjoining Bornstein's office, all standing with the backs to the door, and they all had guns. Guns or walkie-talkies. How could you tell?

They were bent over the side table, hooking up recording equipment maybe — Neil stepped back to the hallway, knocked, then grinned when they turned with muffins in hand, and assorted tray on the table behind them.

"Mr. Cameron," Malhiot said, welcomingly, and Neil relaxed. "Hi," he said, raising his hand to jingle his key fob. "I brought my keys."

"Very good. This is officer Kipland and Sgt. Sawatsky," Malhiot pointed to the men on either side. Neil nodded. Kipland he knew. Sawatsky had dark hair pressed flat by a hat he'd taken off and the stubble on his cheeks was tracked by grooves running down to the corners of his mouth — except for the uniform, he looked like a teacher.

"Take a seat," Malhiot said, and Neil moved around to the chair she pulled out.

The police arranged themselves across the table and Kipland set his phone down in the middle, explaining that they would first state their names. He muttered the date, and time, and introduced each of the police officers. "This will be a conversation with Mr. Neil Cameron, and Mr. Cameron, if you could spell your name for us?"

"It's just like it sounds," Neil said.

"Yes, but if you could spell it for this recording?"

"Sure, okay. I'm N-E-I-L — "

"First name Neil," Kipland interrupted.

"Yes. And last name, Cameron. C-A-M-E-R-O-N."

Kipland smiled and turned to Malhiot who said, "Good job, both of you." Sawatsky rolled his eyes and put a hand on the table. "Mr. Cameron. We specifically wanted to speak with you because you teach both of the missing youth, Melissa Arthur and Jody Bear, is that correct?"

Neil sat up in his chair and nodded.

"You look uncertain, do you teach both of them? And you can answer aloud for — the phone."

"I taught both of them, yes." Neil said. "But, no, I don't know if that's why you specifically wanted to talk with me — I don't know if that part is correct."

Malhiot tilted her head. "This isn't a math test Mr. Cameron — you can paraphrase the question to clarify your answers if you like. Do you understand?"

Which part? Neil wondered. "Yes."

Sawatsky met his eyes. "Do you know where you were on the afternoon of Thursday, September 13th?"

"I was here, teaching."

"We understood that your classroom was empty that afternoon."

"Okay, yes. I have Life Skills students, four pairs of them, but they work all over the school in fifth period. They're doing work placements in the cafeteria, and at the — "

"So you were on the school premises?"

"Yes."

"Until what time?"

Neil thought. "Until probably four o'clock."

"What did you do at the end of the school day?" Sawatsky asked.

"I usually straighten up my class," Neil said. "And then if there is marking to do, or planning for the next day, I would start on that."

"And you'd get your handouts ready," Kipland suggested.

"Yes, if there was printing to do. But everyone does that after school. I try to use my prep."

Sawatsky had begun squinting, and Malhiot looked down at her phone. "What did you copy on Thursday?" she asked.

Neil shook his head, nervous. "I don't know. I could look at my day planner — "

"Do you remember making fifty copies from Tray 2," Kipland asked, "at 4:23?"

That was a very specific question. "At 4:23? Fifty copies of what?" The three officers waited, Malhiot watching Neil's face over the top edge of her phone. "Is there a camera on that?" Neil asked. She nodded. He felt a flush creep up his neck. His fingers were cold, and he curled them against his pulse.

Thursday he'd sat in his classroom and he'd closed a window, he'd sent an email to Melissa and Jody's parents, and then he'd left. "I'm just remembering," he said to the police. "I sent an email to some parents, and it will have a time on it. And I left right after then. But I think it was like I said, right around four o'clock. And I didn't use the photocopier."

Sawatsky cleared his throat. "Thank you, Mr. Cameron. That is helpful. Was the email sent to Mrs. Arthur, mother of Melissa Arthur, at 3:50?"

"Yes, that's right. I can forward you the message," Neil said, then realized that they'd already read it. Melissa's parents must have forwarded it. He'd sent it to Jody's mom too.

"And then at 4:23 you did your photocopying?" Malhiot asked.

"No, I didn't photocopy," Neil insisted. But the police had a printout of the office accounts and showed him his code, at 4:23 PM, printing fifty copies of a scanned PDF file. Melissa smirked, Jody smiled, and beneath their cameos the word "Missing" marched across the page in an old-fashioned Courier typeface.

"Piss-off!" Neil said, and the officers shifted together. Neil raised his hands in defense. "I was buying Piss-off. I was buying this chemical, at the hardware store."

"You were shopping?" Kipland asked. "You were shopping for chemicals? You're a math teacher, aren't you?"

Neil pulled his wallet from his back pocket and riffled through it, but couldn't find the till receipt. "We just bought a house," he explained. "This stuff, Piss-off, is supposed to get rid of cat-pee smells." He felt a bead of sweat on the side of his face and swiped his sleeve over it, embarrassed. The police were staring him down.

Sawatsky sat back in his seat. "It sounds like you got a great house."

Malhiot took out a pen. "This is the hardware store by the grocery? And a little after four o'clock? Can you tell us about the retail clerk, and anyone else who can verify this?"

Neil described the woman at the till as best he could. She'd been older, and she'd told him about her cats, one of them had a thyroid problem — and finally, they let him go. When Neil stood up to leave his shirt stuck to his waist, soaked through. The police shook his hand in turn.

» Twenty-Seven

It was five when Neil arrived home. Tanis was on the front step, the cordless phone clamped between her neck and shoulder. She was closing the top of an orange yard bag.

"Okay, bye Mom — yes, love you too. I will. Okay, yes. Love you too." She dropped the bag, released the phone into her hand, set it on the step and looked up to her husband. "Love you too!"

"I'm glad someone does," he said.

Tanis scanned his face. Was he fighting tears? Neil got angry, not sad, and if he cried, it was in the safety of their bed, in the dark. In their six-year history he'd only done it twice, when his grandparents died. No tears for hers. "Neil?" Tanis asked.

"The girls aren't back. And I'm a suspect, I guess."

"What! Why?"

"They traced the posters, you know the first ones? They traced them to the photocopier in the main office. Then they printed off everybody's copy histories and it looks like whoever made them used my access code."

"Whoever made them?"

"Made them at school. Do you realize how weird that is? They had to be made before Melissa or Jody was even supposedly missing. Premeditated — "

Tanis stood up. "I thought they were supposed to have run away?"

"The thing is," Neil explained, "who'd have my copy code? Bornstein, the secretary, me. That's it, so who?"

"Anyone could have it."

"You mean, they could look it up, then frame me — is that what this is?" Neil threw his backpack down, aiming for the grass, but it bounced off the bag of leaves and tipped them against Tanis' knees.

She propped the bag back up, too calm. "Neil, the whole first week of school you kept writing that code on the back of your hand."

He stared at her. "For crap's sake."

She'd made dinner for once, a squash curry that was ready and waiting. But it made Neil feel worse, not better. His stomach was in knots. After shovelling it down, Neil rooted around for a pen then opened his bag to mark assignments. That was all he wanted to do. Right. Wrong. Right. Wrong. The assignments weren't there. In the midst of Neil's "tantrum" he'd left them at school.

"Are you really going back now," Tanis asked, "in the dark?"

"Walking in the dark, uphill, in the cold. Yes." Neil said, bundling into a jacket. "Do you want to come?"

Tanis shook her head, bent over her phone.

#MissingGIRLS Please forward this to everyone you know, PLEASE!! Two girls named Jody and Melissa are gone without a trace. PLEASE LOOK AT THESE PICTURES CAREFULLY. THEY ARE BOTH MISSING FOR ONE WEEK. All prayers are appreciated!! God will bless you if you share this. It only takes 2 seconds.

» Twenty-Eight

Neil's anger drained in a few blocks. Crossing the commercial strip he looked in at a group of old men in farmers' caps in the window of the Tim Hortons. Outside a dad was hoisting a toddler into a truck, growling in a silly way and the kid was giggling as she protested being buckled into a car seat.

He walked uphill into another stretch of houses, many of them rentals — a house with gravel and cigarette butts for a lawn, another with a door that ended in space, stairs pulled out of the way so you could drop a metre onto the cracked surface of a concrete slab. A few tidy yards down a patchy lawn was decorated by two wheelless bicycles, a cruddy plastic playhouse and swing set with empty, dangling chains. Someone liked his kids enough to buy shit for them but couldn't be bothered to keep it safe?

Neil had read the news reports, and the comments boards, and the multiplying editorials trying to link cases stretching back ten years. Linked by place mostly — here. They freaked Tanis out, and now Neil thought about what it would be like for Melissa and Jody, reading the same news. They'd learn that if a dark minivan pulled up and they yelled and screamed but were pulled into it anyway the only witness would come forward six months too late. That had happened a few years back. Witnesses minded their own business, waiting for the police to break the case with voodoo.

Who should notice a missing teen first? The teachers who marked a week of absences unconcerned, or the parents who might have waited an angry night before calling police? The kids were the ones who'd caught on, and pushed the point of Melissa and Jody's absence before the adults. It was probably one of their classmates who'd printed the poster, Neil thought. Which meant a lot of them probably knew his copy code. They had secrets.

A block from the school, Neil's phone chimed in his pocket, a message from Tanis, and a long one. A streetlight reflected on the screen, blocking the words, and Neil crossed a square of pavement to read in the dark: *Just went up to work in the attic, looked out the window and saw KD in the front of the apartment with a bike. Way too big for her. Then trying to ride it, wobbling on the sidewalk. There is a giant hole in the road and she's in her pyjamas in the dark. WTH.*

Neil tapped the screen. It blinked and chimed again: *There aren't any pylons for the sidewalk. Aren't they supposed to put up construction fences if there is a giant child-eating hole in the road?*

Neil waited, then typed, *I gather she went inside safely?*

It is cold out here. Are you wearing a coat?

Yes, Mom.

Ha, ha. Yes, she went inside. I am going to call the city about a fence.

Good job, you.

Don't fall in on your way back.

Ha, ha. xo

Neil tucked the phone back into his jeans. Tanis was going to be an amazingly helicopterish parent. He had met Jody's mom, Janet, at the school. Karen claimed Jody's parents were "disengaged", but Janet had spoken candidly. She worked evenings, she said, so it wasn't that strange for her and Jody to miss one another, especially if Jody had volleyball. Jody hated volleyball, her mom let them know — the greasy white ball, burned knees, jammed fingers. She went because it was supposed to be fun, not because it was. Janet blurted that out, then looked around the circle of teachers waiting for someone to protest. No one had the heart. It must have been hell, Neil thought, to wake up to a police phone call before she'd noticed her kid's empty bed.

He wondered if Jody, an only child of a single parent, had, like Tanis, crawled into her mother's bed to be sure she was safe — or maybe Jody used to do that but hadn't for a while now. Just as Janet must, at some point, have stopped looking into her daughter's room when she came home late. When did a child earn privacy, Neil wondered. Tanis never had, her mom had her nose in everything, too close. Tanis would have been missed from the moment of disappearance, her mom would have felt it all. The pull of a fist in her hair, the struggle and loss in the van — Neil's imagination was too good. He retched and puked against the fence in the teachers' parking lot, then looked up and gagged. Over the gym, his classroom light was on.

Inside he found his classroom door locked, but the lights were indeed on, without a janitor in sight. The window was unlocked too and Neil re-latched it thoughtfully. The quizzes were as he'd left them, stacked in a pile on his desk, ready to slide into his bag and carry home. Neil's stomach churned audibly and he sat down, coughed back a surge of bile, and powered on his computer. When the screen loaded Neil logged into Facebook, a breach of school policy but the site was only blocked on the library computers. He set up a new account, Stevie Beaner, with tight privacy settings — then searched Taelur Anderson, and Kolton Dueck, and "friend requested" them both.

Neil was sweating by the time he walked home. He fanned himself with the open wing of his jacket in the front yard. The line of bungalows across the street were so quiet, and so often vacant, that Neil felt a flicker of fear when the curtain moved in the front window of the middle house — a white face leaned in close to the glass. Neil stepped back, through their hedge, but the woman was intent on something in her own yard. Her mouth moved, Neil thought maybe she was talking to someone behind her. And then the front door opened and a small white animal flitted inside. A cat. Neil turned on his front path, wishing he'd thought to leave the porch light on. It was dark, full of shadows, inside the hedge.

» Twenty-Nine

Rafts of ice slid beneath the bridge, spinning and bumping against the pillars, and Phidelma walked above them, giddy. The melting river lifted her spirits. So did the orange in her pocket, a gift Mr. Smith had brought back from his trip. A lot of young people were moving west, he'd said, pushing in the door. And taking money with them. Then he'd dropped a cardboard crate down on the dining room table.

Inside there were paper balls, and Mrs. Smith had reached in to unwrap one, revealing a sphere of orange leather. She held it out to Phidelma, and when she didn't take it, tsk-tsked and passed it to Mr. Smith. He peeled it, sectioned the inside and stood by smiling while Phidelma tasted a piece. Apple and carrot together. A sour taste of berries, and a long seed that crunched in her teeth around the juice.

"It's another round of the boom coming, no less than the last," Mr. Smith said.

"Well, it's a blessing you'll be too old for this one, Jim." Mrs. Smith sighed. Phidelma was surprised by the comment. They'd made their money before the Depression, and now that it was lifting she'd have thought Mrs. Smith would be glad to have her husband make some more. His face shifted as chewed, then he stuck a finger into his mouth to fish out the mass of fibrous skin Phidelma had

just swallowed from her own piece. He set the wad of pulp on the tablecloth, smacked his lips and gave an exaggerated blink. "That one was sour."

Mrs. Smith chose the orange for Phidelma to take home in her pocket, squeezing each paper-wrapped fruit to find one just right. A little give, she said, meant it would be sweet enough. Leave it to collect a little sun and it would run like summer tea, she promised.

It wasn't just the river melting. The snow had created a giant puddle at the end of the bridge, and Phidelma had to inch sideways along the railing to get across. Following the road home she hiked the wool skirt up to the hem of her coat, to keep it from mud and splashing. It was hard to dry the skirt in the winter, and she'd avoided washing it for weeks. In summer — well, she wouldn't wear wool in summer — but she could wash clothes when she liked because they'd dry in an afternoon. It was like the song, new on the radio — Summertime, and the livin' is easy. Water and mint and honey, swirled and set in the sun. Summer tea. Phidelma had been hungry for that orange and Mr. Smith had known it. Since Emelyn left Thomas there'd been few treats.

Home to the house, Phidelma unlaced her boots, peeled down her stockings, and arranged them all on the back step to dry. The first smells of summer were coming up in the yard, earth and grass and all those things the winter covered over. The air moved over her bare toes and Phidelma shivered, but felt spoiled. She stepped inside to a pool of sunlight on the kitchen floor and warmed her feet before going upstairs for a pair of dry socks and her moccasins. Looking into Emelyn's mirror, now hung in her own room, Phidelma saw that she'd collected sun on her face. She pulled her hair together at the back of her neck, and smiled. It was almost long enough to perm now and she thought curls might suit her. Soften her face, like the magazines said.

Thomas, home a few days the week before, had stopped in the doorway of her bedroom. She had been smoothing her blouse over the wool skirt and was caught embarrassed between his gaze and her own reflection. She'd thought he'd say something about vanity but Thomas smiled, shook his head and said, "You weren't made to be pretty, Delma, but that wouldn't stop an honest man if he tried."

An honest man. A younger version of Mr. Smith who would work and travel and bring home treasure. Fruit, a fur coat, or a Singer machine. Someone like the men who'd been hired to replace the wooden walkway on the bridge, hard workers who winked and smiled.

Now that there was money moving, Thomas had stacks of furs in the attic again, which Phidelma understood she wasn't to mention. It was nobody's business. When every store sold fur, there was no reason Thomas shouldn't. But he was some kind of middleman in business, she knew, and had trained Robert up to it.

Phidelma pushed the door to the second bedroom open a crack and looked in, to check that Thomas' clothes were still folded clean on the bed where she'd left them. They were, but against the wall there was a new brick of furs too, draped over with a cotton sheet pulled off the window, now stark and bare.

This had been the room where Emelyn stayed. Phidelma had snuck in often. She'd known better than to touch anything, but loved to stand in the room and look — at satin slips, folded over the edge of an opened drawer; glass perfume bottles, and dresses hanging against the wall, weighted hems whispering. The silk brocade had a magic sheen that rippled with the faintest movement. Mrs. Smith had a woman's bedroom too, her dresser decorated by a silver-handled brush, a cut crystal powder jar, and Royal Doulton "pretty lady" figurines. When Emelyn stopped coming home, Phidelma took the cameo mirror into her own room first. Then her dresser. And finally, since Thomas didn't seem to care, the sheer yellow lace-trimmed drapes. She began each day now in a pool of lemon-coloured light.

Phidelma had only just set Mr. Smith's orange under those drapes on her windowsill when the front door opened and something banged down, heavy, on the main floor. Her mirror rattled against the wall and the orange rolled forward and fell. Phidelma knelt, snatching it up as though she could still prevent a bruise. She waited. Thomas was back, but didn't come up or call. What she heard instead was a blubbering sound. A child's voice rose and whined and a low male voice soothed — shush-shushing in an annoyed way that Phidelma knew very well but had not heard for so long that she barely placed it. The child wailed again and Phidelma groaned, then set the orange safely on her bed.

"Papa?" she called. "Who've you brought?"

» Thirty

Neil woke feverish and so sluggishly tired that he asked Tanis to call in sick while he went back to sleep. The secretary sounded skeptical, so Tanis elaborated the details of his headache and retching, recalling as she did that liars embellish, truth states itself simply. "Will he need a sub all week?" the secretary asked.

"Could be," Tanis said, and set the phone down in her office. A cloud of exhaust rose in the window, and Tanis looked out over the yard and saw Michelle's car backing out into the alley. It was a cold morning, then, and would likely be a chilly night. There was going to be a march, a vigil for the missing teens — and Tanis went down to the basement and searched the Rubbermaid bins for her and Neil's winter coats.

The evening before, while Neil walked back to the school, Tanis had looked out from their bedroom window and seen Kaydance out front with the oversized bike.

Then she'd thought Kaydance had gone in. But when Tanis went down the kitchen she saw Kaydance again, out playing in the back lane — where gangs dropped tags and vehicles bounced too fast over the rutted gravel. Tanis pulled on a sweater, went out into her yard with a lawn chair, and made a point of keeping the child at least within earshot. What she heard was a monologue, the little girl chatting to herself. Then silence. Then the chirp of a phone and another stream of chatter.

Curious, Tanis walked to the back of the yard to peek around the stone wall at Kaydance, who darted for the apartment's rear door dragging a stuffed animal on a leash of purple yarn. She had a windbreaker on, but her pants were clearly pyjama bottoms. Pink with spots.

"Hi there, Kaydance," Tanis called. "Is that a dog you're walking?"

The girl stopped at the door and turned.

"Not a dog? Is it a cow?"

Kaydance scowled, not easily won. "It's a girl moose. It's Moosie."

"It's awfully late to be walking a moose, isn't it?"

Kaydance wrinkled her nose.

"Must be bedtime soon, right? *I'm* tired," Tanis emphasized, faking and then falling into a real and wide yawn.

"Maybe you should go to bed," Kaydance suggested.

"Good idea, kiddo. Good idea. You too?"

Kaydance lifted a cell phone. "My mom said five more minutes is okay." She held up the phone and Tanis saw a line of texts, back and forth, about playtime, and Moosie, and bath time. She steadied the phone to read them, scrolling down.

"Five minutes must be up, I'm sure," Tanis pointed out.

"Guess so," Kaydance shrugged, stepping back and yanking the door open to let her and Moosie, dangling on a noose now, through. "G'nite, next door lady."

"Good night, Kaydance."

Pleased, Tanis walked back to the edge of her yard, then did a U-turn back to the apartment. She examined the back door and pulled at the handle. Latched and locked firm. How had Kaydance gone in so easily? Tanis scanned the back of the building then looked left as a car passed the end of the alley. The lane stretched across three blocks to meet the river road. It was a view Tanis hadn't taken in before. A corridor of garage doors framed the river valley and the neighbourhood on the far side. Streetlights and windows twinkled up a dark rise, like embers in a fire left to burn itself low. It was pretty.

Back in her kitchen, Tanis had locked the door and picked up her phone to check for a message from Neil — then jumped at the jangle of the land line, answered, and was surprised to find herself talking to Michelle. Tanis managed, "hi," then froze trying to think of a polite way to explain why she'd been spying on — supervising — Kaydance. But Michelle was calling as a link in a phone tree for the community association that Tanis had only just registered with. They had been contacted about a vigil for the missing girls. Could they count on Tanis and Neil to leave their porch light on? Would they be able to join the march, and were they willing to make a sign?

"Of course, yes. Absolutely," Tanis said. "Will you and Kaydance be joining too?"

Neil barely woke up or managed to eat a thing all day. It seemed best to let him sleep, but Tanis woke him accidentally, clattering things in her office as she hunted for markers in still-packed boxes.

"Tanis," he called, "can I have some juice?" They didn't have juice, only coconut water. She brought Neil a glass, along with two ibuprofens and he swallowed them quickly, laid back, then sat up, gagged, and spat a stream of water at the floor.

Tanis hadn't seen him this sick since he'd got food poisoning in Thailand. "Okay, sweetie, I think you need a bowl up here. I'll get some water so you can rinse your mouth too, okay?"

"I'm gonna sleep," Neil said, rubbing at his face with a fistful of sheets. "I feel gross."

"Yep," Tanis agreed.

She had invited Kaydance and Michelle over to make signs when the girl got home from school, but Neil needed rest so they set to work on the brick patio in the yard. They'd been assigned NO MORE and GIRLS MISSING.

"Hey, now we really can't get on the wrong side of each other," Tanis said, meaning it would mix up the message, then felt dumb saying it.

"Wish we could," Michelle said.

"I hope we can," Tanis said, then dropped her voice to a whisper. "They've been gone less than two weeks, there's time still. Neil said the police have — " She stopped there, because Kaydance was sprinting over. She'd ditched tracing letters early on and had headed off to play in the patch of fireweed around the side of the house. She came back carrying a fluffy bouquet; the flowers had turned cotton and it stuck to sides of her fleece pants, and to her omnipresent moose. Michelle frowned.

"Nice bouquet," Tanis said.

Kaydance *oohed* at their signs. "Nice bubble letters!"

Neil relocated from the bedroom to the front room, finally — and his face flickered, lit in profile by sports on the flat screen, when Tanis marched past outside. Ahead on the sidewalk, Kaydance skipped up to a little friend, and the beams of their flashlights looped through the dust and leaves the procession kicked up in passing. Michelle was a few paces back, chatting with someone whose name Tanis missed during their introduction. She was happy to walk silently, and held both signs against her shoulder as they marched up the hill.

They'd begun by the river, gathering on the grass. A group of women played hand drums, and sang a Cree song Tanis reached for through the screen of another language. A young First Nations couple beside her rose slightly, up and down on their toes, and Tanis wondered if she should too. If it was expected, or if they were just feeling the drum too. Jody's mother stood beside the singers and looked stronger, steadied.

Seventy people walked from the river up the hill to the school, stopping traffic on the thoroughfare to sing again and wave their signs. Then they fell into line again, and the cars swept back along behind them. They'd been a dam in the current, and their energy eddied and pooled as they joined a crowd on the school sports field. Tanis recognized some of the teachers, Declan and Puller, and the very short gym teacher. Also Karen Smith, who gave her a sideways look that could have meant she didn't know where she knew Tanis from, or that she didn't like her.

A group of cadets was handing out candles and Styrofoam cups of cider and there was a good show of students present. They'd picked up on the mood and stood quietly, in small clutches, or sat together on the grass. The little kids, including Kaydance and her friend, played on the pavement that skirted the wall. They set the mouths of their flashlights flat against the cement and lifted them incrementally, tipping them, shape shifting small blobs of light.

Bornstein sat down on a cement planter to watch them, resting his chin on folded hands. At the microphone an elder from the school board gave a prayer, first in Lakota, then in English, and the women circled for another song. Bornstein stood up, straightened his clothes, and stepped past Tanis and through the crowd to read a statement about Melissa, and Jody, and the collective responsibility everyone gathered had to raise children, "it takes a village". Michelle lit a cigarette and whispered to Tanis about a friend from her own high school who disappeared from a house party and never came home. Tanis nodded, but didn't have a story to trade back. A girl at her high school in Edmonton had died of leukemia — but no one had been stolen.

They'd planned to stay to the end of the speeches, but Kaydance's flashlight battery went out. Without her game she became whiny and bored, and Tanis was glad when Michelle gestured that they were ready to go. It was ten blocks back, and Kaydance complained about being tired, so Tanis offered a piggyback ride. Kaydance leapt on to Tanis' back and nuzzled her head against Tanis' neck.

Michelle shook her head, "*Chh-ck.*" She shook another cigarette out of the package in her pocket. She followed Tanis and Kaydance a step behind, first keeping them clear of the smoke, then texting friends she'd promised to report back to about the vigil.

"So, I don't know what to say for how that went, eh?"

"It was good, I think. A good turnout anyway," Tanis said.

"A good turnout, yeah."

Tanis thought harder. "It was a nice combination of things, having the prayers and cultural stuff."

"You ever been to one of those marches before?" Michelle asked.

"No, I haven't."

"Same people always turn out," Michelle commented, and they walked most of the rest of the way in silence. In front of the apartment, beneath the flood lamp, Michelle leaned in to collect her child. "Come on, up with Mama," she whispered to Kaydance, who'd nearly fallen asleep. She mouthed, "Thank you," to Tanis who stepped up to help with the door, expecting Michelle to hand her a key. Instead, Michelle sidled up to the door panel and the bolt turned in the lock, automation matched by a short electric buzz. Tanis jumped, then reached to open the door, Michelle's hands were full of her child.

"Bluetooth, eh?" Michelle said.

"Space age — " Tanis marveled. That must have been how Kaydance had got in the back door the night before, the building was programmed to their phones. Very cool. "Michelle? Thanks for inviting me," Tanis whispered. "If they have another march let me know. And maybe Neil would come when he's better too."

Michelle shifted Kaydance's weight to her shoulder. "Sure, for sure."

"Okay, good night."

"Night."

Tanis crossed the yard, passing in behind their hedge, and reached the front door just as Neil opened it.

"Hey," Tanis said, "you're up!"

"Hey, you're home to take care of me!" Neil joked. He sagged against the frame, still looking grey. "How did it go?"

» Thirty-One

The day Celia came Phidelma heard a child and mistook its cry for her own. In the confusion of stumbling out of her room she fell against the hallway wall and the crash cut short a stream of blubbering she'd recognized as Cree French.

"Father?" Phidelma called out, "who've you brought?"

She came down the stairs to find her brother, Robert, a grown man. And a little girl snivelling, face in hands. "Robert?" Phidelma asked, incredulous.

He left the child and wrapped his sister in a bear hug that reeked of sweat and smoke. His clothes were wrinkly, even his pants creased, and Phidelma guessed he'd come on the train, like Mr. Smith. She eyed the trunk he'd dropped down in the entryway. It was blocked by the child, who had been staring but dropped her head when she caught Phidelma looking back.

"Tanshee, liddle girl," Phidelma tried, mimicking the accent her father fell into with the men he brought around sometimes. The ones who teased her about their handsome sons.

"Don't hassle her, Delma," Robert said, moving behind the girl to square her shoulders with a hand on each. "Celia, this is your aunt, my sister. She is going to take care of you while Papa is working. Do you understand?"

"Robert — "

"Look, they sent her to me but I can't very well have a child."

"Is she your child?"

"You're alone here, and that's really not appropriate for a girl your age either. So here, two birds, one house."

"I'm not alone, Robert, Papa's here. He's here quite often. And I'm working, you know, there's — "

"He's told me that he's not here often enough. And you're getting older and — Phidelma, he wanted to send you out to me but he didn't know that Lily died. And he didn't know about this one. I can't be sitting out to mind children."

Sitting out of what? Phidelma wanted to ask. The child frowned, and sniffed, then released her breath along with a long, bubbly string of snot that slid down over her lip.

"For heaven's sake, Robert," Phidelma scolded, pushing past him. "Who is Lily and who is this child and why on earth would you bring a child this size on a train? She smells like a beer parlour." Phidelma pulled the girl against her skirt and wiped her nose with a handkerchief, then bundled it back it into the waist of her skirt

"Who is this child?"

"You're a natural, Delma. That's just what Mama used to do. You should spit on that thing and polish her cheeks next."

"Robert?"

"She's your niece. Before you ask, we didn't marry. But we might have — I loved her. I did love her and I did mean to make things official only Lily died with the second. A boy. This one's a girl, and that'll make things easier for you. And who knows, if business keeps up, I'll marry and you can get on with your life."

Robert the man was heavier than Robert the boy but he was as insistent, and as nervous, and as hurried.

"What kind of business, Robert?"

"She'll be old enough for school in the fall, Delma, and I'll be sure to keep up paying your taxes so she can do that here. Couldn't

where she was living with Lily's people, Allarys, there wouldn't have been anyplace unless they shipped her off to boarding school."

Phidelma looked closer at the girl. Braids that might have been tidy a week ago were lost now beneath matted swirls that would be torture to brush out.

"What's wrong with boarding school?" Phidelma asked. And then the child raised her face, and Phidelma saw her eyes, grey as ashes. And her round cheeks, red from crying.

"Schmappelle see-see," the child said, plaintively.

"Lily never spoke English," Robert explained.

Phidelma looked between the pair. Her brother, who didn't speak a word of Cree or French that she knew of, had made this child with a French half-breed. Like Thomas had their mother. The apple didn't fall far from the tree, then.

"And I'm meant to teach her English?"

"She's your niece, Phidelma." Robert's eyes were wary, and Phidelma remembered that he could be mean. She was his blood too and he'd left her to Thomas and Emelyn. Now he'd leave his daughter, that seemed clear.

"Where will you be leaving us to, Robert?"

"She'll be seven in the fall," he said, and set a hand on the child's head, spanning it. "It's good timing really, you'll be able to keep housekeeping when she's in school and I can send some for food or whatever it is you think she'd need."

"Schmappelle see-see," the girl said again.

"Like I say, if I get married, you'll get on with your life too. You'll be young enough and . . . "

So this was how it would be. Phidelma crouched to the child's level, and remembered with annoyance that Robert had bruised the orange in her room, dropping down the trunk that she now imagined to be filled, not with gifts or treasures, but with this child's things.

"What is your name?" she asked slowly and clearly.

Robert answered, "Cecilia Agnes Tanner."

"Hello Celia," Phidelma said. "I am your auntie Delma."

Celia looked stubborn, and sulky. But Phidelma would later reflect that it was true, what they said about blood and water. She'd never felt this way about other children thrust into her lap at auxiliary teas. She pulled Celia into the crook of an arm, and set her other hand flat against the small chest and while Robert walked through to the kitchen, commenting on the new pipes and banging open cupboards like the lord of her house, Phidelma whispered, "I am your auntie Delma and I will not leave you and I will not let you get sick and I will not let you be taken out in public with your hair looking like a wasp's nest."

» Thirty-Two

RCity News — Online — Monday, October 1st
Update on Missing Teenagers

Police, Public School Board officials, and the parents of Melissa Arthur spoke Friday at an assembly of students at Russmere Collegiate, two weeks after the girls were last seen outside their school. Students were asked to think back over the beginning of the school year, to see if they could remember anything pertinent in the girls' interests, activities or social connections.

Principal Doug Bornstein said that this is the first time that City Police have addressed a student body in assembly, but that similar events have been held in other constituencies.

Melissa Arthur and Jody Bear were last seen at a volleyball practice where teammates report they seemed happy and were having fun. "Melissa kept spiking the ball into the net because she was laughing like crazy," said Junior volleyball player Jennie Preece. The girls changed into street clothes and are believed to have left the school through the main gymnasium door shortly after 3:00 PM on Friday, September 14th, 45 minutes after their disappearance was first posted on Facebook at 2:15 PM.

Complicating this story, early missing persons messages posted to student Facebook pages have numerous similarities to email spam messages filed by Internet watchdog ABCHoax.com. Senior girls' volleyball coach Lynn Enns said that she was initially hopeful that the girls were perpetrating a prank, but as they have now been gone for two weeks, she is "just plain worried."

Despite the unusual character of early missing persons alerts, Sgt. Glen Wymiss warns that "Invisibility equals vulnerability. The girls are outside the protection of their guardians and, like any missing children, are at high risk." He encourages the public to continue using social media to spread word of the girls' disappearance, but suggests redrafting any message received to include information regarding the girls' physical features, the date and location at which they were last seen, and contact information for the regional missing persons bureau and Crime Stoppers.

As pictures of the girls crossed a whiteboard in the auditorium at Russmere Collegiate today many teachers and students were in tears alongside Cindy and George Arthur, parents of Melissa. Janet McKay and James Bear, parents of Jody, were absent but a handwritten appeal for information pertaining to their daughter was read on their behalf by School Principal Doug Bornstein.

Sgt. Wymiss provides the following for those interested in contributing to the online search for Melissa and Jody:

Melissa Arthur, 16 years old, is described as Métis, with pale skin, 140 lbs, 5'7"with long brown hair, usually worn in a ponytail, which has been previously dyed black, blonde, and pink —

"Don't read that shit," Doug Bornstein said, reaching in front of Neil's face to shut off his screen. The principal's elbow hit Neil's ear and he jumped. "Ow, hey!" He pressed a palm to the side of his head.

Bornstein rubbed his elbow indignantly. "How can you read that crap."

"What crap? It was about the assembly, I was sick. Why does it matter?"

"It matters because the police are watching your computers. And it matters because someone is getting a kick out of this and, frankly, I don't want my teachers involved."

Neil touched his ear gingerly. It would be something on the comment board that had worked the principal up. Neil hadn't got to the bottom of the page.

"I want a week's outline on everyone's wall," Bornstein said. "I want all of the kids to know as much as they can about what's coming. Quizzes, assignments, readings. On the wall." The principal pointed to the whiteboard, then to a blank space on the bulletin board at the far end of the room.

"I don't have any planned," Neil said.

"You don't have lesson plans?"

"No, I have lesson plans but this is a math classroom. We don't have readings and we're between units."

"In all of your classes?"

"Yes," Neil apologized, "I synchronize them."

Doug sighed. "Well, so you don't have to be as organized, I guess. But you'd better be giving them the message that you are."

"Sure, I can do that," Neil agreed. He'd been doing that all weekend. Not for his students, but for Tanis. He'd given making-life-normal his best shot. By Sunday night he'd felt well enough to join her for a walk up the hill. She'd recounted details of the march and vigil, and then they'd gone for dinner at a little Asian fusion restaurant they hadn't tried before. Neil had looked across the table at his wife, who'd been excited that she was going to meet the actual person who'd owned their house, and he'd found himself composing a description of her. *5′7″, 135 lbs, with a fair complexion and medium brown hair worn shoulder length with long bangs. Identifying scar, vertical, on right thumb* — this was not how a date was supposed to go.

It was not how any of the fall was supposed to go. Neil was meant to be hitting his stride as a teacher, and Tanis to land an awesome research contract. Instead he was being creeped and assaulted by his principal, and Tanis was turning into the neighbourhood babysitter. As they'd been getting ready to go for dinner she'd gotten five texts from Kaydance about a moose. Then as they'd been leaving out the front door Neil had heard bell noises tinkling from the back entry. Kaydance's phone was receiving a new text from Michelle to keep in sight of the apartment window, but she'd crawled in through their mystery cupboard door to smear damp sidewalk chalk on the walls in their back entry. Decorations, she had insisted. Lovely, Tanis had said, at which point her phone had also chirped.

"Doug?" Neil said. The principal had headed for the door. "Can you come back for a minute? There's something I wanted to let you know."

He took the principal to the window, and slid it back, and the wind that blew into the classroom surprised them both with tiny pellets of snow.

» Thirty-Three

Neil confessed to a suspicion that "someone" had been on the roof, explaining first to Bornstein, and then to Malhiot, about the lights being randomly on and the window that he kept finding unlatched. A drug drop? They moved Neil's first period to the library, so the police could check out the roof, but after that he was back in his classroom for the rest of the day — and the idea lurked in his mind that the girls might have been hiding up there, though it didn't make sense. There was no shelter, no food. The open window did not necessarily have any bearing at all on Jody and Melissa being missing but someone had clearly been using it. Maybe Kolton or Taelur. They'd both accepted Neil's friend request.

"Why would you do that?" Tanis had asked Sunday morning when Neil tried to explain the fake profile he'd kept refreshing.

"I want to know what the kids are posting to each other. They don't hide things on here like they would in — you know," Neil paused, distracted by a string of "likes" Kolton unleashed. They flagged a series of comments on Melissa's page, and clicking his way to it, Neil scanned to see which ones Kolton hadn't liked — the links to ABCHoax.com. He tapped his screen. "See, Tanis, he's still feeling like people don't believe the girls are in danger. Really missing. But he does, obviously."

"Does he do that in real life, too?" Tanis asked. "Does he stick up for them at school?"

"Not really, no. He's pretty quiet."

"Does he love her," Tanis asked, "do you think?"

"Oh, seriously. Does he love Melissa? I don't know. Maybe he just wants to be associated with the drama. They all think they're in love all the time at that age."

Tanis had fluffed her fingers through Neil's hair, then grabbed it to give his head a gentle shake.

After his fourth period cleared, Neil finally had a chance to climb out his classroom window, which he'd been dying to do since demonstrating the one-way latch that morning. The day Neil shut the girls out, the window had definitely clicked, which meant someone must have got into his classroom to let them back inside, or they had another route to get down. Neil wanted to see for himself. He shut his classroom door, locked it, and turned off the classroom light. Then he hauled himself up and over the window frame, catching his knee on the metal edge.

The air no longer carried snow, but it was cold, refreshing, and the gravel rooftop shifted and crunched beneath his feet. When Neil rounded the corner of the vent casing, where the girls had sat, the air turned warm and sour. The vent drafted the weight room, and Neil could hear Andrew Pulley's voice echoing up, " — you do not do this by yourself," he was saying. "You spot each other. Gavin, what's so interesting about that wall? You spot each other." Neil crouched down in the shadow of the vent casing, and found the tar paper exposed, the gravel worn thin. He fingered his knee where a spot of blood had seeped through his khakis, then knelt and bent his ear to the vent, not to hear better but to sight the roof from where the girls had sat.

If they had left footprints they'd been lost in company. Between his own, and Bornstein going up with the police, and whichever students had been making visits, the roof was a well-tracked space. Investigating the vent itself, Neil saw a collection of stubs thrown in and caught on a metal grille. Store cigarettes and hand-rolled.

He straightened and inhaled the clean wind. He had a fleeting impulse to walk the roof's raised lip, arms out for balance. Peeking over the edge, the girls' escape route was easy to find. Downspouts drained the flat roof, and were pinned at intervals to the brick wall with heavy metal braces. One, close to gym's emergency exit, was more sheltered than the others and on the top of each brace Neil saw mud. On a few near the bottom, dried grass. A person could climb up this way as well.

The girls had been here at least once, perhaps many times. Neil was level with the tops of the elms, which would have hidden Jody and Melissa and Taelur from street view a week earlier. The trees were close in size and age to those down the hill but these ones still had some leaves, protected, he guessed, by their distance from the river and the frost. Below him, Neil heard the gym side door swing open, and two girls' voices broke the afternoon's silence.

"So did you?"

"He did."

"He, not you?"

"No, he totally came on to me."

"Oh my God, your mom would freak!"

"Mega."

"So did you — what?"

"I kissed him, a bit."

"Oh my God, you whore!"

"On his mouth."

"Okay, I don't believe this. You kissed him?"

"I just did that, yeah."

"And he, what, put it away?"

"Oh my god, he got so blotchy, you wouldn't believe it."

"Your mom would still freak."

"Mega."

Mega, that sounded like Taelur. Blotchy and red, that would likely be Kolton Dueck. It was an odd position, to be elevated like this, eavesdropping on their social interactions. Knowing that Kolton could work fraction problems in his head and Taelur might as — well, at least she knew to get him to "put it away". A group called SafeX handed out condoms at the last school dance. It seemed like they were prodding the kids into things, sometimes, but the health nurse insisted knowledge was power. More power to Taelur.

"I can't believe," Taelur's girlfriend went on, "I can't believe he'd even try to take a picture."

"I know. So gross, right!"

Neil closed his eyes. Kolton had taken out his phone — that was what he'd put away. Much less gross, though also disturbing. Kolton had been texting Neil regularly since his classroom visit, short texts like — *news?* Any news? Neil assumed. He'd text back — *hang in there, K.* He'd given out his number at the start of the year and it was supposed to help with attendance and communication with the parents, but they were more likely to use email. Students talked and texted in code, the longest sentences they used were in math word problems.

Neil waited until the two girls, who settled briefly on the lawn, had been picked up and driven away in a CR-V. Then he slipped back in through his window, and pulled his pants free of the scab forming on his knee, which began to sting. Neil powered off his computer, grabbed his bag, and left by the front door to avoid passing the library where the police still had their counsellors waiting for kids to drop by. His phone chirped a block from the school but Neil left it in his pocket; he'd had enough of kids for one day. Time to be home and relax.

The front door was unlocked and Neil pushed it open. "Tanis! I'm home!" She didn't answer. Neil looked into the kitchen, in case she was on the phone and that was why she didn't answer. Her computer was on the table but had gone to the space odyssey screen saver.

"Tanis?" Neil called up the stairs. She wasn't in their room, the office, or the guest room she'd begun setting up for her mom who'd announced that she was coming for Christmas. Neil eyed the eaves space door, the little triangular tunnel. She hadn't mentioned the playroom idea for a while, but — no, she wouldn't be in there with the door closed.

"Tanis?" Neil called into the closet, up the captain's stairs. There was no reply, but his phone chirped again and this time he checked it. Had she had an accident? No — Declan wanted to go biking.

"Tanis!" Neil tried again. He climbed the captain's stairs and stared. The walls were fresh yellow and with the sun shining in the room was almost gold. The vent had been pulled off the little window — it was open and the room was cold and bright. Brand new. An unfamiliar coiled rug covered most of the plywood sheet he'd tacked over the hole where he'd pried up the oil-soaked boards. Finally, Neil heard steps below. "Tanis?"

"Hey, you're back! Did you see?"

"I see, very nice!"

"It's called Golden Wicker."

"When did you prime it?"

"You don't have to shout, I'm right here." Right beneath his feet, in fact. She was at the bottom of the stairs, smiling up.

"Well, seriously," Neil asked, "did you prime it? It won't hold if you didn't."

"They said it would hold. It's all-in-one, paint with primer?" She had wet, raw-looking hands, and held cleaned brushes in an empty yogurt container.

"It'll probably be fine then," Neil said, climbing down to meet her. "Dec wants to go biking."

Tanis shrugged.

"We'll probably stop somewhere. Have you got stuff here to eat?"

"Oh, I guess so. I can make a sandwich or something like that."

"You sure?"

"Yes. Go have fun."

Neil waited.

"Really, that was a lot of work." Tanis waved her brush and a splatter of milky water hit Neil's shirt. "Sorry, we better wipe that off right away. Here. I'm sorry. I'm exhausted, honestly. Give me your shirt, I'll wash it."

Neil changed, stuck a Band-Aid on his knee, and freed his mountain bike from the pipes he'd locked it to in the basement. Tanis had her hands in the kitchen sink when he came up the stairs. She was running hot water over his shirt and her hands. He wanted a hug, and he wanted to hug her, and he didn't want to feel scared like he had coming through the unlocked door into what had seemed like an empty house. Even the open attic window had scared him. He leaned over his bike to peck her cheek.

"If that," Neil said, pointing to the steaming water, "if that doesn't work I'll warm you up when I get home."

"Go," Tanis said again, "have fun."

RCity News — Online — Tuesday, October 2nd

Police dropped early lead in case of missing teen girls

Teenagers Melissa Arthur (16) and Jody Bear (15) disappeared from their high school at 816 Walmer Road around 3:00 PM on September 14th. It has now come to light that the girls were later seen in one another's company on the 200 block of Avenue M South around 3:30 PM. A witness called this sighting in to the police's missing person's hotline on September 15th after reading about their disappearance in the paper. The witness, who prefers to remain anonymous, reported that the girls were headed south on Avenue M, in the direction of the river parkway. "This was a tip, among many," confirmed Sgt. Wymiss, but after receiving this "tip", RCity News 1 reporter James Steward decided to follow the girl's path from the school to the river and discovered a bracelet near a path heading down to the river. Mr. Steward contacted police, who collected the bracelet and presented it to the parents of Melissa Arthur and Jody Bear. "It is Melissa's," Cindy Arthur reported tearfully outside of the city police station, "That bracelet was her favourite bling, but it had a fiddly latch and was often falling off." Prompted by the bracelet or other unknown evidence, fire and rescue boats were seen scouring the city's riverbanks this morning. When questioned, boat pilot Graeme Nelson reported they were looking for personal effects, but could not elaborate further.

<comments on this story are closed due to an ongoing investigation>

» Thirty-Four

In the trunk, there were three dresses that Robert left behind but only two that fit the child. The third Phidelma hung up in Thomas's room, as a decoration, after she moved his things up to the attic. The child needed her own room, Phidelma reasoned, but needed to be close to her aunt at night. She hadn't lived with babies since the twins that died — and knew little about children. Only that they needed to be sung to at bedtime, fed in the day, and kept clean.

Phidelma had Nils and Alexey, the oldest of the boys in the Ukrainian family across the street, lift the double bed frame up to the attic. It was a nice enough room, when Thomas was so rarely there. And if he were to stay longer, as he got older or slowed down, Phidelma could make the large room her father's, as it was probably meant to be. He'd never slept there since Marguerite left, and she couldn't imagine he'd want to now. It had been Emelyn's fabric room for a time, and now Phidelma used it for storage.

The little dress she hung to brighten Celia's room didn't have a single stitch of machine sewing. Even the middy was handmade, not bought and sewed on. It was not too young for a six-year-old, only too small. The bib's square corners had been softened by someone's careful embroidery of flowers, white thread on white cotton so the design would be almost impossible to see unless you came right in close to the child wearing it. Small petals and leaves on a chain and loop vine were worked in stitches tiny enough and tight enough to make it look like a thread, clinging to the fabric, when it was worked in and through.

The clothes that fit Celia were plain, and stained, and Phidelma sent a note to Mrs. Smith, explaining that she was caring for a child now, and asking if she might take a look through the auxiliary box for school clothes. Phidelma set these aside, with school a full summer away — but Celia found them sooner and Phidelma caught her one evening, posing up on a chair, rapt with her own reflection in the glass window on the kitchen door. She remembered her own small self, standing awed in Emelyn's room, watching the silk brocade shimmer.

Celia's hair was dark brown. Not quite the black of her father's, not quite the black of her aunt's. The angled evening light highlighted golden streaks at the girl's temples, but her hair had the weight of theirs. She held a pale blue cotton dress to her chest, one arm cinching it in to her waist.

"My beautiful girl," Phidelma said, and Celia turned, her mouth open. "You are as beautiful as your mother," Phidelma told her and Celia nodded, her face serious. It had to be true, because Robert was not beautiful and Celia certainly was.

"And you are as smart as your auntie," Phidelma added, swatting the girl off the chair and taking the dress to examine the hem. Cast-me-downs were better off big like this. They could be altered so much more easily to fit. Nothing came their way, of course, to match the dainty little dress Celia had come with, but she would have it in her room until she was much older. A little white ghost that proved how she'd been loved. Like the shawl that had never been Marguerite's, not really, but that Phidelma, on longer days, still liked to knot at her chest.

» Thirty-Five

"Neil, check this one out." Tanis flashed her phone over their breakfast of Eggo waffles with ice cream and Saskatoon berries that Puller's girlfriend had brought over in a four-litre freezer bag for a housewarming present.

A chubby girl in a plaid skirt eyed a brown stick, with the caption *FAT EMMA*. An antique chocolate bar. Neil shovelled a forkful of waffle into his mouth and mumbled, "Nice one." His own phone chirped beside his plate, he tapped the screen and saw a new blog post from Bornstein.

Tanis snorted, "Look at this one." Again, Neil leaned in, *THE CHICKEN DINNER BAR*. "Gross," he said.

"Disgusting," Tanis said, "and look at this — "

"Babe, let's put your phone away for a minute, okay."

She looked surprised.

"Do you have a good day planned?"

"Yes, I do. I'm meeting — "

"Good. Look, I might be late tonight because there's volleyball. It's the girls' team and Karen wants extra bodies because it's the first game without Melissa and Jody. There might be some upset kids."

"Sure," Tanis said. "I understand. I won't plan on you for supper."

"Thanks. Just don't eat either of those." Neil tried to lighten his tone, pointing to her phone. Tanis smiled back obligingly. "And thanks for breakfast," Neil said, mopping up the last bits of his waffle. He pushed back from the table and hurried up stairs, stopping on the landing to shout back, "Sweats?"

"Under the window!" Tanis replied.

Neil had unpacked his clothes boxes on the weekend, the sweatpants weren't hard to find. Rooting in the dresser for socks, Neil grinned at himself in Tanis' mirror, then ran back downstairs to brush berry skins out of his teeth. When he came out of the bathroom Tanis had his shoulder bag packed and ready, but she looked worried, and waved his phone. "You've got a text from Kolton? That kid?"

Neil shrugged. "What does it say?"

"Do you normally get texts from your students?"

"Not normally, no, but school hasn't been that normal." Neil reached for his device, stretching his arm out through the sleeve of his jacket. Kolton had written, *M liked T's ass - you tell them?* Neil did a double take. "I don't know, Tanis," he said. "Desperate times."

Tanis crossed her arms over her chest, mug tilting in her hand, about to spill. Neil righted the coffee and kissed her cheek. "I'll find out what he's talking about at school and pass on anything important."

"Okay — "

"I'll be late," Neil reminded, swinging his bag up to his shoulder.

Tanis closed the door behind him, and then climbed the stairs to the attic. She stood on her new coil rug and looked up the street through her new attic window. Neil hurried up their block. With the elms bare, she could have watched him walk farther but she dropped her eyes to the rug. Scraps of bright braided of cloth. The Mennonite second-hand store had been selling the rugs as a fundraiser for a farm in Paraguay and they looked old-fashioned and cheerful. Quaint. Until you bent close enough to see that the braids were made of shredded T-shirts. The flecks of colour were screen-printed band promos and beer ads and sponsored charity runs, spiralling in on their own small galaxy.

» Thirty-Six

Marguerite left when Phidelma was seven, nearly eight — and learning to care for Celia, Phidelma realized just how small she'd been to be left alone. And how much Emelyn had done for her, Thomas' child.

Thomas came home for a few week's span at the start of June and was surprised by the child at the door. He growled at her and brushed past looking for Phidelma, who laughed, "that's Celia" as the child lit up the stairs.

Thomas stared hard. "You've not taken up with a widder, Delma? Un veuv?*"*

Phidelma was as surprised at the idea as he was. "No, Papa — that's Robert's child, I'm keeping her." He still looked amazed and Phidelma stared now, because Robert had said it was Thomas' idea, Celia coming to her. Evidently not. Her brother had been in and out of the house, away for more than a week at a time. He had left some money, but not as much as she'd made at the Smiths'.

"So now I'm feeding another one?" Thomas asked, and while Phidelma scrambled for an answer he tilted an ear to the stairs. He'd heard Celia on the landing too. "She take after that piece of work?" Thomas asked, meaning Robert.

Phidelma shook her head, but school hadn't started yet, and she hadn't realized that the English Celia had been picking up so fast came with an accent that having Thomas back in the house wouldn't help.

The second week of school Celia trailed home to another little girl's house and waited like a waif outside. The girl's older brother brought her back after dinner, and the girl proved to be not so much of a friend the next day at school, telling the story of the orphaned Indian to anyone who'd hear. Celia came home in tears and hid from Mrs. Smith when she came around after dinner.

"She's an odd little duck," Mrs. Smith said, sitting with Phidelma. She'd brought over more sewing, for Phidelma's egg money she said.

Phidelma nodded, agreeing about Celia. "And stubborn," she added.

"A strong will gets a girl a long way," Mrs. Smith said. Then she laughed and passed along that Nils had taken Phidelma for Thomas' wife, and Celia's proper mother. The mistake pleased Phidelma, but not the assumption that she was married to Thomas. She'd rather people thought she'd been married to Robert, who was closer to her age and halfway handsome — either option was silly, though. As for Robert, he was looking to find himself a new wife and then Celia would have a proper home, and Phidelma would get on with her life. She'd explained this to Mrs. Smith before.

"Well, a lot of your girls do marry up awfully old, Phidelma," Mrs. Smith said. "You'll have to set them straight."

Phidelma didn't though. When Nils' and Alexy's mother, Anna, asked outright she told her neighbours that her husband had gone "out to Manitoba."

"You've got people there, then? At Vinnerpeg?" Anna probed.

Phidelma said she did. And maybe they had. In her sleep when Celia called out, she still spoke in the Cree French she'd come with.

The morning after Robert had last been through, the streetlights were out on the block behind Mr. Wing's laundry — loosened just enough not to light, right down the block to make it look like the circuit was blown.

"Have you heard of that, Delma?" Anna asked, wonderingly. "Some prank vaste of money. You know they tell Nils what they are supposed to be doing is putting lights on that new bridge. Just vasting time and money and now, the Vings is done in."

Phidelma frowned, puzzling the story out, but locking on to the idea of lights on the bridge, over the water. Sometimes she could almost remember floating in the cart, with a lantern, because when she told Marguerite's story now it was for Celia, and always at bedtime. Her brother had left in the night, and all the lights were out around the block, and Phidelma slid across the planks of the old cart box, dark water rising.

"Someone," Anna insisted, "did it in to the chinks."

"Did it in to them — " Phidelma repeated. "You don't mean did them in?"

"Did them out?" Anna tried again. "Drives them out?"

"Del-ma!" Celia called, across the yard from the back door. Anna raised her hand to wave, and grasped for the right phrase."Drove them away," Phidelma supplied, turning away. "Celia! What are you yelling about?"

Mr. Wing had brought Celia home once that fall, not entirely unhappy to have been yanked out of a game that had older girls sending her into ditches after tins for a scrap metal drive. Wet and cold, Celia had wriggled free of Mr. Wing's grasp on the front step and then — rather than running inside as Phidelma expected her to — stomped her foot and demanded her treat. He had bribed the girl home with a wind up tin bird that he pulled from his coat pocket and handed to Phidelma.

"It's for me!" Celia protested.

"Is for the day you are good!" Mr. Wing shouted back. He ran a laundromat, or his wife did, and he'd been in the house over the years, with Thomas. Those nights when a younger Phidelma had chased her own self off to bed. She'd never thought of Mr. Wing as funny, nor known that he was kind.

The Wings disappeared with Robert in mid-October. Their building closed and reopened soon as a pharmacy, and Celia made herself a collection from the garbage stacked out back. Cans with gold Chinese writing, pins, and the metal closures from tin boxes, which she arranged on her windowsill and played with in the winter, like a boy would tin soldiers.

Mr. Wing's toy, a red-breasted bird that hopped and pecked, soon sat on Celia's windowsill too. Phidelma gave it over as leverage against chores once she'd taught Celia to make her own bed and walk ashes to the back of the yard. Sometimes the bird's springs loosened suddenly, and in the busyness of morning and evening they wouldn't notice, only one or the other would step on it later on the floor.

Weekday afternoons, when Phidelma sat mending pieces Mrs. Smith sent over, she'd every now and then hear a short woodpecker's call, rat-tat-tat-tat — and then the sound of the bird crashing to the floor. She never picked it up because when Celia came home Phidelma loved to hear the scold she'd give it. And the kisses Celia gave it too, returning it to its nest on the sill.

» Thirty-Seven

Celia followed through to the hilt. Her tracksuit was not only the pink she'd promised Tanis on the phone but also vaguely holographic. Its shoulders danced with dark specks where the plastic fabric reflected her cropped and permed black hair. Straight white roots gave her an unexpected halo. Tanis had been expecting an understated senior, maybe in one of those Navajo patterned fleece jackets, or a quilted button up. She'd pictured getting there first and watching Celia come hesitantly, out of place through the doors. But Celia had beaten her there and, amusing herself, was grinning widely at an iPhone down the length of her extended iridescent arm. When they'd talked on the phone she had seemed so old fashioned. Neil hadn't corrected that impression.

"Celia?" Tanis asked, approaching.

"Tanis! It must be you — look at that sweater!" Tanis had promised to wear green, but her sweater was dull, nearing olive. She should have borrowed Neil's Riders jersey. Pink Celia rose, pulling Tanis into a sudden hug. She was short, and beamed up at Tanis, "It's so nice to finally meet you, dear."

Tanis excused herself to stand in the coffee line. She wanted to know about her house, and its stories, but the reality of this woman had shifted her focus. She shouldn't be thrown. It was the house, after all, she needed to feel easy with, not this friendly but maybe a little strange woman. Glancing back at the table, she saw Celia texting deftly. Tanis hadn't worn a skirt in a year but had pulled one on today, thinking it might make the older woman feel more comfortable. She ordered herself an iced coffee.

"My daughter, you know," Celia apologized as Tanis returned to the table. "She can't seem to keep off of that thing. It's this is happening at the office', 'this is what my granddaughter is doing now'. Any little thing and I've got to know it, right now, or you'd think the world would end. If I don't text, do you know, she'll phone! Now, but you're probably the same way."

"Well, I do have a phone but — "

Celia interrupted, sloshing her coffee against the table. "But you'll be wanting to know about your boots."

Tanis blinked. That was to the point. She did want to know about the boots. "Yes, it was so strange, finding them — "

"Well, they might seem strange to you now, but all men used to wear boots, you know."

"Oh, not that the boots are strange, just finding them — "

"Isn't that the thing? Them being hidden like that."

"We couldn't think why they would be — hidden, like that. Your mind runs off and — "

"I'll tell you the strangest thing about your house, Tanis," Celia said, her coffee clasped to her chest and nearly crushed against the table as she leaned in. "You know it was run by a managing company for years? Well, that was because my husband, Lloyd, he thought it would go up in value, and that was kind of my inheritance, you see."

Tanis swirled the chunks in her Iced Capp with her straw. *Your house,* she'd said.

"We didn't want to sell it, but we didn't like dealing with renters either. It hasn't always been a nice street, if you know what I mean. My aunt sold the other side of the lot — it was a big lot, you know, but after the war with all the veterans coming back you could sell half your lot and they'd put one of those little wartime houses on it. Well, they tried to buy Phidelma's and she held out the longest time and then they paid her twice what they paid the others and built that little apartment on it."

"The green box," Tanis nodded, repeating Neil's name for it.

"It was all veterans that moved in at first. They'd be sitting, drinking and smoking out their windows all day and she did their laundry for some small fee. I don't know how much, but you can be sure it was half kindnesses. A lot of those men were not fit for work. They got relief, you know, some kind of payment."

This was interesting history. "So my house was kind of a housekeeping service, then? Would she have had tenants as well? In the attic space?"

"Oh, there was no attic. Not when I was there. And I said I'd tell you the strangest thing about your house."

My house, Tanis thought.

Celia glanced at her phone, pursed her lips and set it face down on the table.

"You see, I visited over there with my baby a week before my auntie died, and the house was the way it always was, full of things. Men's laundry all over the basement. She ironed everything for them, you know, and there was plenty of food and her dishes and her sewing things all in it together in the kitchen. I hadn't told her I was coming." Celia paused, squinted at Tanis, and spoke for the first time in a way that could be described as solemn. "Do you understand?"

"I'm not sure."

"It was full of *her*."

Tanis frowned. "Your aunt spent a lot of her life in that house, I suppose?"

"And then she died and maybe it did take them a day to find her but not long, you know, because some of those veterans were used to coming and sitting in her yard so they knew something was wrong soon along. But there was nothing in that house. No bottles, no plates, no food. And all the things she'd kept in my old room were gone — not treasures you know, but some toys and blankets and that — even the pioneer quilt — she'd offered it to me when I visited, for the baby. All that was there was the laundry left in the middle of things in the basement. And her bed in her room with her curled up in it."

"Um . . . dead?"

"As a doornail."

Very strange. "And the boots."

"Hm?" Celia had picked up her phone again, was scrolling through something.

"The boots would have been there too. Her body. The laundry. And your grandpa's boots."

"About those boots — "

Tanis sat forward. When they'd spoken on the phone Celia had described in detail how her aunt had her sit and rub tallow into the leather, to keep them waterproof and supple. How she'd gone to bed with her fingers tingling from the nightly chore. It had been a bit walked-uphill-on-glass-to-school-ish, but Tanis had absorbed every word.

"When your husband dropped them off, Tanis — you're married, eh?"

"Yes."

"When he dropped them off, I thought, now here are Pa père's boots. Then I held them and I suppose it's been a long time but something felt wrong."

"The wrong size?"

"I suppose they are about the right size, though my hands are bigger than back then. I'd have one hand on the inside, you know — "

"And one hand rubbing on the outside — "

"I told you there was nothing of her left in the house?"

The woman was going in circles now. Maybe Celia was less with it than she seemed. "There was nothing of her left in the house?" Tanis prompted.

"My auntie never wanted to burden me, you know. She took care of cleaning the place out herself."

"Do you really think so?" It seemed so obvious. The coal chute. The shell-shocked addicts in the apartment next door —

"I know so."

"But what if she'd done that, cleared it all for you — and then she didn't die?"

"Oh, she'd have waited."

"Really?"

"It's what she'd want, to take care of herself like that. Leave things easy for me. So then he called me, this one of them, Taffy. And he says she's gone, and they've called the doctor or whoever it is if they're dead. And then, that same day — so she must have put it in the mail almost right after I left, you see — I get this." Celia had been listing left, and now straightened to the table with a little coil bound book in her hand.

"There was a note card slipped in, about sharing this with Corinne, my baby, so I know it was Delma who sent it." It was a slim album with gold cursive on the cover that promised *Treasured Memories* inside.

"Maybe I could scan it for Corinne," Tanis said, as Celia handed it over.

"What's that?" Celia asked.

"Scan the pictures, make them into a CD?"

"A CD? Is that for Internet pictures?"

"Yes," Tanis said. "Well, they are the same kind of file at least." Celia shifted around the table to sit closer. Her husband's cigarettes rose second-hand from the shiny suit. Celia had complained about his smoking on the phone. Less about the smoking than his killing himself with it. When Tanis looked up, to ask about the people in the first photo, Celia wedged her hands in to turn the pages herself. She flipped them ahead, then back, indexing names and places so quickly that Tanis had to reach out several times to interrupt — the appearance and eclipse of this or that view of Auntie Delma. Phidelma.

This was the woman who chose the flower wallpaper. The hand that had hidden, in the coal chute, an ad for nylons. The hand that hid the boots? Or had that been one of her lovers from the apartment next door?

In one picture Phidelma was a slim shadow cast beside Celia, a scrawny child dressed in frills and clutching a dog. In another — the photos were out of order — Celia's auntie was herself a sombre child at the end of the middle row of a school photo, her middy gouged by an "X" of black pen.

"Who," Tanis wondered aloud, "would cut children's hair so severely?" It really did look as if bowls had been involved. 1925.

Celia flipped through the book, laughing often as the pages clapped together, pulled by the weight of the old photographs. Then she stopped and tapped on a photo of a gathering of girls and women, arms around each other, posed beside a large truck. Three men sat on its hood and roof, ankles dangling from trousers that had been rolled up against the heat.

"You see there," Celia pointed. "That's her smiling."

Phidelma was medium height but slender to the degree of spindly. Her elbows made sharp angles around the shoulders of the women on her either side. Her friends were laughing, open mouthed, and between them, Phidelma was apparently smiling. No teeth showed. Her lips were pressed into a line so firm and straight it looked inked across her face. But her eyes — Tanis thought she could see the smile there. A smile or a squint against the sun.

Celia poked Tanis' shoulder and aped the face, a resemblance to her aunt suddenly and strikingly strong, and Tanis laughed.

"That's at the edge," Celia said. "Across town — over where that big high school is now — a lot of people lived out there after they lost farms or scrip and we'd go visiting. My auntie'd blend right in with the women and I'd try to do the same with the kids. There was always a big bed, and after we'd tired ourselves out running around we'd all lie there listening to the grownups. There'd be music, and cards, lots of jokes."

"The edge? Would that be like the Métis towns in the road allowances?"

"Well, some of the same people, maybe, but they weren't on a road allowance. There wasn't a road. They were past the end of it there."

"But, this would have been Métis people?" Tanis tried again. She'd gathered this much from the names Celia remembered, some of which she'd had to have spelled aloud.

"It would be now, but we didn't call ourselves that then. And lot them were scotch half breeds."

"Phidelma sounds French."

"Grammère, Marguerite, she would have called herself Métis. Didn't you say she's from Rounde Prairie? That was French Métis. They'd just had their rebellion, then."

"The North-West Rebellion? In 1885?"

"She'd have been born after that, I suppose. 1900? When was it they'd all gone to Rounde Prairie, the French ones?"

Tanis shook her head, she didn't know.

"Well, I can just tell you I never got called Métis. Never heard that word." Celia lifted a hand to scratch her cheek. Her hands were almost as creased as her suit.

Tanis looked down at her own. "So, you didn't have much to do with your culture, I guess."

Celia agreed, "Nothing like we saw at Folk Fest last summer."

"Ha. Would Phidelma have, growing up?"

"Well, Delma didn't raise up with them," Celia said. "Your house, that set us outside the rest, somehow. Though we did have girls come. Later, we had girls off and on staying in the house with us. She'd got in touch with an auntie, I think. The girls were some kind of cousins, you know," Celia raised inquiring eyebrows. Was Tanis interested?

"They weren't — what did they call it. In trouble?"

Celia laughed. "Oh no, she was really a kind of chaperone for them if they came in to work, or for the technical school. And they paid rent, I imagine." Celia looked puzzled about something, then shook her head in mock disapproval.

Tanis smiled encouragingly.

"My auntie, when the girls came, she made a real effort. It was our chance to be a bit la-di-da about town, I thought, but she'd drag them into the bush along the river. Getting kindling. Picking berries. Phidelma and me and those girls trailing along, just talking about nothing. Dresses, and who was marrying who and, oh, we were really modern, you know. We went to the movies and all of that. Even my auntie. But those buckets could fill up like something. They've got ranches you can go pick now, all laid out and mowed in between the rows. Corrine says you might was well go grocery shopping."

"I'd rather go to pick berries. Along the river, I mean," Tanis agreed.

"And maybe we'll go looking, in the spring, then."

Tanis smiled, "I'd like that."

Celia did not smile. She bit her coffee cup, scraped her teeth along the rolled rim, squinted at the flattened portion and announced, "No dice."

"I think the roll up the rim thing is after Christmas," Tanis said and felt a blush climb her neck. "Or, I wouldn't have bought an iced drink. If it was after Christmas, and I bought coffee too, I might've won!"

Celia flicked a fingernail quickly off the side of Tanis' cup. "Always time to learn, dear."

She slid the photo album up against Tanis' hand. "You take that for now and see what you see. I've got to get going but we'll set ourselves up to meet again, won't we?"

"Yes, for sure, and it was so good of you to come and meet — "

"Well, someone's taught you lovely manners," Celia interrupted, leaning in to plant a surprise kiss on Tanis' cheek. The old woman's cheek was smooth and soft, and she smelled of Lloyd's cigarettes and coffee and Tanis' own grandma, Kate, who'd used to babysit her Tuesday nights.

» Thirty-Eight

The shape behind the rippled door glass was too large for Thomas or Alexey or Nils. They'd never wait that long between knocking and barging in. Phidelma cleared her throat to say hello, opened the door, and gawked at a man she'd seen only in the newspaper. She felt like she ought to know him and invite him in.

"Hello, ma'am," he said polite as can be, "I'd like to speak with your husband if he's about."

Phidelma blinked. Her husband. Could he mean Robert, or Thomas?

"He's away then, is he, ma'am?" The police sergeant lifted his hat slightly, and rubbed at his forehead. "How long has he been away?"

"Well, it's been a few weeks, sir," Phidelma answered, after too long a wait.

"That's a long time for him to be away on business, isn't it? Do you know his itinerary?"

"Yes, sir." Robert is in Manitoba, somewhere. Thomas is somewhere else, north and travelling. This time of year, fall, he might be buying hides. Deer and moose season is here and he may come back with meat.

"Ma'am?" Realizing that she had not answered, Phidelma flushed.

"It's a bit odd, isn't it, for a wife not to know where her husband is?" The policeman was watching her. Phidelma could feel his eyes on her hands, which were damp, still, from washing up. There would be threads, she knew, caught on the skirt of her dress because she had been darning, she'd taken in more sewing for Mrs. Smith's friends.

"Ma'am, are you all right?" he asked, squinting at her face.

"Yes, sir."

"If he's away, you're taken care of, you've got enough?" Phidelma was no longer sure if it really was the police detective from the paper. The uniform, the jacket, maybe these were all that matched. All the police were tall. All six feet all at least. Robert had told her that. And that he'd never have been hired, even if height weren't the issue.

"I take in," Phidelma said, waving a hand over her skirt. "As needs must."

The policeman smiled oddly. "I can tell you now, ma'am, that there's suspicions about bootlegging through the city, but I can see you are an abstaining woman."

"Yes, sir."

"I can see you wouldn't want to aid and abet."

"No, sir."

"So if you hear from your husband, or if he's in touch, I'd surely like to know about it as well."

"Yes, sir." There can be no way for him to believe that answer. Doesn't he know how a family works? Maybe he truly doesn't because when he's down on the path he stops and he turns around and smiles at her. "You keep well, ma'am."

That night Phidelma climbed to the attic room and sat on Thomas' bed. It had been many years now since they moved into the house and her father had carried furs in and out in broad daylight. That secret had been in the open a long time. If there was something new, maybe it had to do with Robert, who left with the street bulbs wound out. Phidelma would have liked to go to Mr. Smith, to let him know about the policeman's visit and ask what to do, but if Robert was in trouble Phidelma needed to make sure first of all that she and Celia will not be. She had already asked, quietly, through a woman at the auxiliary and if Lily's family made a claim for the child it would be regular by law for Celia to be sent back.

The little girl had taken to sleeping with Phidelma's floral shawl, the one they'd become used to pretending was Marguerite's. Celia wraped it around her stomach, pulling the droopy nightgown Phidelma sewed her into a cinched waist. After she was tucked in, she lifted the tip of the folded triangle up, to rub the soft frayed corner against her cheek.

She looked so peaceful, asleep, that it was hard for Phidelma sometimes to remember the little girl's tantrums straight on. The most recent had come when Phidelma hadn't let Celia take a spool toy Thomas had given her along to school. The teacher would have taken it away, or some other child.

"A thing, if it's so hard to keep safe, should stay home," Phidelma scolded, taking the toy away. Celia screamed and Phidelma froze, caught on a memory of Marguerite. Wanting a thing took such power over you. Phidelma had looked at her mother's emptied eyes and understood, a lesson learned early.

Celia jumped at her aunt's closed fist and screamed, frantic and furious. Phidelma gripped the child by her shoulders, took a kick to her shins, then pinned the little girl's arms to her sides, the toy a knot under her hand.

"Do you want your face to stick that way?" she asked Celia. It took four tries before the child seemed to hear, and another two before she gasped for breath and looked up, confused. Phidelma took Celia by the hand then and led her up the stairs to find a place for the spool among her treasures on the windowsill in the little bedroom.

Celia rubbed her eyes, then turned the spool so it could face out at the yard. "He's watching for Pa père," she explained wearily.

Did the girl really think that the face Thomas had carved into that wooden spool could see? Phidelma had caught Celia calling it by his name, Pa père. And she had overheard that whispered as Celia slipped it into the front of her sweater. A guardian against the children at school?

» Thirty-Nine

After visiting with Celia, Tanis felt tired. Inspired, the way she did anytime she met old people who stayed so alive, but also just tired. She was remembering her grandma Kate, and thinking of her own mother coming soon, who would cluck and shake her head at the socket boxes that Tanis doubted, somehow, they would paint. Back at home, she slipped out of her sweater and skirt, and fell onto the bed and into a heavy dream where her conversation with Celia kept going, and Tim Horton's shifted dream wise — the trays of doughnuts behind the glass changed first to books in a library, then to racks of wine over a pool. She woke, confused, close to four.

Tanis stretched, wondering if she'd caught Neil's flu or if this was just an ordinary kind of foggy and tired. She slid down under the duvet, pulled it above her head, and squirmed off the mattress sideways — the very best way to make a bed shoved up against a wall. She smoothed a hand over the bed, turned to face the clothes she'd dropped on the floor, and pulled the skirt back on.

Before meeting Celia, Tanis had tried a property query with the City Archives, submitting an online request form. Now, checking her email, Tanis saw that the archivist had got to it quickly — sending a ZIP attachment with original files on the house, including a building permit, issued to Thomas Tanner, an electrical connection order, and two sanitation orders related to septic connections. The pipes seemed so old it was hard to believe that they hadn't always been in the house, but as Neil pointed out they would hardly have placed them so low in the basement if they'd been in the original plans. Tanis wondered if they were lead. They'd have to find out — among the archivist's attachments was a statement that the pipes went into the house in 1939, just before the war. And, shortly after:

A TRIBUTE — published in the pages of — THE STAR Memorial Obituary: TANNER — The Death of Mr. Thomas Tanner, aged 67 years, of 723 Avenue L South, occurred at his late residence last week, Thursday November 10, 1941 at 11:00 PM. A Requiem Mass will be held with his family, of Morden, Manitoba, where he will be interred. Surviving are his loving daughter, Phidelma Tanner, his son Robert Tanner, and his granddaughter, Cecilia Tanner. He is predeceased by his wife, Marguerite, daughter-in-law Lily, one daughter, and three sons.

Amazing. Celia's Grandpa Thomas had died right here in this house as well. Maybe he'd hidden his own boots first? Old houses, old ghosts. Not ghosts, Tanis corrected herself, smiling. Lives lived. She reached for the phone and tapped Celia's number, which rang without an answer.

There was a text from Neil, though, which must have come in during her nap: *Hi — P w vball x*. Pizza with volleyball. Kiss.

Tanis had taken the afternoon off, basically, meeting Celia, and would otherwise have started on the box at her feet. Three fat files of suspect purchases from the university's department of financial services. The money would be handy, Tanis supposed. Evenings were supposed to be couple time, though, and here she was. Neil had only gone to Karen's practice because of the missing girls, she knew that too. For the non-missing girls. They deserved to feel safe and she didn't really begrudge them his supervision. She replied to his text, *OK. Later, x.*

Then reconsidered. She should have said *good luck to the girls!* But the game was bound to be over, or close to it.

Tanis put the phone on her desk and went downstairs to slap together a peanut butter sandwich. She carried it back up and stalled on the top step. A spray of white plaster dust had appeared in front of the hall closet, again. She'd swept one up the day before.

Now that the attic was open to the rest of the house it was sucking air in interesting ways. Tanis felt the draft move past her bare arms. The bedroom door clicked in its latch, and the fan of white dust restructured itself against the floor.

"Phidelma, what's the trick?" Tanis asked aloud.

It seemed very likely that a woman who had, by Celia's report, kept a wood stove pristinely clean of ash and soot would know what to do about leaking plaster. Google was rather reliable, too. Settling back at the computer Tanis learned that plaster in 1920s-era homes could be made of anything from pure asbestos to barium weighted flour or cow dung — none of that sounded great to breathe.

"Are you in here, Delma?" Tanis asked, typing "Phidelma Tanner" to Google. There was one result, but from Vital Records of East Bridgewater, Massachusetts. Not the right Phidelma. "Thomas Tanner" yielded 1 million 200 thousand. "Tanner Saskatchewan Métis" fourteen entries, and at the top of the list *Tom Tanner Interview, Métis Oral History files.* Unbelievable. Available online. The computer spooled, downloading a PDF, clearly scanned from a typewritten document. Tanis bit her sandwich and read.

Descharme Lake Oral Histories, at resettlement – 1979 – Paul Langlois, Local 47, interviewee Tom Tanner

P.L.: So you're not taking them up on a house in La Loche, Tom?

T.T.: No. <inaudible>

P.L.: Is that because you're still living, as they say, on the land?

T.T.: Still living, sure, you'd think a man would notice that. <laughter>

P.L.: I mean, are you staying because you make your living from the land. Hunting, fishing, this sort of thing.

T.T.: Making a living, I did that, you know, I'm an older guy now, Mr. Langlois.

P.L.: Have you lived here your whole life?

T.T.: No, I've been here a while, though.

P.L.: Since the war, Louise thought?

Tanis put her sandwich down on her desk. It'd been a bit too good to be true — Thomas had died in 1942, during the war. Still, she kept reading — the Tanner family didn't seem to be very big, it could still be one of Celia's relatives.

T.T.: Mm hm. I came up here and they were glad I did, too. I wasn't so old then, and the younger men were going overseas. I did some hunting, fishing, and this sort of thing then. Took care of some women, this sort of thing. <laughter>

P.L.: While the younger men were away? How old would you have been then?

T.T.: Well, forty maybe. Maybe forty-five.

P.L.: So you weren't married, I'm guessing, when you came here.

T.T.: No, I was on my own. I did that when I was young.

P.L.: You got married quite young?

T.T.: Sure, twenty-two. She would've been sixteen. Maybe. That's how they did it then, the Catholic ones, marrying really young. Not that she had a choice about it, mind you.

Phidelma's parents had been married when she was eighteen, not sixteen. And Marguerite hadn't been knocked up, she was a widow. It was a similar age gap, though — which nowadays would be an illegal age gap. Interesting.

P.L.: Was it an arranged marriage?

T.T.: No, hew. She was cranky about it but those Catholics, you know. <shooting sound>

P.L.: Got ya .<laughter>

T.T.: Took a while, eh. Then they give me a horse and she looked like a stuffed pillow by then. Gave her pots and a quilt. That's what we had, and her brothers helped me build a house. That first one was small, hide windows even, and I'd grown up with glass. Going back in time, it felt like. We ended up with the quilt on the wall to keep out the wind. But that, with just the first girl, that was a good time for us. Hard work, for both of us. I worked with her brothers.

P.L.: Were there many children?

T.T.: Sure, we had five.

P.L.: And where are they all now?

T.T.: Well, she died, my wife. And the three of them died small, infections. Before her, though. TB probably, and that was hard on her. Losing the first girl, and two other little ones. Then Robert, he grew up and died. Needed a big grave, that one. He was a big man. That was in Saskatoon.

Robert in Saskatoon? Tanis pushed her chair back to from the computer, went downstairs to fill a glass of water, and carried it promptly back up. Thomas and Robert were both very common names, add William and John and that was probably half of the men in the province at one time. A big son named Robert — buried, not missing in action overseas — but it was an interesting coincidence.

P.L.: Saskatoon? Is that where you were from? Or the road allowance south of the city? Or Eastside?

T.T.: Well, where I was from wasn't there. Spent time around Prince Albert and Portage at different times, but then I did go to school right through. <pause> Got you, eh? I wasn't raised in the bush like some of them here. More of us old ones did more school than our kids, I can tell you.

P.L.: <inaudible> and were you in a war, Tom?

T.T.: Not overseas. But that was exciting times, spent a long time away from the family. <inaudible> <pause>

P.L.: What were you working at, Tom?

T.T.: Always got to work. <pause> Wasn't easy to find, we rented rooms out sometimes too after I built the house. I had three languages coming out of school. Thought I'd work in government but I ended up working under them.

P.L.: You mean black market work? Drink?

T.T.: Oh well, or furs. They were stingy with the Indians like now, right. Just about anything you could get on to the reserve you could trade up. <pause> You know, Paul, they'll tell you there's a few of them in La Loche that might as well be mine. That's another reason to stay here, right.

P.L.: Sorry, Tom?

Tanis pushed herself back from the keyboard again, shaking her head this time. This old Métis guy had three languages, had survived off the bush for decades and presumably had a wealth of knowledge of the land, a unique perspective on history — and he kept coming back to bragging about womanizing. Tanis skimmed down the file, and stopped at something about fishing, and read more.

T.T.: They were great women, you know, they worked with the fishery. Drying them, that was for women, but catching, filleting, packing, making gardens, they did all that too in the war. And they didn't let those kids get away with a thing.

P.L.: Now those kids, they would've been at the mission school?

T.T.: Right. Never been Catholic, see. My kids, I had to pay tax to get them reading and writing. That was hard on my wife, her kids not going and all that.

P.L.: A lot of families might have thought that was a good thing, you hear —

T.T.: And lots of kids died, right. Well, mine died anyways.

P.L.: It sounds like you did well by your kids, Tom, getting them to school. Do you have advice for young people about that?

T.T.: I'd say what my father said. You've got blood on you, you'd better have killed a deer. Mind your own business that means. And your kids, you got to make them work so they know about it when they're young or it'll be real hard on 'em later.

Good advice, but pretty generic. Tanis had heard Neil say something similar, and disparaging, about the parents who called in excuses when their kids didn't finish work. She pressed CTRL-F and typed Métis.

P.L.: Do you consider yourself Métis, Tom?

T.T.: Reckon that's why you're interviewing me. <laughter>

Tanis hit the search again.

T.T.: I had cousins in between the wars that were stooping, thinning wood, digging roots, all those things you'll have been hearing about for Métis eh? <inaudible> Good people most of them too but they worked too hard. Don't see them around to interview, do you?

P.L.: <laughter> So government work was a health choice then, Tom?

T.T.: Sure. Now here I end up on a trap line. <laughter> Sold furs through the Indians, they were getting better prices after the war.

P.L.: I've heard a bit about that from some of the other old timers too.

T.T.: Sure, that made work for them.

P.L.: This has been home for a long time, eh? <pause>

T.T.: <inaudible> <laughter>

P.L.: I don't suppose you're considering retirement?

T.T.: Kill me first.

P.L.: Well, no thanks. <laughter> Thanks then, Tom.

<inaudible>

<end of transcript>

Tanis spun her chair first to face the hall, and then the window. She stared out into the dark, through the twin orbs of the streetlight in the alley and its reflection on the glass. Forty-five-ish years old in the war, and this had been recorded in 1979, Thomas Tanner would have been eighty at least. Still going strong.

» Forty

T*'s ass — u c it?*

Neil opened Facebook page on Tanis' computer, signed himself in, and opened a pop-up frame that displayed a low angle booty shot with a lacy thong sticking out the top of a pair of skinny jeans. Tanis reached over his shoulder to coast down the forty likes the picture had already received. It jumped out — *Melissa Arthur.*

"Do you think it's real?" Tanis asked, feeling a surge of anxiety.

"I really hope so," Neil said, and then tapped the mouse, liking the photo.

"Seriously, Neil — are you insane?"

Neil stammered, "I liked seeing Melissa's name, not the butt — "

"That was idiotic. What do you think the police — "

"Oh come on," Neil put a hand on Tanis' thigh and held on to her leg to keep her from leaving the room. "I used Stevie B, not my account. And look, Kolton liked it too."

"Well," Tanis said, "that makes forty-two."

"I just got the text from Kolton. I have no idea what the police think about this, Tanis." Neil gripped her leg. He'd gone kind of white and Tanis chewed her lip, "go back to your profile."

"What?"

Tanis shoved him off and gestured for him to get out of the chair, which he did. Then he knelt beside her while she clicked through the world of Stevie B. He'd liked a few bands, but posted nothing else identifying. In the real world, like the online, Neil had always made it a point that he could banter with students. Make himself available and comfortable to them. Fine. But this girl, Taelur, would not want her math teacher liking her panties. "Neil, you do see how dumb this is?" Tanis asked. "Especially right now."

Neil stood up quickly.

"Because there's an investigation, and they'll think this makes you involved and — " Tanis was working up to an explosion.

"Because," Neil interrupted, "right now there could be someone stalking kids at my school, and I want to know what they — oh, fuck it Tanis."

"Excuse me?"

"I have to get dressed. Look at Melissa's profile while you're on there." Tanis clicked on Melissa's name angrily and her wall opened with post after elegiac post. It read like an open eulogy, but at least Stevie B. wasn't her friend. Tanis logged out, and back in through her own profile and felt her stomach release, tension lifting just enough for tears to leak through. She blew her nose into a Kleenex, balled it up, and threw it across the hall. "Neil!"

"What?"

"You need to get rid of that account — "

"Okay." That came quicker than Tanis had expected.

"Or — is that a good idea?" Tanis asked anxiously. Neil's head appeared in the doorway of their bedroom. "Would that be suspicious? Can you just let it go inactive?"

"I think that they never actually delete it. I'd have to request that, from a valid email address or phone line. I can let it be inactive, though. I can deactivate it."

So Neil would be permanently linked, and implicated. All for one stupid impulse to spy. To care, really, but it was still dumb. "Imagine if these old records I've been going through had stuff like this, Neil. Pictures, links connecting people, what they liked . . . " it would have made it quite a bit harder for a person like Thomas Tanner to disappear. Neil came back to the office, dressed for work. "She called actually," he said.

"Who, Mom?"

"No, the boot lady."

"Celia?"

"Yes, she said. What did she say . . . " Neil took a deep breath, trying to remember. "She said something about thick soup. But then she asked about school too . . . " In fact, Neil had found himself giving the old woman a play-by-play of the staff meetings, and the neighbourhood search the police had done. Block to block, through everyone's yards. Celia *tsk-tsked*, then reassured him oddly, saying there were no secrets in a police investigation. Then she added that the neighbourhood hadn't always been so run down.

"Did you tell her?" Tanis asked. "I left a message, but does she know we have the obituary now?"

Neil backed away to lean on the windowsill of Tanis' office. He squinted at her. She squinted back. He was stalling, confused. Celia had said something about the first girl who'd gone missing. Not an obituary, a girl some years back found behind an empty house. It sounded like something he'd heard before. Jody's flash fiction assignment.

"The obituary for Tomas Tanner?" Tanis prompted.

"Sure, she said she'd be glad to talk to you when you were back." Neil pushed up from the window. It was nearly seven-thirty, time for him to head off if he was going to make the morning staff meeting. He stopped at the doorway and turned back to Tanis, who'd spun in her chair but not risen to follow him down.

"Have a good day, okay?"

"I — " Tanis hesitated. She'd been going to say, I will. Instead she asked, "When will you be back tonight?"

"Right after work."

Tanis nodded but still didn't get up, so Neil stepped back into the room and bent to kiss her, setting a hand on her thigh. He squeezed, and the rolling chair shifted away from his weight.

"Yeesh," she said, and put a hand on either side of his face to stabilize it.

"Right after work," Neil promised.

"Tell them about this, and Bornstein, okay?"

"I will." Neil said.

But when Kolton texted again as he walked up to the school, Neil felt an anxious vertigo. He was supposed to have already reported Kolton's text breach of teacher-student boundaries too. He should have done that a week ago. The new message read, *You see it?*

Neil stopped on the sidewalk, turned his phone sideways to make the keyboard expand and thumbed out: *We have a staff meeting this morning. I am going to make sure that this is highlighted and taken seriously. Thnx and hang in there.* >SEND

"At this point, we are relying on reports from the public," Malhiot told the gathered staff. The chairs weren't even half full this time.

"What about social media?" Bornstein asked, pre-empting Neil's report. "Did you see what they've been doing on there? You see what they've been saying about very young missing women on the RCity comment boards?" He was angry.

"Yes," Malhiot replied calmly. "But it takes a lot of resources, policing those."

"Did you see the — the buttocks?" Neil asked, and the officers and a healthy handful teachers turned to stare at him. "On Taelur's Facebook page there's a shot of her rear end and — "

"No there's not," Karen cut in, phone raised. She showed the group a picture of Taelur pouting out of her profile picture box.

"This morning there was a picture of her rear end," Neil said.

"Do you often look at — ?" Malhiot began.

"Melissa *liked* it," Neil added. Silence fell over the library and when Sawatsky crossed his ankles under his chair, his shoes dragged over the industrial carpet with an audible hiss.

"What exactly did Melissa *like*?" Malhiot asked.

"She *liked* it. I mean, her name comes up in the list of people who clicked that they liked Taelur's picture."

"Did we know that?" Malhiot asked her partner, her face expressionless.

"Yes, we knew that," Sawatsky replied, staring Neil down.

Neil imagined them stepping to either side of his chair, hoisting him to his feet. Slamming him into a wall. The room was tense and Malhiot's response now was to lean back her chair in a bizarrely relaxed way. "Well," she said.

"Can I talk to the two of you in private after this meeting?" Neil asked.

"Sounds like that might be a good idea," Sawatsky said. He kicked his legs out in front of his chair, still crossed, and coughed. When Karen didn't pipe up, he pointed at the phone on her lap. "You after him, I think?"

"I have classes all morning, he has prep," Karen shot back.

"You first, then."

While Neil waited in a chair between the doors to the principal's office and the boardroom, he sent Kolton another short text: *I'm on it buddy.*

Tanis had dropped a line as well: *Coffee with C again, ur on supper.* You're on supper, as in making supper? Neil tapped his wife's name, heard the beginnings of the first ring, then hung up the call and pocketed the phone quickly when Karen flew out of the meeting room, cheeks red and wet with tears. At the reception desk, Adrienne put a hand over her phone, "Karen!"

"Karen?" Neil echoed.

Karen reached for a Kleenex from the box on Adrienne's desk and blew into it, then sniffed. "I want a sub, can you tell Bornstein?"

Adrienne looked nervously at Neil. "Will you be needing a sub too?"

He shook his head. "I think they're stuck with me today."

Karen glared and Neil attempted a smile.

The police accused him of trolling for youth porn.

"That's not what I was doing," Neil said.

"Is this the image that you referred to viewing at the staff meeting?" Sawatsky asked, lifting a streaked computer print out.

Neil covered his eyes. "She posted it!" he protested, eyes shut tight. "I wasn't trying to see anything — I'll close the account, unfriend her, whatever you think."

That wasn't what they wanted him to do. In fact, they'd been watching both his real and "assumed" Facebook accounts, as well as his phone, and they asked Neil if he might like to tell them what he had been trying to see.

"I just wanted to try to find out what's going on — the students were all talking as if they knew more and I know that's partly just a youth thing. Wanting to be part of everything. But they were friends with the girls too, so you never know."

"You didn't think that we could be trusted to monitor that activity?"

Neil paused. "I don't know."

"And what's up," Malhiot asked, brushing her bangs back from her face with a smirk, "what's up with the murder in your attic?"

Neil's chin dropped. "There's no murder in the attic. We found boots. My wife is kind of creative."

The two officers spoke at once. "That's not what you texted to your friend Mr. Puller." and "We've put that together from her emails, actually."

Neil gawked. "Is this legal?"

"We contacted your 'informant' too, the former resident of your house."

Neil blinked.

"The old lady," Malhiot clarified.

And now Neil remembered Celia on the phone, her strangely worded phrase about secrets in the course of the investigation. He leaned back in his chair. "So does she know something?"

"Do you?"

"No."

"Yeah, we know that." They laughed but it was oddly stiff, like their posture.

"Now, however," Malhiot said, "we do have reason to believe that Kolton Dueck has had contact with Melissa, or someone with access to her Facebook account." She tipped her head to Sawatsky, who shifted forward in his chair. "You've put yourself in a very unique position, Neil."

"And Karen, her too?"

"No comment," Sawatsky said.

Neil hadn't heard anyone actually say that aloud before. He glanced between Malhiot and Sawatsky and repeated, "No comment?"

Grassfire

by Jody Bear

The clay banks are bare after spring, the muddy water opaque, except near the bank where the water fades clear, stained the red brown colour of rust and dried blood. Beneath is the imprint of a child's hand, at the tips of small fingers sharpened claws stole a grip on the river's bottom. Green teeth of willow ripple underwater, thin fangs yellowing at tapered leaf ends. It is not a time for winter storage, this spring they will spoil. The handprint lies under the water and thunder cracks, an animal breaking through the brush. There is a smell of sweet new sap, dripping from leaves cut by insect teeth. The field was mown short, to guard against grassfires, but there is a wet popping sound and, underground, roots explode with heat, flames burrowing through the damp soil. The cut grass smudges the river, burning wet. It smokes, flares, twists on short stems. The beaver's print, the kid's hand, untouched in the water.

[Jody, I don't know what to say. This is a very moving piece, with authentic detail but I am not sure that it addresses the theme of "surprise". Come to see me and we can discuss your grade for this piece.]

» Forty-One

When Celia checked her messages Wednesday afternoon she barely recognized Tanis' voice, it was so excited. "Celia, I think we've found her. Delma. Your grandpa, Thomas. And also your mom." Celia called back in the evening to find out more, but by then Tanis was confused. Thomas Tanner had died twice, she said.

"Well, I don't suppose it would have been an uncommon name," Celia said.

"The details seemed right though, and names — I'm sending this to you anyway."

"Well, all right, dear."

"And the war records — there's veterans records, and missing-in-action, and killed, and no Robert Tanner, at all. And that would be a common name too, wouldn't it?"

"I'd expect so, yes, that one too. What about Lily?"

"I thought I'd found a lead," Tanis explained. But Lily Tanner (née Allary?), Celia's mother, failed to appear in any record except as witness on a baptismal registry. She probably had another name too but Celia said she didn't know.

Light panned across the wall of Tanis' office. A glare off a car door, then headlights from the back alley that blinded Tanis when she crossed to the window. Behind the apartment

Kaydance was climbing into their car, being buckled into a booster seat by Michelle, duffle bags and pillows shoved in around her feet. 8:30 PM. Another mystery, but Michelle had mentioned Kaydance needing a break. With Michelle managing the Community Association website they hadn't been able to get away from people calling, paranoid people. Intolerant people, Michelle said.

Celia had continued talking, but Tanis watched Michelle go back in for something, leaving Kaydance alone in the dark backseat. "Did you notice, dear?" Celia repeated. Kaydance grinned and kicked as Michelle reappeared with Moosie and Tanis sighed with disproportionate relief. "I'm sorry, Celia, what should I have noticed?"

"The boots in the picture?"

"Just a minute, which picture?"

"The funny smile."

"Okay. It is a funny smile, isn't it?"

"It's the boots. Look, at Pa père on the roof of the truck and look at his boots. Laced up. See the top, all wrapped around and crossed over?"

"Hang on just one second." Tanis carried the phone across the hall and sat on her bed to flip through the memory book. "Got it."

"Around the eye holes, you see that?" Celia said.

Tanis examined photograph. It was small to begin with, and the boots were hanging dangling off of pretty skinny legs. "I think you might need to help me more, Celia."

"See they're crossed at the top."

"Like skate laces."

"Like skates, that's right. He always did them like that, you see."

"He had skinny legs."

"Damn skinny. So you see now? These boots you gave me have got no marks like that."

Tanis felt a nudge of frustration, and heard a beep that sounded like the Forester. Neil was probably waiting for Michelle to move ahead so he could pull in. Tanis forced herself to focus. "They're not Pa père's boots."

"They are not," Celia said. "No, see she told me he'd died but I never did believe that. She said I'd dreamt it all, you know."

"Dreamt it all?"

"It's him. That other Thomas Tanner you found. That's Pa père, see, he must've escaped, gone on the lam."

"Gone on the lam from what?"

"Makes you think, doesn't it. Why die twice? Why'd he want to be dead the first time? And who'd send the obituary? Phidelma had to have been in on it. With her dad and my dad and the Wings probably too."

"The air force?"

Celia laughed, "The Chinese family."

"The Chinese family?"

"Sure, there was a family up the street. People like that had a real hard time back then being outsiders, so we can't judge. I told Corrine that when I told her about how you'd been looking into us for connections to Al Capone."

"Oh, Celia, I wasn't — "

"See, Pa père and Robert, they probably had to clear off and then they were sending money, for me and Delma. Taking in from the veterans couldn't have kept her too well, all those years."

"I don't know."

"You see now, don't you?"

"I'm not sure."

"They'd — well, it sounds terrible, doesn't it. But it's obvious enough. They'd offed a man up in that attic of yours."

Tanis laughed. That had been her first thought about the oil stain. But it had been oil. The old boards let off clouds of black smoke when Neil and Declan lit them, breaking in the black metal fire pit she'd bought at a Labour Day sale. Michelle had made Kaydance wait until the fumes burned off before they roasted marshmallows.

In the picture of Phidelma with her funny smile there were two other men. The one, face shaded by his hat, was noticeably heavy set. Had the hat disguised him to his daughter? The same man was posed a few pages later beside a tiny Celia. At "the edge" he'd perched behind his sister, up beside his father, and had probably dented the roof of the truck. Robert's legs dangled identical boots to his father's, without the wraparound lace.

"I'll keep looking into this," Tanis promised, though, at the moment she'd run out of steam — it wasn't fun, the nervous compulsion she felt toward the dead in their home. The back door banged open, and Neil was back.

"Take care of yourself," Celia said.

"I will, and you too," Tanis said, carrying the phone downstairs. The kitchen door swung in and Neil pushed a pile of overflowing grocery bags through along the floor.

"Could've opened the door," he mumbled around the Forester keys, clamped in his mouth.

"They're old stories, and they are not going to change too much if you're busy, you know," Celia said.

"Thanks, Celia," Tanis replied, reaching out to relieve Neil's mouth of the keys.

"Bye for now, dear. I can hear you're busy there."

"Yes, bye, thanks." Tanis set the phone on the kitchen table and moved to help with the groceries. The bags were wet and she realized, as Neil came in with second round and a waft of fresh cold air, that it had begun pouring since she'd last looked out.

Neil shook rain out of his hair with two hands, spraying her face. "Kind of gross out there," he said. Then, "are you seriously still in pyjamas? Did you get dressed at all today?"

"I just — "

"School was good, yes."

"It was good here, too, I got some — "

Neil kissed her quickly, "Guess what, I'm a spy."

"A what?"

"A P.I. A dick — hasn't your mom always said I'm a dick?"

"What are you talking about?"

"I've been seconded by the police." Neil grabbed Tanis in a damp hug, then set a hand on each shoulder and met her eyes. "Don't worry, the wire's not on tonight."

Forty-Two

Kolton stood nervously in front of Neil. Then he slouched down, half-sitting on the top of a desk in the front row. He was trying to look relaxed. "It just means what it means."

"Which is?" Neil asked.

The newest text had read *They got no clue.* More tellingly, it had been sent to Melissa's phone. The police had gone into Kolton's files and made it look rerouted, accidentally sent to Neil.

"Who has no clue about what?" Neil pressed.

"You know man, you listenin'."

"Listening to what?"

"You always listening, you think I don't know that. I know that."

"Kolton, this is a pretty serious situation with your friends. If you know anything, you'd better come out with it." The boy bent his head and scooted his fingers over the brim of his hat.

"Was that a yes."

"Un-hunh."

Math nine was gathering outside the classroom door. Neil shook his head, asked Kolton to let them in, the boy responded with a practiced groan, and that was it. Whatever it was.

At lunch, Neil went down for coffee in the staff room and was ambushed by Karen. "Neil, they're saying you had some kind of rendezvous with kids on the roof."

"What?"

"Look, I didn't mean to be listening but you know how they are. They want a reaction, no way I couldn't hear it. Supposedly Melissa told Kolton that you'd been creeping them on the roof and on Facebook."

"Well, no."

"We all know the roof access is in your classroom."

"Who's we, exactly?"

"Just, it's kind of obvious. So tell the cops before they hear it somewhere else."

"Tell them what?"

"Whatever you heard the kids say that made them think you were creeping them."

"Nothing."

"Nothing like you listened to them and you heard nothing, or nothing like — "

"Nothing like I . . . " he couldn't say that he closed the window. "Nothing like there's nothing to this. This is Kolton wanting attention, okay? He been creeping Melissa, you know that."

"He been?"

"Whatever. Can I have some coffee now?"

"Whatever? Just don't let this bite you."

An odd choice of words, Neil thought. Karen hadn't been forthcoming about her own session in the boardroom — Neil guessed it had to do with exactly this. Rumour spreading. But he was clean. He'd confessed the roof part a week go. And now he'd be helping finally, on the down low.

Thursday afternoon the police sent Neil an email with text to send, to plant, to Kolton: *You are right to be worried about Melissa's "secret". It suggests that she may have placed herself in danger. Let me or another teacher know if you hear anything more about Melissa's plans.*

It was too wordy for Neil, who communicated in short texts even by email. Tanis pointed that out, adding that she couldn't imagine the boy missing it. But he did. When he read it, Kolton fell back inside another secret. Her hushed whisper, when they'd looked down through the opening in the crawlspace over the gym at the Welcome Week Dance. Miss Smith had been calling their names, "Kolton, Melissa, now!" Now, shake the giant plastic tube. They had shaken it hard, both of them laughing as they freed a waterfall of balloons. He'd bundled the empty plastic back into his lap, winding it into a ball, and felt Melissa's body moving beside his. Moving against him, warm and soft. Her face had disappeared, lit only in pieces by light shining off the disco ball dangling beneath them. "Kolton," Melissa had whispered, looking down, "we're so above this shit." Was she making a pun? He had laughed and she had grinned, her teeth shiny in the sweeping light. They'd each sat back, separate again and mostly invisible in the dark. Then Melissa had put her sneaker down into the hole, and Kolton had jumped to grab her and she laughed like crazy. He'd thought she was going to do it then. Jump right through.

›› Forty-Three

Children were meant to be out of sight, Phidelma had learned that well. And in this house that meant the landing — the half up, half down place. It was where she came to send Celia to stand and think about her mistakes. And it was where Celia ran to hide when Thomas showed up with the dog. Phidelma was nervous too, but held out her hand and the dog came to her, nails clicking against the floor. It had the black and tan colouring of a German Shepherd, but it was smaller and scruffier than most of that breed. Not a pretty sight.

"He'll keep you," Thomas said. He was drunk, and propped himself up with a hand on the wall. "You'll keep her," he repeated, in a growl, to the dog, who stared up at Phidelma and gave a tiny wag.

"Not likely," Phidelma said. Another creature to care for. But she was surprised how she felt safer once the dog lay in the yard, sleeping on its rope. He barked when men arrived, giving her warning before they came trudging up through the house. And he was friendly enough, though Celia took to the dog before it took to her — she named him Bingo and crushed him with round-the-neck hugs that he'd whine and duck away from. He startled when she ran in the house. Outside he got excited if she threw a stick, but

wouldn't fetch. He'd take it off to a corner of the yard, and lie down, growling, to chew it.

Phidelma showed Celia how to call him, a two pitched whistle. How to give him a scratch, under his chest, to make his back leg kick. And she sent her out to the yard with a boiled egg one day after school. It was soft in the middle, the yolk dripped down around Celia's feet and Bingo came to lick it up. She reached for his soft, uppy ears and the dog worked his head out of reach as usual, then sidled back to clean her fingers.

"Delma!" Celia shouted. Bingo sprang back, alert. "Delma! He likes eggs!" Celia held her hands out and Bingo came back with more kisses. Phidelma came to stand in the door behind them. "Eggs, hm. He likes you, I think."

Bingo slept in the yard, but crawling into bed that night Celia smelled his fur on her hands. She sucked salty egg from under her fingernails, snuggling down. Delma's quilt was so heavy that Celia could feel the horse in it — and she pictured its hide sparkling. Flecks of hay rising like gold dust when he shook out his mane. Celia's dream horse was a dark horse, for a night rider, the one they read about at school.

Late at night when the moon is out, he gallops and gallops — up to the door, where Pa père came and went with his jingle jangle of coins and keys. Candies on the table in the kitchen were prizes and apologies both for the shifting and emptying, the feet on the stairs. Celia woke confused.

There were voices raised in the yard, a man swearing, and Bingo barking. She snuck through the hall to Phidelma's room and found her sitting up in the bed already, a Bible open on her lap.

"Celia," Phidelma said, patting the mattress. "Listen — The angel of the LORD came a second time and touched him and said, Arise and eat, or the journey will be too much for you. He arose and

ate and drank; and with the strength from that meal he walked forty days and forty nights as far as the Mountain of God."

Celia heard a car door close hard and, she thought, Robert's voice, calling someone out. Bingo whined, then barked again, and Celia crawled in beside Phidelma. Taking her cue, she whispered, "Where's that mountain at?"

"Listen," Phidelma said, "When I was small — " The dog yelped, then growled. Phidelma held Celia at her side, keeping her from the window. "When I was small, Celia, our house was small and we had — " Phidelma pointed around the room " — we had no table, no chair. We children sat on the floor to eat, and we slept on the floor as well, rolling up the mattresses every morning and tucking them out of the way."

The stovepipe rattled inside the chimney — something banged down on the floor in the kitchen and a heavy tread crossed the main floor.

"Shh," Phidelma whispered. "Everything we had fit in our quilts. Your quilt, Grammère Marguerite's wedding quilt, carried all the clothes, rolled and tied up tight." Phidelma drew Celia in closer. "All the tin dishes, all the clothes, spilled out when they unrolled. And then we'd take the cords we'd used to bind them and Mama and her friends would take the ends and your auntie Meline would jump. And their girls. I was so little, Celia, smaller than you. So I would sing. And we liked the one — all in together girls, never mind the weather girls, when I call your birthday, will you please jump in!"

Together Celia and Phidelma whispered, "January, February, March" . . . all the way through — "November, December!" The main floor was still. Phidelma asked, "Do you remember how you used to steal chalk from the sisters and we'd put it in the fire, right at the edge of the stove door. Then it came out so warm, and we'd wrap it in the tea towel, for our toes all night. Do you remember?"

That had been Meline but Celia answered, "It was so warm." The window was dark and Celia thought that Bingo was probably hiding too now, in his dug out place by the coal door. She cuddled in to Phidelma, and her auntie took her hands and wove their fingers together. Men's voices rose again in the yard, loud but level this time. An engine started, and moved out of the yard, and then there was a jingling sound, keys. They heard someone whistle, high and clear — the never ending song that had caught on with all the boys at school: Oh we pushed the damper in; yes, we pushed the damper in, and the smoke went up the chimney just the same. So we pulled the damper out; yes, we pulled the damper out — the whistle ended mid-line. Celia looked at Phidelma, who shook her head.

"I think it's time for you to be asleep," Phidelma said, switching off the lamp. "You can stay here. There we go, let's lie ourselves down." She pulled the blankets up and Celia curled her knees into the warmth between them. "Now," her auntie whispered, "Do you remember the bedtime rhyme — how many miles?"

"Thirty," Celia said, then whispered the proper line. "Three score miles and ten."

"Seventy," Phidelma corrected, gently. "Can we get there by candlelight?"

"Yes, and back again."

» Forty-Four

Celia called again in the later evening and Tanis answered just as Neil finally got the gas mower to choke. The machine coughed, then gurgled like a motorbike and Tanis slipped inside, away from the noise, explaining, "Neil got this second-hand lawn mower — and a leaf blower. So it's yard work night. But — did you get the files I sent?"

Celia had. And though Tanis hadn't found her father's records, Celia was excited to have remembered that in the war, when there was no coffee, her aunt had gotten barley from the edge and made coffee with that. Blackening the kernels in a frying pan to make a thick tea that was bitter as hell but caffeine-free. "And that was my first taste of being grown up," Celia laughed. "Didn't like it one bit!"

"I'm tempted to try it out," Tanis said. "I've got soup barley in the cupboard, would that work?"

"And stink up your whole house blackening it," Celia said. "I wouldn't bother. When can we meet at Timmy's again?"

"Anytime," Tanis assured her. "Though this week is so busy."

"You clear your business, dear. Then we'll meet and I'll invite Corinne too, she hasn't seen that picture book in years. Did you scan the whole of it?"

Outside Neil had begun experimenting with the leaf blower, and Tanis tilted her head to the window. The sound of the motor was faint, as though he'd moved beyond the yard. Was he blowing leaves out of the alley, too?

"I'll see about scanning it tonight," Tanis promised, signing off. But Neil's piles of leaves drew her outside. There was no point letting the wind undo his work and Tanis was nervous, she realized, about sharing her research with Corinne. She did want to meet Celia's daughter, but was worried about how she'd come across — and how Celia had made her out. The house, in another version of history, would have been Corinne's inheritance. She had a condo though, Celia said. A strata condo with a pool and underground parking. It sounded nice, and also easy. No Polyfilla. Fewer strange sounds.

Tanis went to bed with a novel, intending to read, and lay listening to the house knock. They'd turned the heat on finally and the vent covers rattled every time the furnace fan adjusted.

Neil came to bed exhausted and unshowered. He flopped down, smelling sour, muttered something unintelligible when Tanis suggested he listen to the vents, and rolled himself into a cocoon of bedding.

Tanis felt tears pool unexpectedly in her eyes and rubbed them away. She was exhausted herself. Neil was working for the police now so the drama, the copy code, and the lack of boundaries — that was all just confusion. But Tanis felt kept in the dark, and resented his easy slide into sleep. He'd begun wheezing, his congested snore rising from a dark cloud of duvet that Tanis poked at ineffectually. She patted the shape, then gave Neil's shoulder a shove. He snorted, then muttered, "When we catch him." The police didn't know if there was anyone to catch, though. Neil smacked his mouth, then breathed more quietly. "When we find them," Tanis whispered, closing her eyes.

She ran her fingers along the dark wall, feeling her way toward the closet door. The lamp cord snaked up the ladder. Tanis heaved herself over the lip of the attic floor and the coiled rug slid away, baring the plywood sheet, the hollow space. She turned to face the work lamp and Robert groaned from a corner beyond the light. His head rose, he sighed, stepped forward, and Tanis gasped. A black gash began on his forehead, cut his eyebrow, and marked his cheek beneath a swollen eye. She raised a hand to his face and he shook her off, turned away. She followed him to the sagging bed, beneath the window. His hair brushed the angled roof. She knelt, fumbling at the laces on his boots. He dropped a hand to her head and she grasped it, pressed it to her cheek.

Robert's fingers slackened. His head drooped, then started up, and Tanis set her hands on his chest. "You're tired," she told him. The wool blanket was folded across the foot of her own bed, where the child slept, curled so small. She lifted it carefully, and when she bent to cover Robert his eyes opened strangely, pupils dilated to black pools. He closed them and she touched his cheek — the blood was tacky, drying to seal the wound. The window needed a covering. Winter was coming and the bed would be cold. There was frost on the grass in the yard already and when she looked up at the eaves, she felt afraid. The dog crept, whining from a shadow at the side of the house — Tanis woke and felt for Neil, then tucked her feet against the warmth of his calves.

The furnace vent clattered at the foot of the bed and the lilacs rattled outside the window, insisting their presence. Neil breathed softly at her back and Tanis watched the streetlight's potassium flare fade behind their bedroom curtain, yielding to morning.

» Forty-Five

The frost that stripped the trees backed off. Friday was warm, and the weekend promised a reprieve. The kids came to Math ten relaxed. Neil greeted them with a fun introduction to irrational numbers, those that can't be represented by fractions.

Phones chirped during his lecture and Neil reminded the class about Bornstein's social media ban. It was a veiled threat that sent fidgety hands to bags and pockets, but most of the kids focused on the worksheet he passed around. A column of numbers and shapes they had to identify as rational or irrational. He asked them to find examples in the textbook, and then in the classroom. Alexa had reached already for one of the magnetic fraction apples on the windowsill and separated it on her desk, whispering an explanation to Stephanie who'd twisted around to watch from the desk ahead.

At the back of the class Taelur scooted into her seat and picked up her pen. In the far corner Kolton had his hat on and chin down. Neil walked through the desks and made a show of glancing at everyone's work, nodding and giving encouragement where needed. At Kolton's desk he found the worksheet half done, and a series of doodles in the margin. The golden rectangle, a nautilus shell — art on topic.

Neil tapped the page. "This is right on, Kolton," he said, and caught a movement from the corner of his eye. Taelur plopping quickly back into her seat again. Kolton scowled in her direction and palmed Neil a crumpled note. *Mel Facetimed you yet, boyfriend?*

Neil looked down, Kolton dropped his face and shook his hat. Two desks away, Taelur had her fist at her temple, hard at work now.

It was "becoming clear" to the police, apparently, that Kolton knew something. Neil had been asked to meet the boy at the skate park by the river after school. To bike by and "just happen" to see Kolton skating and "just happen" to engage him in a chat freed from student-teacher constraints at the school. Neil was very aware, as he pulled on his windbreaker, of Tanis perched at the bottom of the stairwell.

"Isn't 'gaining trust' what Yannick and Kipland are supposed to do," she asked.

"*Yanis* and Kipland," Neil corrected. "I don't know — well, they are supposed to be liaisons, but they've kind of merged in with all the other police now."

Tanis nodded. "But why do they think you can do this?"

"They just need to grab every straw they can," Neil explained. What had Sawatsky said? "In the course of an investigation like this, everything is important."

"Everything can't be important," Tanis protested.

"Everything could be."

Neil rode first, looping several times around their own block, to look authentically exercised and also to calm himself down before he went to "happen upon" his student — which turned out to be easier than expected since Kolton was not on the skate ramps, but sitting, parked, on a bench beside the bike path.

"Hey, Kolton!"

The boy met Neil's eyes with his mouth hanging open, head flexed back to see under the brim of a new square-fronted ball cap. Fluorescent wires dangled down either side of his neck. Act natural, and casual, they'd coached Neil, so he reached out and yanked a wire, pulling an ear bud free. "Hey, Kolton!"

"Hey, what!" the boy protested, gathering the wire into his hand.

"Mm — what you listening to?"

The boy mumbled the name of a band that Neil had never heard of, but he nodded to indicate interest. He wondered if he should sit down. He was straddling his bike and it felt weird. Kolton looked down at his ear bud and the song, heavy on the bass, rose up between them.

Neil bent and rubbed his quads. "Look, Kolton," he said. "I had a girlfriend too once, I mean before my wife. Not in high school actually, when I was at university. Her name was Stacey and she had a lot of things going on in her life that she didn't want, you know, broadcast? Okay. So I get that about Melissa. It doesn't mean that she doesn't deserve to be safe, right?"

Kolton was listening. Looking very uncomfortable, but listening.

"So, I'm glad I saw you here because I wanted to tell you about Stacey. Do you get why?"

"No."

Neil looked up, what next. He squinted down at the top of Kolton's hat and the boy mumbled, "I guess so, yeah."

Neil swung a leg over his bike, walked it to the grass, and opened the kickstand. He gave Kolton his space, settling at the far end of the bench. "Okay," he said, "why?"

"I'm supposed to think you know what I'm all about and then tell you where Melissa is and shit like that."

"I didn't think you could tell me that."

The boy looked past Neil to the skate park.

"Can you?"

"Nope."

"Okay. So look, Melissa and Stacey, I'm thinking they actually are kind of the same and the thing is that I don't know what ever happened to her."

"What, she ran away too?"

"I guess so, from me, at least."

"Melissa's not — she not doing that, okay?"

"Well, she's not here and you are."

"She gone."

"Run away?"

Kolton's mouth twisted.

"Let's just walk, okay, just walk a bit."

A teacher in spandex leggings walking a mountain bike, and a student with a longboard under his arm. Neil had no idea where he was walking Kolton to, but the cops were the ones who'd told him to cross the line so he started for home. Halfway up the block they ran into Tanis, standing on the sidewalk, arms crossed, staring at the New Free Church of Christ sign-of-the-week: *Forbidden Fruits Make Many Jams.*

"Look at that," she pointed, "Delicious right? And who is this?"

"Kolton, meet Tanis. Tanis, meet Kolton." Neil sensed things getting awkward but his wife switched to her friendly interview mode. A random stream of trivia flew out of Tanis' mouth. She'd been in the garage and found a hole in there. A mud pit thing, covered over by the pressboard they'd taken for temporary paving. She'd found an enamel bowl, and somehow made that sound interesting. Also, she rescued a Rainbow Brite doll that probably belonged to Kaydance. All the old toys were coming back. Rainbow Brite was from her own childhood. Hers and Neil's, in the 80s. "Really, Kolton," she said, "would you guess we're that old?"

"Yeah," the boy teased, and Neil saw that the boy had pushed his hat back. It opened his face. Tanis dove in, commenting on the stickers on Kolton's longboard, asking the inane "what are you going to be" questions that adults drop on kids — but the guy was answering. Telling her he'd be interested in physiotherapy.

Neil wanted to interrupt and tell Kolton how key math was to getting into the health sciences, but Tanis was asking if he had any other dreams.

"They've been kind of weird lately, actually," Kolton said.

Tanis didn't miss a step. "Do you journal them?" she asked. "Dreams are so important, you know. They give us so much direction."

"What have you been dreaming, Tanis?" Neil asked, curious, and she shushed him. Kolton, encouraged, told them about a dream where he saw a kid getting followed by a car, driving up behind it, and then the kid actually got pulled in through the window.

"Oh God," Tanis said. "That's scary."

"But then it turns out it's his dad," Kolton explained quickly. "And then, in the dream, I'm just standing there, 'cause I'd started running, you know. To it. And I'm feeling stupid and stuff."

"Oh, that's not fun either," Tanis said. "It reminds me about those missing girls from your class."

"Yeah," Kolton said, "None of the kids at school can stop worrying about them but the teachers, like Mr. Cameron, have been so great."

Tanis put an arm around Neil, and smiled, shaking him gently.

"I'd better get home now so my mom and dad won't be worrying about me," Kolton said.

"Ride safe," Tanis said. "It'll get slippery soon."

"Bye," Neil offered, and they watched Kolton turn the corner of the block, a hiccup in his lanky gait when he stopped to drop his board.

"Well?" Tanis asked, as the boy pushed and carved away over fresh black asphalt.

"Well, nothing."

"I kind of hoped not. Do you have to call the cops now?"

"I guess so, but there's nothing really to say."

"The road's done, I didn't even notice the machines go," Tanis commented. She admired the new road, unlined so far, but scattered with yellow leaves. "I guess they'll be back for the next block soon enough."

"I guess," Neil nodded. His phone buzzed against his kidneys, muted in the phone pocket of his cycling shirt. A text from Kolton — *U got a hottie!*

» Forty-Six

"How's 'staging a disappearance' any different from disappearing if no one knows where they are?" Tanis asked Neil, late Saturday afternoon. She perched on the edge of their bed, where Neil had thrown himself more heavily.

"It's not getting lured into a car by a lollipop," he muttered, lifting a pillow and squashing it over his eyes.

"I wasn't thinking a lollipop, Neil."

"Smokes, beer?"

"Or money for favours."

"I really don't think so."

But there are only so many ways for women to levy power, and that was one of the most obvious. Historically, one of the most useful. Tanis watched Neil lift the pillow off his face and shove it under his head. "Do you need an Advil?" she asked.

He'd messaged Bornstein about the note Kolton received, the handwriting so very similar to Taelur's, and the principal suggested Neil rearrange his seating chart. To get rid of the too obvious, too empty desk between the two kids.

"It can't hurt to change the seats, can it?" Tanis asked. "There'll still be the same number, if she comes back."

Neil shrugged. Jody's seat bothered him, actually. The students treated it like it was haunted, or toxic. The other thing bothering Neil was the boys. The same ones who'd been swearing and barking at girls during Welcome Week had turned solicitous, offering to walk girls home.

"But that's good, isn't it?" Tanis asked.

"It's like a switch went off, Tanis. They talked that way because — well, because it was them and the girls could take it." Tanis frowned, and Neil put his hand up, just listen. "Now they're all getting this impression that girls have to be protected, shit like that."

"Respected, maybe."

"Well, that's the thing — that's not what this is."

"So, what is it?"

"It's objectifying women."

"Really? I thought that would be the barking part."

"No, that's just dumb. But it comes out of them being attracted and not knowing what to do and, yeah, it's not respectful — "

"Seriously not. And not okay."

"But it's not objectifying them as breakable objects either."

That was interesting — but if girls being targets for "harmless" cruelty was a sign of things being "okay", Neil hadn't come full circle to sense. "I hope it's habit forming," Tanis said, and tipped herself sideways to lie on the bed. The lilac hedge raised its skinny bare branches through a band of golden afternoon light and Tanis sighed. They were supposed to be shopping for groceries. They'd been invited to a potluck by Puller and Noreen, an early Thanksgiving thing.

Neil tugged at Tanis' shoulder, rolling her to face him. "The parents have been emailing me — about exams, provincial exams. Melissa's mom sent me an email asking if she'll get an exemption, she'll have missed so much. As if that were the first — "

"I'm sure that wasn't the first thing that came to her mind, Neil. She'll be looking for anything she can do. Anything to help. Like you are, right?"

Neil frowned. "Why aren't you?"

"What do you mean?"

"I mean, these girls are missing and you're wrapped up in some weird decorating the house history thing, misleading the police."

"I wasn't meaning to mislead the police," Tanis protested. "They wouldn't have been misled at all if they weren't spying. What could I do, search and rescue — volunteer with the community association and get harassed like Michelle?"

Neil shrugged.

Tanis didn't know what to say. She had been circling the girls in her heart and mind, holding on to the two of them, laughing on the curb. She knew she couldn't bring them back. She had read about women gone missing from their area, and she had walked up the hill to the yard where a body had been found. Six in ten years was a lot of murdered women for a city their size. It shouldn't be, and wasn't, a statistical expectation. The women had been mostly First Nations, the cases — not all — but many unresolved. The first murder in the city, something that felt important, was a baby girl. A "developed infant" whose body was wrapped in calico and snuggled into the side of a manure heap at the stockyard. There weren't more than a hundred people in that early settlement and it still went unsolved. There was something wrong on the long, long term. A story Neil's students had walked into, purposefully or not.

Faced with Tanis' silence, Neil had closed his eyes. Now she reached for him, shifting into the curl of his arms. She didn't kiss him. She slipped her fingers under the hem of his T-shirt and pulled it up, then up again, and Neil opened his eyes. He squinted at Tanis, frowned until she did, then cooperated, pulling his T-shirt up over his shoulders and head. Tanis bent over her husband, hands on his torso, cheek against his chest to hear his heart. Pressed against Neil, she remembered dreaming of Robert upstairs, and she wondered how Phidelma would have got him down. She was about to speak, but Neil's fingers moved into her hair, stroking it back from her face. He was living and warm. His chest was soft. She turned her lips to it, then down his body.

So this, Neil thought, holding Tanis afterwards, *this is trying.*

A name, Tanis was thinking, *a good baby name is Jessamyn.* It was not the time to discuss names, but she would save the question. Ask Neil in the morning — now she was ready to sleep, and closed her eyes just as he remembered the potluck.

They showered, dressed and were out the door in the nick of time and, despite finally having a functional kitchen, greeted their friends with a tray of doughnuts from the Timmy's drive-thru. Neil won Trivial Pursuit. Tanis weighed in on Noreen's upholstery options for an inherited sectional, the ugliness ante climbing until they were both laughing on the kitchen floor.

They left their car parked out front of their friends' house and stumbled home, every-so-slightly drunk, along the river parkway.

» Forty-Seven

"Well, it was a smart thing to do, of course, selling the half lot. A lot of them were doing it, then, after the war, and the government could just throw them up, those little houses. Two bedrooms up, one down."

Celia had told Tanis this part a few times now. And she'd come this afternoon in the same shiny pink tracksuit as before, with the addition of a white fleece toque. The Tim Horton's was nearly empty but Celia had picked a table next to two fifty-something women, who were listening in.

"There are quite a few in the neighbourhood," the woman facing Tanis said. "Lots of infills." She shook her head, swinging giant brass hoop earrings under a greying bob cut. Her friend, plainer in a black scarf and jean jacket, raised her cup and added, "Those little houses were so much better than the boxes they're putting up today."

"I know," Celia said, giving a dramatic shudder. They all laughed and Tanis smiled politely. The recent infills were plain and spanned the entirety of their twenty-five-foot lots. Grey walls. She knew what they meant.

"We'll leave you to it," the hoop earring woman said, eyes on Tanis. She winked and Tanis suddenly wasn't sure who had intruded on whom.

Celia tapped at her arm. "Those veterans," Celia said, "lots of them retrained for a trade after. Those ones next door to us weren't retraining. Veterans Affairs was paying just to get them on their feet."

Tanis nodded. "They were shell-shocked?"

"Well, I suppose," Celia said, "coming home from *all that* overseas, but it wasn't something we saw, you know. Well, there was one or two that were queer, but it was different days then. You didn't go around mooning like now — no. They were mostly cheerful, and mostly had no family, and me and the kids across the street, we'd hit them up all the time."

"You hit them up?" Tanis smiled, curious.

"Oh yes, for treats. We'd walk with them and they'd end up getting us, oh, I don't know, an orange crush or something like that. There were these chocolate bars, Fat Emma. Delma's favourite. Fat Emma, hoo!" Celia laughed.

"I read about those — "

"Did you? Lots of malt in the middle, they were a nice treat. I used to save half — oh, maybe a little less than half — for Delma. We didn't say we loved each other then, you know. But we did plenty for each other, more than families have to do now."

"I'll bet," Tanis prompted.

"She made every piece of clothes I had, the longest time. Underpants too." Tanis laughed as Celia squirmed in her seat, miming pulling bloomers on.

"Did she teach you all that too?"

"Well, some, I suppose. But I was in school, you know, and they taught us a different way there. Patterns and electric machines. Elastic came along — "

"Right! Elastic."

"I went all the way through, though. Right through high school, first one in the family since my grandfather. Then the boarders, some of them went to secretary school. Or radio and switchboard training. There were opportunities for that kind of thing in the war, but after it a lot of girls married real quickly."

Tanis considered that, and waited for an ice grinder to quit squealing at the counter behind them. "Not Phidelma?" she asked.

"No, not her. Though she was young enough. Not even twenty when she got me, you know." Why had Tanis imagined Phidelma as incredibly old? "She had the house," Celia continued. "A way to keep herself, and a child too. No reason to get married, if you see things that way. Oh, I suppose there might have been some men from next door she was friendly with, over the years. That would be my guess. But never any marriage or children, just me. And just as well for me, probably — I'd have been lost in the shuffle."

The grinder started up again. The people at the drive-thru window were hanging onto summer, milking the menu before Iced Capps gave way to Pumpkin Lattes. Tanis had ordered a coffee to match Celia this time, and turned her cup on the table. "I guess Phidelma was pretty smart," she said.

Celia's eyes crinkled. "She didn't know much at some ends. And some old ways weren't good, not telling things, you know. But everyone had their business. Not like today when they announce everything to who knows who."

"They were more discreet?"

"A person had their business, then, and kept it, yes. But it was more than that. Even asking about my parents — well, maybe she didn't see me having a right to know where I'd come from." Celia dropped her voice. "Do you know, anytime I had a cold she used to find a cigarette and light it in my bedroom, wouldn't ever explain why. Old, old medicine, but I didn't know it was anything special until my kids were grown up and got interested. Now they're wanting to know about the things she and Pa Père did."

"You mean, Métis cultural stuff? Or old ways like you just don't talk about things, and you try to pass and be white."

"I couldn't have fooled too many with that," Celia said, patting her hair. She'd re-dyed it and lost the white roots. The curls were blackish-blue. "But if you want to know about cultural stuff, you're better off talking to Corinne."

In the oral history transcripts — the veteran's oral histories that Tanis had gone fishing for Robert in — the men shared much more than Tom Tanner. Tanis had found audio files, MP3s, and listened attentively, absorbing the cadence of the old, slow voices. They answered the historian matter-of-fact, detailing life on their farms, on the land, in the wars. Many came home to make a living off summer fishing and winter furs, like at Descharme lake. The old timers told about how to keep the traps, where to hide them, set them, spring them. Tanis pictured furs piled high on a sled, dogs harnessed, ready and panting. *Muskrats practically jumped into the traps,* Thomas Tanner claimed, and he could sell them anywhere. He had abandoned his family for that life. Not an uncommon thing Celia didn't think, in those old families that history shuffled around. The uncommon thing was the house in town, Phidelma in it alone, and all the little pieces Celia knew that stepped the story up to the present.

Tanis lifted her laptop to the table, navigating free Wi-Fi to the website of a local heritage fund. There was a grant program, she explained. Together, she and Celia could make an application to write up her family history. An urban Métis experience, set after the homesteads had been reclaimed — unfarmable lands deemed "unimproved". Scrip paid out as land, stolen back through the homestead act. It was a story not a lot of people knew, her great grandfather's story.

Celia put her nose the laptop, frowning. "I never heard of these people," she said. "You give me a minute here." She lifted her phone, took a picture of the screen, and sent it off to Corinne.

The restaurant's side door chimed and a pair of farmers came in, talking at each other: "Southeast they've had so much rain they're going to have to plant rice instead of wheat come spring — Oh, I don't know, our rain last spring though, wrecked my gloves, dried so hard I gave them to the dog. Lorraine, you know she's got two big dogs — she leaves 'em in the house all day, that's terrible — "

"Tanis — " Celia had her phone at her cheek, "when's the deadline for this thing?" The deadline was approaching, and they would need twenty sample pages, but as Tanis saw it they'd already begun. She'd traced the family's genealogy as far as they could, and two nights earlier she'd recorded Celia on speakerphone. She'd wanted to collect Celia's memories of the original kitchen, how it'd been when she was small. The black iron range, and the ashes that had to be drawn out from under the firebox very slowly, so they wouldn't just float up and get all over the place.

T.C.: What did you do with them?

C.M.: The ashes? Oh, they went in the tomatoes, dear. Yes, they'd do wonderful things in the tomatoes.

» Forty-Eight

Janet watched herself walking in between the school and her car, chin tucked against the wind. She'd been crying and the news cameras had caught her looking terrible, which felt about right. A newswoman's voice-over shared that Janet walked the blocks of the neighbourhood every night, and many mornings too — and Janet watched her car dissolve into a photo of Jody. Her school picture from the year before. She had rounded up better, more recent photos from the summer, but the police liked the school portrait. With the background and face size standard the generic shots encouraged the public to look for details, they said. Janet had never considered Jody's school pictures mug shots before, and didn't like it.

It was true that she had walked the neighbourhood every night the last four weeks, but she wasn't holding her breath for some new clue like the newswoman made out. It saved staring at the empty chair in the living room. It didn't save having to walk past the empty bedroom every night, though. Janet was reminded again and again how she'd taken for granted that Jody was there, sleeping, the night she disappeared.

Janet had been trying to keep in mind that Jody had a good head on her shoulders. Had always been resourceful. But her girl slept the same way she had as a toddler. On her belly with her head pressed up against the pillows instead of on top of them. It had been a long time since Janet knew Jody's every move in the day but she'd always known where she slept. Janet muted the newscast, which had moved on to the weather, and went to the doorway of Jody's bedroom. She closed her eyes, willed herself to open them again, and met the eyes of the teenage vampire that pursed his lips on a poster over her baby's bed. He was very feminine, Janet realized. And incredibly young.

She walked back down the carpeted hall to the living room and pulled her phone off its charger. She texted: *I can't sleep, can U? U OK?*

She ran her thumb up the phone, rereading the messages she'd sent, increasingly frantic pleas for Jody to get in touch. Her phone made the double pop that signalled incoming texts — something from James, probably. She swiped her messages to Jody away and tapped on the bright rectangle at the top of her text feed and saw: *Mom, I'm OK.*

Janet backed her legs into the couch and sat down hard. Her thumbs shook as she tapped: *Where r U? I'll come. Where?*

U working tonight?

No. You're safe?

How can I pick U up?

Will U meet me at Esso.

Stay put.

I'm sorry.

Melissa with U?

I'm sorry Mom.

Janet dropped the phone to the counter and grabbed her jacket, shaking it to check for keys. Jody was okay. Jody was okay and Janet was trembling so much she had to sit down to get her boots on. She picked up the phone, watched it vibrate in her hand, and hit the phone icon beside James' name.

"Jody texted, she's at the Esso, I'm going to get her — yes, we'll wait. I don't know who she's with. I don't know what happened. I have to — " *I have to go,* Janet wanted to say, but James was asking if she hadn't actually talked to Jody. Should he try to get her on the line? What if something happened before they got there — what if someone else had her phone? Had Janet called the police? He was frantic and it wasn't helping Janet to calm down. "Meet you there," she shouted, cutting him off. In the car she tapped Jody's name, turned the ignition. *On my way.*

» Forty-Nine

At the highway Esso station Jody was caught in her father's embrace. James shielded his girl from the sweep of headlights pulling off the highway, and from the wind that blew so strong and cold across the open edge of the city.

Janet's red Civic bounced over the service road. James didn't wave, but kept his eyes on the car as Janet crossed the asphalt lot. In the weeks of searching, Janet had dropped not only weight but the softness she'd had since Jody'd been born. Now she fought her door open against the wind and James pulled their baby tight against his chest and whispered in Jody's ear, "Mommy's here, love."

The police had told them what to do when Jody made contact — no blame, no anger — Janet wanted to scream. The wind whipped her hair across her face and she snatched it to her neck. Her girl's face swam behind a flying curtain of hair too and Janet reached a hand to clear it back. Jody had always been careful. She looked up from James's chest, waiting. *I must not scream*, Janet thought. "Thank God," she said, and Jody flew into her arms, burrowing her face, and it was all Janet could do not to shake her. She bit the inside of her cheeks and steadied herself, bracing against the wind. James' arms circled them both, catching Jody up in the smells of Daddy's smokes and Mommy's shampoo, and a sharp smell of diesel that blew off the pumps.

They stayed close, bearing her up for the police when they came, a parent on either side. They promised to take her in to the station, and a clinic, the next morning — tonight they took her home. Janet made them all tea, and Jody a sandwich, and it was still early — barely ten — when James lifted their girl up from the couch and walked her to bed. Janet watched father and daughter move down the hall, then stepped outside with James' cigarettes.

He found her on the driveway. "Since when do you smoke?"

Janet held out the package, nearly empty, and James saw paper casings roll against the cement. He caught a fist on his chest, lifted his arms and caught another, and a third before Janet backed off, swearing, and sagged against her house. She'd gotten crazy. He didn't blame her.

James caught her elbows and stood her up. "She wanted her light on," he said. He walked Janet inside and down the hall to Jody's room where the door was open, the desk lamp on. Jody slept in her clothes, her head pushed up into her pillow.

"You've had enough I think, eh?" James said. "Too much heavy lifting." Janet had a hand on the door frame and stood staring into the room. James rubbed a hand over her shoulder, then stroked it down her hair. "I'll sleep on the couch, okay? Go back to Dan's for tomorrow — sound right?"

That was what she wanted, what she needed. Back to normal.

"I'm sorry," Janet whispered, but James couldn't tell if she'd aimed it at him or their girl.

» Fifty

Tanis read the RCity news update twice. She mouthed the words, the second time through. *Thank God.* Neil had left for school twenty, maybe thirty minutes before and Tanis reached for her phone and saw: *Welcome home, Jody Bear!* It sat beneath an earlier message that Tanis had missed: *BBQ needs propane.*

She texted: *Yay!!!*

No shit!

Tanis hit the phone icon, and Neil picked up. "Babe, Math nine is just about to start. I don't have any details but I bet there'll be a staff — Heath, what the hell! — yeah, well excuse me — what the heck, then, sit down — Tanis, gotta go."

Tanis set her phone down grinning. A manic Neil was a happy Neil. She wondered where the girl had been. Three and a half weeks — she bit her lip and turned back to the screen. The update had just been posted and there were seven comments already, but no real details. Tanis spun her chair away from the screen and felt a rising tide bearing her up. Neil was happy, Celia was excited about their collaboration, and Jody's return felt like a part of both. She wondered if she should text Michelle. Why not!

Neil came home both giddy and snippy, the way he got once the worry of something, the need for calm and control, had passed. He fixed himself a sandwich, then headed out to fill the propane tank arguing that they *would too* be barbecuing all winter long.

Tanis settled in to her desk, thinking that she'd get a little start on the sample pages, and they ended up coming together quickly. She'd filled her ears up with Celia's ramblings and putting her hands to the keyboard felt like tipping a Yahtzee cup.

circa 1939 — Rocks to a River:

Every morning for the last six months he's been sitting there when we go down. He gets the coffee ready on his own and then he sits waiting so that when I come down he can say, "There's your coffee — I'll have eggs." I'll fry him toast too, when we have bread and bacon. I'm Thomas' daughter so I'll cook for him, never mind him being away so long. I didn't ask where he'd come from, just took care of things. I washed the clothes he set on the chair in the attic room, and I made a chore for Celia of cleaning up his boots. I don't see a reason for us to be up making breakfast before six, but he did this same thing to Marguerite. The same to Emelyn.

He'd be away freighting or cutting trees, and he did a bit of the army too. All of those things, I'd guess, made him get up early, and he'd be sitting there waiting at the table any morning home. The time Celia found him in my kitchen, growling "I'll have eggs" — well, I fell right into my mother's skin . . .

I've started warming milk in the morning for Celia now, too. Her teacher says giving a child coffee makes it hard for her to keep still, and could stunt her growth. Celia's shorter than the rest already. I'll buy a can a week of the sweet condensed stuff she likes, and cut it with tea that's had a good boil. There's fresh milk delivery, and some on the street get that. But I don't trust what hasn't been canned. The law never stopped them from watering milk before — there's been typhoid spread at the edge that way. It's no wonder my mother nursed us on tea. Meline, after she was sick, always had a cup in her hand. And I was jealous of that — imagine thinking dying was something to be jealous of . . .

For Celia's school dinner, I build jam sandwiches with store bread. It feels like waste but the girl won't eat the crusts. "For Pete's sake," I say, and she bursts into tears. So she's off at school, eating her triangles without crusts — and I wonder, are there other grown women left like I am, eating dried out crusts with butter for lunch? Or do they just throw them out for the birds? There are fat pigeons in this neighbourhood, I can tell you. I've shared her castaways with the dog. It's a wonder how stubborn the child is. Her Pa père could sell rocks to a river, too, and he was always proud of that. He sold himself to my mother and that can't have been easy . . .

It was rambling, but it caught the spirit of the thing. Of what they could do. Tanis pasted the text into an email, hit send, then called Celia so they could read it through together.

"You're sure Corinne will be okay with this?" Tanis asked, double-checking.

"Well, I'm never sure with her, but she is," Celia replied. Beyond the phone she was clinking something, getting set to cook. They'd eat when Tanis brought the rest of the files over for Phidelma's grandniece to read.

›› Fifty-One

The night that Jody came home safe, Neil washed his car, bought propane, and dug through a Rubbermaid bin in the basement for tools to connect the new tank to the barbecue. The tank was cold and his fingers felt thick, fumbling with the coupler. When his phone chimed he was tempted to leave it in his pocket. Tanis would be home soon enough, he guessed. Couldn't whatever it was wait?

But it was Kolton, not Tanis, texting: *J's back but M is still missing!*

Neil tapped the screen to reply, and then he reconsidered and tapped the phone icon. Kolton picked up out of breath, "Mr. Cameron, I did kind of a dumb thing." The boy was practically panting into the phone.

"Okay," Neil said. "Well — breathe."

"It's on the news," Kolton blurted, and Neil checked his feed. *RCity News — Friday October 12: Friend of Melissa Arthur admits to planting girl's found bracelet.*

"Seriously? Is this you?"

"Yeah, dumb," the kid's voice was wheezy, scared.

Neil saw text pasted from a comment feed, a header to the article: *Posted by Neigh_boy — The police are not taking this seriously. They didn't even search the river until I put her bracelet there. Just coz Jody's back it doesn't mean Melissa is safe. We were covering but now I REALLY DON'T KNOW WHERE SHE IS.*

"Neigh boy?" Neil asked. Kolton breathed heavily, and Neil chose his words. "What exactly did you do? What do you mean you were covering?"

The boy had planted Melissa's bracelet, on a bush, by the path.

" . . . her bracelet — *Jesus*. Why?" Neil asked, and Kolton practically whined into the phone — the police *had* to keep looking for Melissa.

"They're still looking, Kolton. And I bet Jody will be able to share something to help, but — you planted evidence? How did you have her bracelet in the first place?"

"She gave it to me."

"Why?" Neil demanded. Kolton wouldn't very well wear a rhinestone bangle.

"She just did." And the boy had promised to give Melissa two weeks to decide whether she'd "do it" before he gave it to anyone else.

"Do it, Kolton? You're fifteen!"

"I mean do it, Mr. Cameron. Like do herself in."

"Kolton, maybe you've never heard this before but — " Neil stared at the back door of his house. *Friends don't let friends think about killing themselves. Friends don't let friends disappear.* "When a friend is in trouble," Neil began, then snapped " — that's when it's time to tell a fucking grown-up."

The boy clammed up, then hung up, and it was at that point that Neil heard Tanis' feet on the path at the side of the house. He'd taken the car, she'd ridden his bike to her meeting but he hadn't heard her cycle up. Had she heard him swearing at a child?

"Hi, Hon," Tanis said. "Do you want this in the basement or the garage?"

Neil watched her face.

She lifted her eyebrows, waiting. So she hadn't heard him. Neil looked at his bike, swore again, "shit," and her face snapped shut.

"I'll take it in," she said, and wheeled the bike past the tools he'd scattered on the concrete patio. "I gather you need a minute?"

Neil turned and paced to the back of the yard, out of her view. He pocketed his phone, tried a deep breath, and slammed his palms against the side of the garage. Instead of absorbing his anger it swayed. Neil stepped back, out of range. Had the siding actually rippled? The graffiti tag, censored by shadows, looked like a bruise. A bad tattoo.

Neil turned to the house and saw Tanis' silhouette recede from the kitchen window. The hook and chain they'd bolted up to seal the milk door looked terrible. It would do for the winter, for security, but in the dark the black zigzag looked like a sloppy set of stitches. Neil ran his eyes up the back of their house. A light came on in Tanis' office. The roof angled up above the window and Neil calmed, considering the unfinished side of the attic. With Tanis' loft looking so good he'd nearly forgotten the mess of paper insulation and mouse shit behind the sliding wall — the wiring that snaked through it was insulated now, though.

Neil lifted his phone and reread the kid's message. Now he typed back: *Hang in there. Jody being back is good news. We'll find M.*

The girls had not been abducted, Melissa's bracelet had not truly snagged on a bush by the river, and Kolton hadn't trusted Neil after all. Neigh_boy — an alias for everyone.

Declan had already talked to Jody's dad. The man had said that Jody was okay, had been safe but lonely at some cabin, and had "learned a lot from her mistakes." It was a vague answer, the scenario weirdly bucolic — but Declan didn't think they'd get many more details. Non-missing persons had a right to privacy.

Neil put a hand on the corner post of the garage, pushed, and felt the structure shift. It needed to come down. He looked up at the garage's battered roof, and gawked at the sky. A bright abundance of stars were revealed in darkness over the alley. The streetlights washed them out.

Neil bet that Tanis had found the RCity article by now. She'd gone to her office — and he tapped at his phone to read it the rest of the way through.

The teen's comments above were posted within a discussion on Melissa Arthur's Facebook page regarding whether or not Melissa had in fact been wearing the bracelet police found snagged on a bush along the river parkway trails. While her mother confirmed that Melissa was wearing it the morning of her disappearance, her friends could not remember her putting the bracelet on after volleyball practice. "If she'd had it on we would have known," explained another youth online, "she always had to get someone to help do up the clasp." "She had two," another post reads, "was it the one with the heart and the teddy bear from her mom or that blingy one?"

"At least the comments are closed!" Tanis' voice came across the yard. She'd come down to the back entry. Neil crossed the yard and she pulled him inside, into a hug. Neil rested his forehead on her shoulder, then pulled back.

"I'm sorry," he said. "I'd just got off the phone with Kolton when you came back. He's the teen, of course."

"I guessed — " Tanis said. Neil scanned her face. She looked sad but not upset.

"How did your night go — better?"

"A little surreal, actually," Tanis said. "Guess who Corinne is?"

Neil frowned. "Celia's daughter, that's who you were meeting?"

"Yeah. And she's the Riverbend MLA also, Corinne Laurie."

"No way — "

"And she knows Michelle, from the Community Association."

"Small world," Neil said. "And what does she think of you and her mom working together? The dirty boot project?"

Tanis tipped her head. "She seems to like it. Though, there's a lot of historical context, and political context — she'll have a lot to say, I think, before we publish anything. It was pretty obvious that Celia's excited, though. Her daughter definitely liked that."

"And you're excited," Neil smiled. "And this funding, is it a good bet?"

"I think so, actually. I called to check the guidelines and the grant guy said the fund wasn't even accessed last year. And he likes the sound of our project. And, he knows Corinne — " Tanis paused, then grinned. "She has this other idea she wants me involved with too, a princess dance. Kind of like a girl power party, for the little girls. I guess they have them on some of the reserves. This would be a multicultural one, for Riverbend. Just everything fun — door prizes, 50/50, a piñata . . . "

Neil nodded. "That sounds fun."

Tanis sighed, "Yes."

It was a clear night, all those stars. They had wood leftover from the wheelchair ramp. There was at least one beer they could split in the fridge. "Tanis," Neil asked, "you feel like a fire, babe?"

She went to change into warmer clothes and Neil pulled the metal fire pit away from the house, to the centre of the concrete pad. A light came on in the apartment and spilled down onto the rolls of newspaper that Neil was tucking in under broken kindling. He looked up at Michelle's window. So, they were back now too. Kaydance would like a princess dance party and Neil doubted it would take Tanis long to tell her about it.

"Do you think I should be drinking this?" Tanis asked, stepping out from the back entry to hand Neil a jar of beer. She'd split the bottle between two mason jars, and sipped daintily at hers.

"Probably not," he said. "Better give me that one too."

» Fifty-Two

"What, now you *want* me to check their walls?" Neil teased, but he settled without additional protest into Karen's desk chair. Kolton had already texted — Melissa had liked a picture of Taelur in a tube dress, and posted: *Smokin' hot, baby biatch!* Which, details aside, was awesome news.

He logged in to Facebook as Neil Cameron this time, not Stevie B, all above-board. "You know her wall is public — " he told Karen.

She groaned.

" — you could check it out yourself."

She reached for the mouse and slid the screen down.

Posted by Jody Bear: Mel, Bullyshitta, Blud Cozens don't fight, don't wear tights. Poke your nose outta pantyhose, draw this side of the law, land. This beach ain't sand, grand stand. Voice it, you got choice coz — be safe. x.

Neil read the post twice, and guessed Karen was doing the same. Was this really a rhyme from Jody? It didn't read much like what she'd turned in to Karen, but that had been for a teacher, this was for her friend.

"That's pretty heavy," Neil said. "Sweet sixteen gangsta' rap." He tapped his fingers on the edge of the desk, trying to see how you'd sing it.

"It's not heavy," Karen said. "And she's fifteen. Smart ass."

"What?"

Karen shoved at Neil's shoulder, "Not you." She hit a bookmark on the address bar — Etymology. She typed quickly, hit enter.

Cozen (1565–75); perhaps < Old North French coçonner, to resell, dupe, verbal derivative of coçon, retailer (< Latin coctiōnem, accusative of coctiō, cōciō dealer), influenced by Middle French cousin; literally, cousin.

"I'm not sure I get it," Neil said. "What?"

Karen took in a breath — then let it out and pointed at the clock over the door. Neil looked up, then shrugged, there were five minutes left until class. Karen sighed again and held a palm out to the screen. "She's smart enough to write that, but not smart enough to spill it?"

Neil frowned, still waiting. Karen knew as well as he did that Jody had met with the police — and some change had happened for Melissa's parents too, at least they'd stopped asking to talk to the school. Jody had told them something, he guessed. Now Karen didn't want to be caught on Facebook and Neil wondered why. The police hadn't even banned him from it, though he had got a lecture from Bornstein and deactivated Stevie B. Karen obviously knew something more about Jody and Melissa's "adventure". *Not smart enough to spill it* — right. She was trying to distract him from whatever she'd been about to accidentally say.

"Yeah," Neil said, rising. "I can't read your mind, Karen. Relax."

RCity News — Online — Monday, October 22nd
Teen Melissa Arthur still missing

Two weeks after the safe return of her friend Jody Bear, local teen Melissa Arthur remains out of contact with family and friends. James Bear, father of Jody Bear, released a statement that his daughter is cooperating with police and social services to provide information relating to her friend's whereabouts.

Police have now identified "the friend" who met Jody and Melissa the afternoon of Friday, September 14th. Twenty-five-year-old Andrew Gangier, a student in a community building trades program, confirms that he spent the weekend with Melissa, before parting ways. "We dropped the other girl at the lake. Then we watched movies and videos and partied a bit," said Gangier. They stayed in his basement apartment, ordered pizza, and watched an early missing persons' announcement on the news. "Monday I went to classes and when I came back she was gone and her bag of stuff and some money, too." Pressed for the exact sum missing, Mr. Gangier said, "Not that much, maybe sixty, or a hundred dollars." Melissa was recorded boarding a city bus midday on Monday, September 17th, and has not been seen by friends or family since. Police caution that harbouring Melissa would amount to obstruction of an investigation and that criminal offences for endangering a minor would apply. Anyone with knowledge of Melissa's activities over the past weeks is encouraged to contact city police promptly.

COMMENTS (62)

1) Prayers for Melissa. Prayers for the rest of them.

2) <comment removed by moderator>

3) Nice account from Mr. Gangier but a bit late to the airwaves. This Jody kid was in a cabin close to town for a month and no cop never found her — wtf?

4) echo previous post

5) Parents should give her a lesson. Let me tell you what I'd do to my daughter — oooh, public forum. Grounded for life.

6) It's not enough to live off the back of the masses. No tax. Free school. Now they want a special investigation — Regular police not good enough, eh? I got better ways to spend my money, clean up your own damn mess.

7) I wonder if these kids know about Home Free? They'll pay free fare on any bus to get kids home, from anyplace, they just have to go to a bus depot and ask for security.

8) I completely buy this — seems like something teenagers would do — ill thought out plan that spirals out of control. That the girl Jody turned off her phone to save a battery is both funny and sad, but accurate, I'd guess.

>What do you mean, ill thought out plan? What battery?

>Running away isn't a lifestyle choice, 'something teenagers do' — it's a symptom of some f — ed up situation they don't know what to do about — not funny/sad

9) <comment removed by moderator>

10) HEY NOW One's still in the bush, don't be casting stones

NEXT PAGE >>

» Fifty-Three

Kolton pushed open the door of the bakery and the bell over the door jingled. He looked around and almost didn't see Jody. She was at the coffee counter but tucked in beside her dad. Kolton saw the poster up on the wall behind them. Then Jody waved and Kolton felt a knot jerk up in his throat. Melissa was still there on the poster. She should've been coming out of the washroom behind him or something like that. Slipping her hands under his jacket and he'd close his eyes and shiver and she'd be like, *warm my hands up, stupid.* The door chime jingled again. That was Kolton's mom and dad coming in.

Jody stood up from the counter.

"Hey," Kolton said, and she kind of dove in for a hug and surprised him. "Oh, hey," he put his arms up around her head. She was a lot shorter than Melissa.

"You two have a lot to talk about, I guess," Kolton's dad said. "We'll sit ourselves here at the counter, son." He reached out to shake hands with Jody's enormous dad, and Kolton's mom scooted around to sit on the far side of her husband, staring at Jody. On the drive over she'd called her a little shit.

"Yeah, we'll go sit," Kolton said, and he followed Jody to a table across the bakery.

"You mad at us?" she whispered.

Kolton shook his head.

"Did she tell you?"

Kolton raised a hand to his head, so it would look like he was leaning on it. He pulled the brim of his hat sideways to cover his face. "Tell me what?"

Jody stared at Kolton's hand. His fingers weren't yellow from smoking anymore, but it looked like he'd been chewing on them. The nails were barely there. Kolton licked his lips and there was white stuff at the corner of his mouth. Like he'd been running. She swallowed, "Mel was going to tell you about her and me — "

Kolton shifted his hat back. "You guys scared the shit out of me, actually. How come you never texted?"

"I never had my phone charger." She had tried to save the battery, checking it once a day. It'd got harder and harder to read her mom's texts. Kolton didn't look like he believed her.

He leaned across the table and whispered, "Where the fuck is she?"

Jody wiped at her face. "Yeah, I don't know now."

"You're shitting me."

When Jody closed her eyes she could feel their parents staring. And she could feel her own self staring off the stupid poster. She'd already told her mom and dad, and the police, and the counsellor. She wanted to explain but it was hard and she felt like Kolton should already know. He'd hung around Melissa lots. He'd remember how she talked about teaching everyone a lesson. If they were going to be treated like they were invisible, they might as well be *#Next*. Maybe he'd remember why it had made sense — and Melissa had dumped Kolton too, he'd know what that felt like. Jody opened her eyes, expecting to meet Kolton's, and found him staring down at the table.

"They're saying you just did it for attention," he muttered. Then he looked over her head, right through her, and Jody turned and caught the look on his mom's face.

"She kinda hate me?"

Kolton dropped his head, temple to his fist. He leaned into his elbow and his phone chimed in his jacket pocket. Taelur wanting to know what Jody was like now, probably. When she'd be back at class. He'd stopped jumping every time it went off; he didn't expect messages from Melissa anymore. Kolton looked up at Jody waiting on him and straightened his back. "She's just my mom. You gonna be at school?"

» Fifty-Four

The trail at the river's edge was wet, and at the break of the bank the path became a river itself, a bloodline for melt trickling down. At night the trail froze. In the morning it was white, and crunched underfoot where windows of ice stretched over empty space.

Melissa's sneakers beat on the asphalt path, crumpled softer on the frozen grass. Past the trees every step broke glass. At the river's lip the path became slippery, the mud soft — and the risk of sliding into the water was very real. Melissa pressed the toe of her right shoe into the path, testing it. She examined the print, the ridges of her gym shoe stamped in.

A log rested on the bank nearby. A largish branch, maybe pulled down by a beaver, or pushed up by a raft of ice. The bark had swollen, split, and peeled away from the wood, which was pale and smooth underneath. Melissa set the heel of her sneaker against the bared wood. She kicked out, threw herself off balance — and crab-walked backwards, clawing at dried grass.

She was shielded by an overhang of willow. The leaves were dry and silver but still clinging on. The log responded slowly beneath her, slipping off the bank into the water with a tug from the current. It dipped under and the river burped it up to spin away downstream. Everything was quiet — and suddenly Melissa's idea of leaving the footprints, of walking backwards so carefully that they would assume she had fallen in, became impossible. The river swallowed the dead branch and Melissa was muddy and cold and the first she knew about her terrible crying was Mr. Cameron, crashing through the bushes on his bike, shouting, convincing, "You're okay, you're okay!"

Neil cried aloud and Tanis woke pinned under the weight he bore down into a clenched fistful of duvet. He released it with a sob and Tanis eased herself free, unsure whether to wake him. She smoothed his hair back from his face. It was damp; he'd been sweating. A nightmare. She let him rest.

» Fifty-Five

The children had been skipping with a piece of laundry line, but in a wind the line was too light to twirl properly, even when they wheeled their arms at top speed. It seemed like a good idea to tie the washers on. The weighted line flew hard and fast, to the girls' startled delight. They jumped, excited, again and again. When one caught a shin, she hopped out with blood on her stockings and the next jumped in. They should have stopped, but it didn't hurt much, and it upped the ante. It made them jump higher, and they were good skippers, all of them. Elspeth Murray didn't get a scratch, but it was her mother who was the most worked up. Celia brought home a nick on her ankle herself. Even if it had been Celia's idea, Phidelma argued at the teacher, it was the other girls that had joined in.

Tanis nursed a coffee and read through the sections she and Celia had underway — they fell into three time periods more or less. The link to the present day was the boots and it was going to be hard to get them right. When Tanis pressed Celia for a plausible interpretation the story got stranger — it might be better to leave them as random a find in the manuscript as they'd been in the attic. Tanis wasn't sure.

When the policeman came knocking, Celia heard something. The man asked for Thomas and for Robert. That was the morning after the fight in the yard, and they'd come down in the morning to find the kitchen a mess of muddy footprints, the dog with a bloodied ear. Of course the furs from the attic were gone.

The policeman came round again a day later, looking for Thomas specifically, and Phidelma told him that her father had gone "to his people." The policeman looked at Celia, who'd peeked out from the stairway, and he said with real pity in his voice, "I think I hear what you've said."

It was another week before Phidelma found a pair of men's workboots tucked under her back step. She was alone when she found them, Celia off at school, and she looked around the yard to see who'd left them. She lifted them up and the boots didn't answer, but shed clots of dried mud — a mess someone hadn't wanted to track in.

When Neil woke, the smell of coffee met him on the stairs, exhaled by the new bubbling drip system on the counter. He realized that he hadn't been assaulted by cat pee or nicotine smells for quite a while now. They were living it out, or the cold was settling things back into the basement floor.

He'd expected to find Tanis in the kitchen and looked into the front room, but it was empty too. Perhaps the attic. He was about to go look when the toilet flushed and water ran. There she was. Tanis came around the bathroom door and Neil reached for her, grateful. "Thanks for the sleep-in."

"You are welcome, my dear."

"My dear. You've been working with that old lady's stuff already, hunh?" Neil grinned. "Will you take some coffee — one lump or two?"

"Black like my heart," Tanis said.

Neil laughed, "Is that hers too?"

Tanis shook her head, smiling. "Did you look out the window yet? Come see."

They stood at the sink and looked out at their yard. Snow had frosted the grass, still green, as well as the garish yellow play structure that sat, newly assembled, beside their garage. An uncle had gifted it to Kaydance but Michelle had no room for it in the apartment, obviously. "It's big, *shee*," she'd said, heaving the box into her car. Kaydance and Moosie had looked on, despondent, until Tanis stopped Michelle and called Neil, who'd had to call Declan, in the end, to help assemble the thing. It was 8:00 AM and it was snowing, and looking over at the apartment Tanis saw Kaydance at their window, drawing with window crayons.

Tanis knew now about the heat vent beneath that window. She'd been up for coffee with Michelle, when Kaydance was off at school. Their space was warm and messy — little fingerprints on every shiny surface. This morning Kaydance was tucked in behind the curtains, foot warmed by the jet of air that billowed the cloth out behind her. She was drawing a line of animals again. Ponies, maybe unicorns. Either way they were appearing in an orderly rainbow spectrum, Mr. Roy G. Biv.

In the course of Neil's leaf-blowing extravaganza he'd discovered that Kaydance had been creating art on the side of their house. Tanis did not especially mind — the little girl had crouched down below the stone wall, so her colouring was mainly out of sight. She'd drawn an interesting scene beside the dryer vent showing five stick people, all wearing skirts, arranged in a big circle around a little circle with a heart on it. The singers at the vigil, Tanis thought. Neil squinted down along the parging where their little friend had tagged the house repeatedly with variations of her own name: *Kaydanz. K-Dance.* In one small bubbly cloud, the mysterious *KD & P.*

Tanis had imagined P, a boy in grade three with an action-hero T-shirt and one of those faux-hawk hairdos that cool parents let their kids get. Why's that cool? Neil had countered. How would a kid whose parents dressed him like that rebel? How would Kaydance rebel, he'd pressed, if they let her scribble freely on their property — graffiti? They had presented the window crayons as a gift, and it looked like they'd do the trick.

Tanis looked back to the yellow play structure collecting snow and elbowed Neil. "We'll have to get her some Sharpies, so she can decorate that thing."

Neil grunted, and turned away to find milk in the fridge. Tanis had let him sleep in, right through her "procreation schedule". He hummed absently, remembering the night before last, Tanis coming up fresh from a shower after her run. She'd mapped herself a five kilometre route so she could claim personal bests. It ran west, then south, then back along the river — Neil shut his eyes. *River, mud, Melissa.* Neil couldn't remember what the girl had said, and a sense of utter loss stabbed through his chest. "Tanis?"

She'd reached for the tap and held her mug at the faucet. "Hm?"

ACKNOWLEDGEMENTS

This novel draws on a history of place and am I indebted to the Saskatoon City Archives; the Gabriel Dumont Institute oral history project; and to my late father-in-law, Lee Baker, whose stories, spirit, and creative mentorship I am so very grateful to have known.

I have many people to thank for their support completing this novel — David Carpenter and Lori Pollock (first responders); Mike, Merrill, Shannon, Kathy, Alison, Graham and Chelsea (critical cheerleaders); Liz Philips (editor extraordinaire); and my family, especially Ena (motivation unlimited!).

Thank you also to the Canada Council for the Arts and Saskatchewan Arts Board for assistance through their literary grants programs; and to Thistledown Press, Al and Jackie Forrie, for bringing the manuscript forward in its present, published form.

Sandy Marie Bonny is a writer, visual artist, and science educator whose short fiction has appeared in literary journals and anthologies including *Prairie Fire*, *Grain*, and *The Danforth Review*, and was featured in *Coming Attractions 11*, Oberon Press' annual anthology of up-and-coming Canadian fiction writers. Her first book of short fiction, *The Sometimes Lake*, was published by Thistledown Press in 2012. *Yes, and Back Again* is her first novel. Bonny lives in Saskatoon.